The *Shores* of Lake Marie

AJ LeBergé

PAGE PUBLISHING
Conneaut Lake, PA

First originally published by Page Publishing 2022

ISBN 978-1-6624-8664-7 (pbk)
ISBN 978-1-6624-8666-1 (digital)

Printed in the United States of America

Acknowledgments

A very special thank-you goes out to Skyler, my spouse, for all the love and support and for him helping me make my dreams a reality. I also thank my fans, whose continuing support and positive, public book reviews make this ongoing series possible. To family and friends, I wish to thank them for all the memories and their help in life.

Chapter 1

Driving leisurely through the scenic countryside of Southern Wisconsin and Northern Illinois, Laura, Caroline, and Cheryl were happy to have reached the charming little village of Antioch, Illinois. It was a relief to have finally passed through acre after acre of dairy farms with cow manure permeating the air. Quaint as the area was, the three young women were on a mission to reach their final destination and agreed they would have plenty of time during their vacation trip to explore the surrounding territory. They were already running much later than intended, and there was some work to be done once they arrived at their reserved woodland campsite.

Passing the old Come on Inn Lodge and Tavern, a sign pointed the way to their desired location: Camp Lake Marie. Laura thought that the lodge would have been more comfortable than staying in a tent in the woods, but the decisions made for this trip had not been hers alone to decide. All three of the young women had discussed and negotiated their vacation plans before booking. The important thing was that she was looking forward to having a great time with her best friends. That was all that really mattered to any of them when it came to any particular details.

Pulling up to the main campground gate, which was the only visitor access gate at Camp Oak, the women cheered. Rolling the driver's-side window down, Cheryl brought her sports sedan to a stop while allowing the engine to continue purring. The security guard exited his guardhouse and approached the three lovely women and their ride. He greeted them appropriately and smiled.

While speaking to him, Cheryl could not help but notice that the right side of his face had been burned and scarred. Not only were his looks unusual for other reasons, but his personality and behavior also disturbed Cheryl somewhat. While the man did his job professionally, he had a creepy, giggling laugh. After every sentence he spoke, he chuckled when nothing he said was even the slightest bit humorous. More notably, he stared at her specifically for what she felt was an uncomfortable length of time while assisting them. His eyes never blinked, nor had they moved even a fraction of an inch in their sockets, as one would have expected they should have.

The unusual man spoke slowly while collecting their campsite cash fees, issued Cheryl a receipt, issued a *Camp Oak Park Regulations Manual* and *Antioch Visitors Guide*, and provided a gate access card to use during off hours. Cheryl's conversation with the gate guard was longer than she would have liked. He apparently wanted to verbally discuss details contained within each brochure he handed her when the literature would have spelled everything out for them anyway. Cheryl deduced that the camp officials probably couldn't count on anyone actually reading everything and believed that some of the information might have needed to be verbally presented for the illiterate, but dumb she was not.

The only real bits of information the women wanted to know at this specific moment was where their campsite, the ranger station, and the public clubhouse were located. The guard descriptively directed them while pointing in various directions with finger gestures. Then he made a comment emphasizing that the forest ranger was off-site for the time being. For their safety, the guard promised he would make sure that the ranger knew they were there to check in as soon as he returned to his office.

While the grounds had a clubhouse, it was actually just his and her separate public showers with filthy toilets positioned off one tiny common area gathering room. Outside the clubhouse, a playground suitable for small children and a tennis court adorned the property. An aged, tattered net was strung across the court and did not resemble what potential visitors would have observed in pictures on the campsite's website. All the beautiful photos posted online made the grounds look like a five-star facility. It must have been years since the website pictures had been updated. In general, nothing about the clubhouse would appear appealing to any traveler expecting more than the fact that the amenities actually existed.

In the case of Cheryl, Caroline, and Laura, the drive had ratted their bladders. Being as though they wanted to relieve themselves quickly rather than waiting to stumble upon one of the randomly scattered outhouses around the campgrounds, the nearby clubhouse option appealed to them for now. In most cases, one would expect that clubhouse facilities in these park areas would be somewhat better maintained than any stinky old outhouses. With the clubhouse looking the way it was, one could be certain that the outhouses were definitely horrid. At Camp Oak, that was certainly the case.

From a short distance away, a man cloaked in black remained well-hidden behind the lush landscape. Preoccupied with their conversation, none of the women noticed his being there. But had they noticed, nobody would have questioned his presence anyway. He listened but was mostly interested in the physical appearance of those arriving. It was evident these females were special. They were just the type he had been hoping to scout out. All were youthful, wholesome, and pretty enough. They would be perfect for his diabolical needs.

Deep inside his mind, he was bothered by a sense of awkwardness. It had been a while since he had planned anything such as he had on his mind. He attributed the feeling of butterflies in his stomach to that lapse in time. Yet somehow, there seemed to be another unsettling feeling lingering in him. It was the feeling that he would regret ever having set eyes upon these three particular women. It was a feeling of doom he had never experienced before. But he would not allow this opportunity to pass by. They were too suitable to let this opportunity not go acted upon.

Upon the guard opening the gate to allow them access, the women drove immediately to the clubhouse. Once there, they rushed in, searching for the commodes. Upon discovering them to be in an utterly disgusting condition, they jokingly chattered about probably having preferred relieving themselves in their pants. Not only were the commodes wretched, but the entire areas surrounding them also reeked from a variety of waste biohazards. The porcelain was speckled with a highly toxic mold.

"Imagine what the outhouses must look like if this is the clubhouse facility," Laura commented while scrunching up her petite nose. Most disturbing, Laura thought, was that there were no privacy walls around the commodes. Others in the area would get a clear view of whatever she was doing. While there was a shower area, it was just a rusty, open-ended pipe coming out of a dingy, peeling block wall. There were colors of stains on the walls and floor that none of them could begin to guess what had created.

Currently, there was an extremely overweight woman showering with her two very small girls huddling together under the single pipe of streaming water. The setup could not have been any more primitive or uninviting, yet it was available should someone require it. Fortunately, the women had made other portable toilet arrangements for during their stay at the camp and hoped they would be able to bathe in the lake water by their campsite. But none of them had considered if the lake water would not be sanitary for that purpose. Toxic algae made the water unhealthy most times. Visitors never seemed to consider that.

Furthering their ride to their campsite, the women continued to crudely discuss the guard at the front gate. Laura was sympathetic about the way he had looked and acted. Caroline and Cheryl did not hold back on their objectionable thoughts. Without any consideration for people with such handicaps, they made fun of him relentlessly—not in a realistic manner but in more of a surrealistic, joking fashion.

Cheryl found humor in declaring that he was the previous gate guard at a vampire's castle and that he would be coming to get them during the night when bats would be flying about. Women would be abducted and delivered to a mad doctor, who would be performing ghoulish experiments upon them. "He'll be coming for you, Laura," Cheryl said in a horrific-sounding voice. While Laura did not like that they were making fun of the man, she knew that it was all in jest and that they were just having private fun among themselves. None of the women would ever be publicly unkind to any person, and they knew how unfortunate it could be for a person to be handicapped or less fortunate.

Laura suspected this trip would bring about a lot of silliness, as they all had what they perceived to be a sense of humor that knew no boundaries. Jokes would sometimes go too far, but they understood one another well enough to know there was no real cruelty ever intended. All of them were often in the habit of speaking without thinking when talking privately between friends. Any thought on their minds could and would just slip out of their mouths without concern. They would soon be finding out just how much potential reality there was in their jest.

Having finally arrived at their rented space, having pitched the tents, and having become situated, they appreciated that dense trees would be shading their site from even the most intense midday sun. Laura never really had much interest in camping, but this trip was something Caroline and Cheryl had been planning since long before high school graduation day. It was expected that they would soon each be going away to different educational facilities come the fall semester. The thought of being away from one another was a disheartening topic.

While camping wasn't something any of them would have actually preferred to do on a vacation, this was the getaway they all finally agreed upon. The cost was relatively inexpensive—next to nothing—and each needed what little money they had for the future. Antioch, Illinois, was not far from the state border where they lived in their parents' homes in Salem, Wisconsin. The road trip was only a mere six miles from home. That made for a short commute to the site by car and was another topic discussed in having made the decision to camp here.

Although many things were considered, there was one major selling point that helped Caroline and Cheryl agree to make Camp Oak their final, decided-upon destination. In fact, it was enough of a selling point to have entirely based their decisions upon. Antioch had been the scene of rather recent murders reportedly committed by a local man. Additionally, Camp Oak had been the campground from which several campers had gone missing over many years. It had yet to be determined by investigators if the two scenarios were in any way related. When Caroline and Cheryl managed to secure the exact campsite from which four young campers had supposedly gone missing from last summer, they were ecstatic. That group of four campers a year ago had been the last reported incident of people to have gone missing. They convinced Laura that they simply had to come to Camp Oak and check the place out for themselves.

This piqued Laura's interest too, as she was going to pursue an education and future career in criminology. Criminology had always fascinated her since she had grown up adoring a crime-solving cartoon dog and his gang of amateur sleuths. Caroline, however, was going to study occult and paranormal phenomena from a scientific perspective. Cheryl had other ecological and geological study interests in mind. Combining all their interests, this forest preserve in Antioch was the perfect travel destination for all of them to appreciate.

The three women were longing for a place to put their textbook studying minds to rest since having graduated. Their goal was to have fun and enjoy a passion for the macabre while spending their time together—sort of. Contrary to the way Cheryl and Caroline felt about a relaxing time away, they got Laura to agree to this trip by misleading her into thinking it would be an investigative adventure of sorts. They promised her it would consist of interesting tours of local crime scenes, of which there were many in the area, and men!

Antioch drew the men in by busloads in the warmer weather—men who enjoyed all the water activities the lakes had to offer and men who showed off their physiques in nothing but skimpy swimsuits. For anyone interested, men and women were sights one could expect to see on the lake this time of year. Should the right man—or woman, for that matter—come along for any of the three, the other women would possibly be on their own, which they joked about that. They also assumed none of them actually had the personality to hook up short-term with any stranger. While attractive enough to easily land a guy, none was really known for being that sexually precarious.

For kicks, they made a bet pertaining to which one of them would have the gumption to score first. If any of them was slutty enough to hook up with a stranger on this trip, that person would have to kiss the gate guard on the lips while grabbing his crotch sometime before they departed. These women had never reneged on a bet and hoped the penalty for this one might help keep the trio together in their group for the entire trip duration. Each knew this was to be their special time together.

Having arrived at Camp Oak only an hour ago, the young women had managed to become nicely situated. Their larger tent was a deluxe green structure that was large enough to accommodate several adults. The design flaunted a large canvas space big enough for five sleeping cots if needed. An attached but separate smaller compartment was completely screened in for lounge seating off the front. Additionally, they brought along a small tent that they would equip with a portable camping toilet to be used as their private outhouse. The toilet was nothing more than a supported seat with a dangling plastic bag underneath, but it would do. Fortunately, their brothers all enjoyed camping and had provided them with the equipment they required for a modernized camping experience. That included folding sleeping cots, sleeping bags, folding chairs, a large food and beverage cooler, mobile firepit, and a small gas cooking grill in case a natural wood campfire wasn't suitable for their cuisine.

It didn't take long before Laura figured out that she had been suckered into a weekend of fighting off bugs and that little else might interest her at the campsite. Caroline and Cheryl were simply happy to be there, spending time together, and Laura knew she would be shamed by her friends if she didn't appear happy for that reason alone, so she would grin and bear it. It was only Caroline and Cheryl's intent to make the trip a relaxing one.

Laura was not as pensive as they were and knew she would become far too antsy if they didn't plan periodic adventurous excursions. She liked to keep busy. It would not please her to spend her time just sitting around a campsite counting the minutes or bugs until the trip was over. From where they camped, not even night stars would be able to be counted through the thick umbrella of trees. Just in case it rained and they chose not to leave their shelter or if Cheryl and Caroline could not keep Laura adequately entertained, Caroline had brought along several books for reading. She loved to read anything she could get her hands on. For this trip, she had mostly selected books based upon Antioch's legends and folklore.

No matter the topic, sticking their noses in books since graduation was not something Laura and Cheryl had hoped to do during this trip. Still, a couple of books in this selection were something Caroline hoped they would take some time to peruse. Neither of those two was of the published variety. Both were scrapbooks that had been assembled by Caroline's own hands. One was an ode to their friendship and contained all sorts of clippings and pictures of their fun old times together. It showed how much she truly valued their friendship. Another was a scrapbook of everything she could find of interest pertaining to Antioch. Any other person could see it predominantly focused on the occult interests she was fascinated by, but she would not have noticed that herself.

It was simply based upon how she personally thought and viewed the world around her.

One of the best features at their campsite, Laura observed, was the lake they had a view of if standing in the location nearest to it: Lake Marie. During daylight hours, boaters could be seen partaking in a multitude of activities, which included swimming, waterskiing, and fishing when dangerous water alerts were not in effect. At this time on a prime weekday afternoon, the sound of motorboats whizzing around near and far was still noisily audible at the far reaches of their campsite and even deeper into the woods. However, the area was not as noisy as it could become at peak times. While some campers might consider the boats a noisy distraction from the wilderness experience, Laura did not.

More so attention worthy of their particular campsite, they had the luxury of having a clean stretch of pebbled shoreline beachfront between the treed area where they were camping and the water's edge. It was the next best thing to having their own private beach. While campers from other sites and other people coming by water to the land could access the shoreline there, nobody else was occupying it at this time. It went unspoken, but Laura was pretending in her mind that it was all her own private beach.

Bugs would still be a nuisance in that area, but the air fogging devices and body repellent sprays they brought would remedy that situation quite a lot. Cheryl was a bit apprehensive about the use of any harmful chemicals given her ecologically friendly mindset, so hoping to please her, Caroline had also brought along more environmentally friendly citronella candles although the idea of lighting a few candles to protect them against the veracity of the local insects only made Laura and Cheryl laugh. Their own hometown, not too far away, was not immune to bug infestations.

Whatever had made Caroline think a few candles would be of any good use in the wilderness was beyond their comprehension. Caroline had really only intended for them to use them in the tent at night for added protection, not to use them with the intention of ridding entire areas of pests. But being that the girls joked about most anything, Caroline and her candles were a fair game topic.

Cheryl looked at Laura and commented, "I bet they are some sort of occult candles Caroline lights to pay homage to Deskari, the great and powerful insect god." The girls chuckled.

"Yep! We are probably going to end up her sacrifices to the bug creatures. She is probably one of them, as she bugs me all the time," Laura added with a giggling homage to her own wit.

While the forest was cooled by treetops blocking the sun, the beach area also received a cooling breeze from off the open lake water. Each area had pros and cons, and Laura seemed obsessed with analyzing and discussing them. Cheryl and Caroline didn't pay any mind to the conditions until Laura pointed them out one by one. They tried their darnedest not to care. Bugs, heat, or noise—it all made no difference to them. They were just appreciating being there, wherever they might be at any given moment. Rain or shine, good times or bad, they would always make the best of any undesirable circumstance.

As the others had also done on their own, Cheryl had researched the area's geography before making her final decision to make this their vacation destination. She had a plethora of knowledge; and it did not matter where she had been, was at, or was going to be, she knew her facts about the surroundings. Antioch and the Lake Marie area were no exception.

For such a small village with acres of lakes, there were so many facts one could learn. Lake Marie was a nice-sized lake covering approximately 480 acres. It featured many points of interest. A few private homes were scattered on the shoreline on the opposite side of the lake across from the camp and again at the opposite end too. All the homes had been customized, and each was unique in many ways, but they were all older.

Lake Catherine was the next lake over and was accessible through a waterway channel. An acre-or-so-sized island was situated in what was somewhat near the center of Lake Marie although the island would shrink and gain in size dramatically depending upon seasonal water levels, which were known to vary greatly. Camp Oak and other conservation area forestry surrounded much of the lake, except where a couple of small bits of shoreline touched local farmers' fields.

Chapter 2

Cheryl was diligent in pointing out the peak of a rooftop barely visible in the distance across the lake and alongside a short waterway channel. The rest of the building it was attached to was obstructed by several rows of large trees. "That building," Cheryl said while pointing, "is the Baskin Boat Shop. There is a diner at the shop, and an outdoor dining patio backs up to Lake Marie. The shop is accessible by water off Lake Catherine over in that direction." Her finger continued to point, directing their attention. "Lake Marie and Lake Catherine are connected via a river channel over there," she continued to say while pointing to another area. She didn't want to stand around discussing too much about it at this time but managed to give a pretty good although brief, description.

Cheryl stated, "I know a boat shop might not ordinarily be of interest to most people, except those who utilize the lake and areas surrounding it. In this case, the Baskin Boat Shop has history here and draws in more and more visitors annually. Its main purpose when it opened many years ago was to store about a hundred private boats in the colder seasons and gas up motor vehicles from on and around the connecting lakes. Not every lake has a gas station for such vehicles, and watercraft come from other areas through the channels to fuel up at Baskin's dock pumps. Over the years, the establishment has grown larger to include watercraft sales and a general store selling groceries, gifts, hardware, fishing bait, and boating supplies.

"Most recently, the Baskin family expanded the facility to include a small indoor/outdoor café with tables and seating overlooking Lake Marie and gorgeous scenery. Even that food service has been in existence for several years now. Despite its growth over time, visitors claim its original charm manages to remain unblemished. Because of the multitude of diverse services Baskin's provides, locals and tourists who are in the know have left positive online reviews. The Baskin Boat Shop is one of the few local businesses not located in the heart of town that remains open all year round. Recently, business there has reportedly boomed with the establishment's affiliation with local crimes, which we can discuss later."

"Which crimes in particular?" Caroline questioned.

"We can tell ghost stories around the campfire tonight," Cheryl replied. "In general, within the last year, Eli Charter, who ran a charter boat service from the docks there, was found dead in one of his boats.

Dan Baskin, son of the Baskin Boat Shop owners, was arrested on suspicion of murder for Eli's death—not just Eli's but other murders and crimes as well. Dan was found to be mentally incompetent, I've been told. Since then, tourists apparently want to visit the shop even more so."

"I read about some local crimes," Laura added. "They fit right in with my criminology interests. Unfortunately, many people were not happy with the decision labeling Dan as being incompetent. I've since heard of some very bad incidents and protests occurring at that shop. Not everyone sang its praises online. Still, it best be on our tour list of places to stop in. I can't wait to visit there. It sounds so macabre, but it also sounds charming in a small town sort of way."

Laura, Caroline, and Cheryl were each somewhat aware of the various aspects of crime stories, ghost stories, legends, rumors, and history involving Antioch and Lake Marie. It had already been decided that their information would make for intriguing conversation to share at night once settled in near a roaring campfire. For now, they had completed the finishing touches around their campsite and planned to fog the area with bug spray—despite Cheryl's ecological protest—before embarking on a short hike. That would give the bug spray smell a chance to clear while they explored nearby.

Cheryl was completing clearance of a small circle of dirt at the center of the site before lining the circle with a metal firepit and a perimeter of rocks.

AJ LEBERGÉ

While most previous campers had been following the campground guidelines for precautionary fire retention, the burnt ground clearly indicated that some campers had been lighting open fires directly on the ground. Doing such was considered a fire hazard. Maybe those people had not read the regulations or just did not care. It disturbed Cheryl to think of how easily they could have started a forest fire and burned down all the beauty it had taken nature so many years to create. Then to the best of her ability, she prepared the metal pit with twigs and logs of various sizes, prepping it for their fire to be lit come sundown.

While bending down, a bright object, which had apparently been unearthed during the shuffling around of the supplies that day, caught Cheryl's eye. Picking the item up and dusting it off, she was quick to show her friends the nice metal cigarette lighter she had just found. It was of golden tone and not particularly of cheap quality. "Look!" Cheryl said. "I just found this cool lighter. It's got a name engraved in script. It reads Julie." Cheryl pondered over her find. "Too bad it has already been engraved. That's okay anyway. Perhaps I can have the name buffed off and polish this up as a souvenir for myself." She was pleased and believed it would make a nice possession.

Having completed their campsite to each of their approvals, they sat down for a break to take it all in. Everything seemed perfect, they agreed, except for the noise. At this time, the motorboats seemed distant and not so loud, but a group of motorcyclists had descended upon the campgrounds and had obviously taken over the lot nearest to them. The roar of their engines was a distraction from what could have otherwise been a harmonious balance in nature. The cyclists' lot was somewhat distanced but still near enough for the women to hear the many sounds emanating from it, especially any of the loud noises. But it was discussed that the motors would soon quiet down once the cyclists made camp and the motorboats left for the night, so they were not going to complain about the current loud, rumbling sound conditions, which would only be temporary. Loud sounds should have been anticipated upon selection of such a site, positioned as it was, and it could have always been worse.

Knowing that there were still a couple of hours until dark, Laura requested they depart on foot to take a hike around the nearby area. She wanted to explore what was close by. That was her way of saying that she did not feel totally comfortable in unfamiliar surroundings and wanted to check things out before she could be fully at peace. The sun would eventually begin to set, but with a few hours of daylight remaining, they all agreed they had enough time to explore. The setting of the sun would be an appropriate time for them to be returning to their lot, they concurred. It seemed it would be an enjoyable way to appreciate the remaining daylight and accomplish some activity campers would engage in.

Not that any of them cared about the time of day on this trip, but time was passing quickly for them. They would have been at the campgrounds much earlier in the day had Caroline not had an unexpected medical appointment come up, which detained their original departure from home. No matter, they had arrived, created a nice camp, and still had the time to enjoy a hike. All things considered, the only thing they had anticipated doing and had not accomplished on their way to the camp was to stop at the Baskin Boat Shop. To conserve time today, it was decided they would go first thing in the morning tomorrow being that they had enough supplies to get through their night.

There was to be no rushing around anticipated on this vacation. There would be much time to see the town and the places they wanted to at a later time. Anyway, since each of them had their own knowledge of the area's history, they felt it best to discuss their knowledge of the sites before exploring them. That way, there would be more appreciation for the sites if they fully understood what to expect upon exploration. The boat shop was one such particular place with lots of history to discuss.

Strolling peacefully through the flora, the trio followed cleared pathways to the best of their abilities. From the looks of things, it was obvious that people had often strolled these paths and had worn the vegetation down into adequate walkways. Only rarely did one of the girls stray from the perceived clearings to get a close-up look at something. When doing so, insects would rise up from the low-growing plants and swarm in a frenzy, enticing the three to stick to the clearest of areas as much as possible. Creepy, crawly things were not appreciated much. At this time of day, the insects seemed to be resting, awaiting the cooler air of evening, when they would be certain to fly about the countryside in large gathering masses. The walk was nice, they repeatedly reiterated along the way, as long as the bugs remained undisturbed. They found it of interest to identify all the different types of bugs they could spot and, as well, the various foliage varieties.

Mostly, the hiking trio made small talk and discussed things they were seeing along the way. Several small animals scurried about under blankets of dead, drying leaves. They seemed to make for an especially hot conversation topic. Cheryl loved all animals and was happy to see any of them. Caroline didn't mind the critters' existence but was alarmed when they would unexpectedly run or fly out in front of her. Laura would rather not have any close proximity to any wild fauna. She simply felt bad because the animals seemed too startled by the human intrusion into their environment. As Laura said, "We don't live here. They do. We are intruding in their home territory."

While observing a chipmunk, Cheryl stepped off the beaten path and watched as it burrowed down into a hole between two exposed tree roots. Taking a closer look, she spotted a particularly unusual rock. Upon closer examination, the realization struck that it was clearly an Indian arrowhead. They were not an uncommon find, if one was lucky enough, but any found would likely be very old. Pleased with her discovery, she picked it up and brought it over to Laura and Caroline. Cheryl just knew it had to be authentic and stated that she would be happy to later share the information she had researched on the local Native American tribe. "Looks like another souvenir for me," Cheryl said with a smile as she slipped it into a shirt pocket.

At that moment, Caroline was working up the nerve to discuss another matter completely off topic that had been weighing on her mind. She needed to get something out in the open that weighed heavily upon her conscience. While there was some happiness in her voice, she was starting to cry for no apparent reason that Laura and Cheryl could figure on their own. Caroline wasn't the type to just break out in tears, and she was unable to conceal that she had a real problem.

"What is the matter, Caroline?" Laura stopped in her tracks to question.

"I have been very emotional lately," Caroline replied. "You know, I was at a doctor's appointment today. And, well, he said that I am pregnant."

This was some big news for Laura and Cheryl to process considering that the three of them had always discussed their lives so openly. They did not even know Caroline had been sexually active with her most recent boyfriend, Dale. Caroline and Dale had only been on two or three dates that Laura and Cheryl knew of—that is, if one or two of those encounters could even be construed as official dates.

"The condom broke when Dale and I had intercourse. As we know, these things happen," Caroline explained. Tears eased up as she felt relief from having spoken about it aloud. "My mother and Dale want me to keep the baby, and I just don't know how I feel about that. A baby was not what I expected out of my near future," Caroline said with confusion in her voice. "I need to do a lot of thinking on this trip and will hopefully come to some logical and rational conclusion. It was only three dates I had with him, you know? I haven't come to know him well enough at all yet. It was just a casual encounter."

Laura and Cheryl each made an attempt to be as supportive as they could, given the unexpected announcement and assured her, they would be supportive of any decision she made. This was not something they expected to hear, and it wasn't something they could ignore. They just didn't know what else to say at this time. Neither of them could envision Caroline being unwed with a baby at this point in her life. At this very moment, Caroline was not exactly glowing radiantly, as an expectant mother often did, or so was their observation and opinion.

"Guess I could've brought a third less alcohol with us on this trip," Laura said with a smile, trying to lighten the moment. She knew Caroline's announcement would be taking all the fun out of any anticipated wild party time.

Since Caroline had been bold enough to discuss her dilemma, Cheryl decided to share a secret of her own. "I did not want to tell you both sooner because I did not want you to worry about me and also because you both have been so happy about your education plans," she said before taking in a deep breath and adding a pause to her words. "My father was forced to close his company, and now my parents don't have all the money they promised me to get me through the school year. I don't know what I am going to do about it. I can't see a reason to start school if I can't finish what I start."

Laura and Caroline both consoled their friend and attempted to assure her that everything would work out the way it was meant to. While they might not have meant what they were saying, it was the best they could do to offer their support. Laura had nothing disheartening to share and felt a bit out of sorts over the predicaments her friends were in.

"Whatever will be," Cheryl responded. "I'm not going to let my situation ruin our trip. I'll figure it out for myself when it comes time to make any decisions. Maybe some rich, handsome, single guy will cross our path out here and sweep me off my feet," she said with a big smile, which showed off her impeccable pearly whites. Those were things that could be said about Cheryl—she always had high hopes and a big smile.

While the women huddled in a supportive three-way hug, Caroline glanced up and noticed someone watching them from an afar distance before darting off. She pulled from the huddle and gazed away intently while squinting.

"What is it? Did you see something?" Laura questioned.

"Someone was watching us. I'm not positive, but it looked like a Native American man from this distance," Caroline informed them.

"Well, this is a public park, and we are out in nature. I'm sure there are people all over who could be wandering about and observing us at any time. This isn't the place for privacy," Cheryl said, stating the obvious.

"It's not that, you twit!" Caroline said in reply to Cheryl's obvious answer. "It just seems overly coincidental that you found an Indian arrowhead and then I thought I saw a Native American. Tribal people really are not common here these days, certainly not dressed the way he was—in ancient garb—at least. It was like I was seeing someone dressed up for Halloween in an Indian costume from the old Wild West days. If he wasn't really Native American, it seems kind of racist for him to be dressed that way, don't you think?" Caroline added, "I may need new glasses, but he looked rather transparent to me. The apparition appeared and disappeared so abruptly that perhaps I imagined the whole thing. Whatever or whoever I saw is definitely gone now."

Making their way back to their campsite before dusk, the women were rather exhausted from even such a brief excursion. It had been a long day of preparing for the trip, driving, setting up camp, and hiking. No food had been consumed recently. Top priority was debating over who would be the first to utilize the portable toilet. Cheryl won in a two-out-of-three coin toss. Laura wasn't about to hold her water in and went into the trees behind the toilet tent.

"Hi!" Laura could be heard by Cheryl through the canvas tent as they peed in unison.

"What are you doing there?" Cheryl inquired, expecting some prank would soon be played upon her.

"I'm peeing too!" Laura said with a giggle. "Since I couldn't go to the women's room with you, I'm doing the next best thing. Seriously, though, I had to go really, really bad and was scared to go off too deep into the woods by myself. Here, I take comfort in knowing you are near. I'm not even sure what I will do at night, in the dark, if I need to come out here to potty all by myself."

"Don't you dare awaken me during the night because you need to relieve yourself! Ask Caroline," Cheryl suggested. "Only wake me if something is in the area—you know, spiders, snakes, bears, a guy with a chainsaw," she joked, hoping to give Laura the heebie-jeebies. Laura didn't usually scare easily and was a very rational person. Dangerous critters were a real possibility, though. Rattlesnakes and venomous spiders were rarely spotted, but they could very well exist here, as well as dangerous large mammals. Within moments, Cheryl came out of the toilet tent, just as Laura came from around the back of it.

Caroline was a few yards away, lighting a campfire. She looked up at them and immediately announced that Laura had a couple of ticks on her shoes. "I hate to say this, but after I go to the bath-room, we all best strip down and check each other over. I've got better repellent we can apply," Caroline suggested.

"Maybe we should all go into the tent, where nobody could possibly see us," Laura requested.

"I don't think so," Caroline responded. "If we have any ticks on us, bringing them into the tent isn't the best thing we could do. Besides, it is still lighter out here for us to see them more easily. It's not only about ticks. Look for anything unusual. On the two of you, we could find just about anything," she joked. "Start stripping down and looking each other over. I'll be back in a couple of minutes after I use the toilet and get the bug repellents. Check your clothes and each other very carefully. Don't have too much fun without me! I'll be right back."

From within the trees, a shadowy figure watched from a secluded site. As Cheryl and Laura undressed, the observing figure began breathing heavily. Reaching his hand down between his legs, he pulled his thick prick out of his trousers and began fingering his exposed, enlarging member.

Within little time, Caroline returned with the repellent and joined her friends in removing her own clothing. Upon naked inspection, all three anointed one another with salve from head to toe. None of them were actually enjoying the experience. They were all rather disgusted by the possibility that a parasite could be affixed to their flesh, sucking out their blood. From a nudity perspective, it was not as if they had not seen one another naked before. It had been a common experience during years of locker-room showers at school and friendly sleepover parties. They had touched one another before while applying body and suntan lotions, so this didn't seem much different from any of those times.

Nudity exhibited around the campsites occurred rather frequently, and the guy spying on them knew it. He had seen just about every possible scenario of kink one could imagine. It was a matter of being in the right place at the right time or loitering at the right campsites long enough. He was not the only one who frequently cruised the woods seeking perverse enjoyment. Stroking himself feverishly as the women rubbed one another, the hidden observer climaxed a load of his seed on the tree bark in front of him. He stared with an evil smirk as he watched his load drip down the tree onto the forest floor by the toes of his boots until the women began putting their clothes back on. While the females were engaging in dress, the man slipped away quietly knowing he would return to see the nymphs again.

"Let's just hope that's the last time I ever have to lay my hands on either of you two skanks," Laura said, partially being truthful but mostly jokingly. She would do anything for her friends, but this had not been something she was expecting. The repellent seemed sticky on her hands. She just wanted to move on with any other activity possible and begin a new conversation.

"It's just part of ecology," Cheryl said with a professional, dignified justification. "At least we are all bug-free for now. That does not mean that something can't crawl or slither its way onto any one of us at a later time. I'm sure this will not be the last inspection we need to endure before departing for home."

Laura and Caroline were not pleased with that observation. It wasn't that they were not aware of nature, but this was their first situation confronting any of nature's potential wickedness. Ticks were not too serious, except for the possibility of carrying disease and the fact that they are gross. Unfortunately, some other dangerous creatures had been known to exist in the Antioch region. Even a mosquito bite could prove deadly. Mosquitoes were known for being one of the deadliest creatures on the planet, but not so much around Antioch, though. Mosquitoes were just more or less a nuisance in these woods, a very annoying pest at that. After a discussion of the dangers, Laura and Caroline were more on edge and aware than ever.

"Thanks, Cheryl," Laura said. "Now my skin is going to crawl. I'll be jumpy all the time we are here."

"You think you are jumpy over that? Just wait until we tell our stories around the campfire," Caroline replied. "I'll have you so scared you'll be awake all night! The stories I plan to tell are horrifically disturbing."

"Thanks to both of you," Cheryl said under her breath. "I'm starting to really regret coming to this camping trip."

"Starting to?" Laura verbally questioned. "I regretted coming since the moment we arrived. Don't tell me you two didn't lead me here under false pretenses. You had no intention of making this about crime research. As you knew, I would have enjoyed that much. It's going to be all about you two in your swimsuits, tanning your fat chalky-white cellulite ripples, isn't it?"

"That's just mean," Cheryl replied knowing very well that Laura was joking. "We don't have fat ripples." She continued. "You've already been told we'd take you over to the boat shop tomorrow morning. There is quite a lot to explore in town too. We can spend the whole day touring this gore fest they call a village tomorrow. What more were you expecting in the middle of nowhere?"

"Yeah, Laura!" Caroline exclaimed. "Besides, I will keep you entertained enough tonight with my astute knowledge of Antioch folklore as soon as I get the fire blazing on high. We'll be needing a roaring fire to help keep the bugs and critters away unless we intend to sit in the screened section of the tent into the night."

"If we do that, we can't sit around the campfire and roast our treats," Cheryl said with protest in her voice. "It's something I have been looking forward to all along."

"Exactly! We all have, I'm sure," Caroline agreed. "But before we do that, I have something to reminisce with you two over. Remember this?" She pulled from her backpack an old scouting manual that she had saved over the years. She was not one to ever get rid of anything. That was even more obvious when she also removed her childhood scouting vest adorned with an eclectic variety of pins and patches. It was a personal possession she had worn at one time in her life, and she took pride in boasting about it. She had always been the most accomplished scout in her troop, but that hadn't mattered much to anyone since she ceased her association with the scouting organization years ago. Even now, her friends did not seem to be as jealous of her scouting accomplishments.

At one time in life, they had been very jealous of Caroline's many achievements when she had originally been honored with awards. Back then, it seemed to all the involved children that every reward, pin, badge, and title had been a major life milestone. Making her friends envious now was not Caroline's intent by showing them her collection. It was merely a means to start a discussion about their past and to invoke memories. Caroline, Cheryl, and Laura had all worked feverishly, often as a team, for the same accomplishment awards back in the day. Upon reminiscing, they all relived the days in their minds as if those days were only yesterday. Many of the awards had even been issued for acts of wilderness survival.

Having reminisced about their past in scouting, Cheryl wanted to talk about a thought she had been thinking about all day since the cigarette lighter had been found. "I was thinking about the name on this lighter," she said. "Julie—Julie is the name of a woman missing from this area, isn't it? What are the chances this lighter belonged to her?"

"It is a common name, Cheryl," Caroline answered. "We may never know. Strange things have happened around here. What if it is her and she is still around these woods? What if she's dead and her corpse is buried here? Her bones could be right under our tent. What if her specter haunts this very campsite?"

"Unlikely that it would be the same Julie," Laura responded as she passed around fire-cooked marshmallows on a stick and began preparing some wieners for roasting. At this time, the fire was at its peak intensity while extreme darkness filled the land beyond its glow. A chill in the air wafted by and made the flames dance in cryptic motion while sending a shiver down Laura's spine. Not that it was very cold, but the air struck her in an odd way and cooled her to the bone. "I did a lot of research on the atrocities committed around here and on missing persons. Julie was not one of the missing persons known to be affiliated with this camp. She is—or was—a friend of a homeowner across the lake. There is not much to Julie's story, except that she vanished. It's the backstory of her acquaintances, which you would find very, very interesting. Just wait until I tell you—if you don't already know, that is."

Cheryl and Caroline were aware of Julie by name, but neither knew much about her or of her friends. It was mostly just common knowledge that Julie was a young woman around the age of twenty-one last year when she went missing from the lake area last summer. She had been visiting a friend and went missing. Her car was later found abandoned. News reports had stated that there was a search for the missing female. Julie never turned up. That was all people heard on the subject.

Seated in folding chairs surrounding the blaze while munching on delicacies, the friends listened while Laura briefly discussed Julie in general.

"But first, listen quietly," Laura requested. "What do you notice?"

"Crickets?" Cheryl quickly said. "Crickets, frogs, and toads are all I hear. The crackling of the firewood too. Thank goodness for no mosquitoes buzzing around us near the fire!"

"No," Laura answered quietly. "It's what we don't hear which I was referring to—no motors from cars, motorcycles, or boats and no civilization, just nature. The man-made noises had stopped."

"Nice," Caroline commented with a smile. "Isn't it? Not much different from home. It's just that we don't often take time to appreciate it. Except the feeling is different here. Have you felt it? It's unfamiliar—dark and ominous with all these trees blocking out the light of the moon and stars. No distractions. No family to come out and disturb us like when we are sitting on our parents' patios. Yet I still get the feeling we are very much not alone here."

Cheryl and Laura nodded in agreement. After a brief period of silence to appreciate nature, Cheryl and Laura broke the mesmerizing tranquility and quietude at the same time. Laura wanted to speak with embellishments about the story of Julie. Cheryl talked over Laura and began with a history lesson, causing Laura to stop speaking and to let Cheryl take center stage.

"Antioch was once inhabited by Native Americans until 1832 when they began to leave the area. What is now the nearest highways were once Native American trails. Back then, they all didn't mind being called Indians, as some people today might argue is racially inappropriate. The Indians fought in the war of 1812 here and the Black Hawk War of 1832 too. There are still many Indian artifacts that are found each year. Finding that arrowhead today was a cool find," Cheryl believed. "I think it is a real one but could just as easily be a souvenir shop trinket. I'm certain we'll see many souvenirs just like it when we go into town. We can ask local people there to tell us about it tomorrow."

"That has nothing to do with the topic we were discussing, but thank you for that boring history lesson," Laura said with a sarcastic smile following her words. "I was in the middle of building to a haunting story about Julie, and you cut in with a history lesson?" she asked with amazement and wonder. "What gives, girl?"

"I'm building a story too, Laura. Just go along with my flow!" Cheryl responded. "We have plenty of time to hear about your goblins and ghosts." Her story continued. Taking time to embellish the details, she attempted to weave a hauntingly intriguing tale. Local facts about the village and lake were being entwined into her demented tale. "In 1939," Cheryl continued, "a sawmill was built here, and it made Antioch a shopping center for commerce at that time. The waterways made it easy to transport paper goods and lumber. That was when bad things began happening around here. The more people who came, the more stories were created and passed along from generation to generation."

Laura and Caroline were becoming bored with this history lesson and felt as if they were all back in school, but both their interests were piqued a bit when Cheryl began explaining about a mysterious, ancient Indian burial ground on the island in Lake Marie. It was reportedly on the very island they had viewed earlier from the lakeshore nearest their campsite. But while interesting, it still had nothing to do with the story of Julie as far as Laura could figure.

Caroline interjected and began speaking after Cheryl finished giving them their history lesson for the trip. Caroline preferred her choice of topics to discuss much more and felt she made a better storyteller, or at least that was her opinion, and she was entitled to it. "I researched the legends and folklore of the area, as we are all interested in them," she stated in a mysterious voice, but cutting off speaking her words midsentence, she stopped and stared blankly.

"What is it?" Laura asked. "You look like you are having a stroke or something. Is everything okay with you? Not that you don't often have that dumb expression on your face!" she said, attempting to joke while making a crazy smile and loony, contorted look upon her own sourpuss.

"I thought I saw a figure over there in the woods. It was just a dark shadow. It moved, and I didn't have time to make out what it was," Caroline answered.

Neither Cheryl nor Laura took her seriously and was certain it was Caroline's way of trying to spook them before telling her gruesome tales in a manner only Caroline could. "Seriously," Caroline said before crossing her heart with her fingers. "I am sure I saw something in the trees, probably even a person." But no matter what she would have said or done to get her friends to believe she had seen something, they would not have believed her. They knew how well she could pull a person's leg, and this was the perfect opportunity for her to build mounting suspense.

After they all finished talking about many other topics, Caroline got her thoughts back on track with the telling of the story of Julie and Julie's affiliation with Lake Marie. "As I was saying, my dear friends, I studied the truth and folklore of Antioch." Caroline had many stories to tell. Several of them coincided with that which they had already discussed. But that did not make her tales any less intriguing to her listeners. There were, however, many tales that could not be proven as fact or fiction, as many tales contained both real details and legends that had been distorted over time. Some had even been embellished upon over generations of time.

Caroline spoke of ghosts, devil worshippers, murdered people, and people who had disappeared. Tying her story to Laura's history topics, she told more of the island in the lake and how an old Indian burial ground on it was said to be cursed—that is, it was cursed to outsiders who invaded the sacred land. It also reportedly had the power to resurrect the dead who were buried there so their spirits could seek vengeance upon their enemies and their ancestors. More recently, the ground on the island had become very unsettled geographically and spiritually. Geographically, the ground was now very saturated with water, rendering it unstable. Spiritually, it was rumored that too many trespassers had been violating the land, taking what archaeological treasures they could grab. Whatever a person decided to believe as the truth—in human spirit or in nature—something there was very angry. Ghosts of local dead were said to wander the very woods they were in.

Cheryl laughed. "That's not even scary. And how do they get from the island to the mainland woods? Don't tell me there is a ghost ship catering to their travel destination desires? Get real!" Cheryl teased Caroline. "I will give you credit for reporting the truth in what you researched. I read some of that as well. The water composition combined with sediment, sand, soil, and plant life all somehow mystically combined to create natural mummification of the Indian corpses there, just in that area. Nobody knows exactly how or why. It just happened naturally with ecological changes over time.

"But before it was even known to have happened, the Indians somehow knew that area was different and that it would someday happen. Imagine that! They were not ignorant folks for that time. Supposedly, there are Indian symbols around the island warning trespassers, protecting the dead, and protecting whatever else is there. It is believed that anyone who has been there and upsets the mojo will be cursed. That rumor apparently has been disproved—for the time being, at least. Not that I believe in any of this hocus-pocus and mumbo jumbo in the first place."

"True. It has been somewhat debunked. Many people affiliated with Julie had been there," Caroline said, jumping back into the conversation. "The sheriff, Dean, had a crew comb the island for any signs of Julie or clues. If you didn't know, Dean is still reportedly having a fairy-tale romance with Janet, Julie's friend. Janet seems to be the center of traumatic news reports surrounding those Antioch mysteries last summer, yet she remains at the lake, holding her head high within the community."

"That is true," Laura continued with some more of her criminal knowledge of the case. "Janet was only twenty-one last year when she obtained what was previously a vacation home on this lake. It had been owned for generations by her family. She moved from Prospect Heights, Illinois, into the lakefront home to be on her own as a full-time local resident and creative artist. I enjoyed viewing some of her canvas and sculpture works online. Her brother, from California, Steven, showed up in town last year to allegedly visit his sister, Janet. Being in the wrong places at the wrong times made him a suspect in local crimes. In particular, the murder of a hooker, Kim Kinski, drew attention to him from local authorities.

"In the meantime, a couple of Janet's Prospect Heights gal pals came to visit. One was Julie, of whom we've been speaking. Julie went missing and was never heard from again. Bless her soul. Here is the really bizarre part of the story. Sadly, Kim's corpse was found chopped up in a basement freezer at Janet's house. Janet's brother was cleared of any suspicion when the son of the owner of the Baskin Boat Shop, Dan, was believed to be the guilty party in all the crimes. As we discussed earlier, Dan was considered mentally incompetent. We all know what happens in such cases. Meanwhile, Janet reportedly has remained here in the house with her new love, Sheriff Dean."

"I don't know how Janet managed to build a life here after all that," Caroline said, providing her own thoughts and opinions on the crimes. "I'd be too upset by it all to stick around. Just imagine living in a house where someone was found chopped to pieces while you were living there. I can't picture what type of person Janet must be."

Laura continued providing even more background information. "Not only that, but that wasn't the only murder affiliated with Janet and her sphere of influence. Remember, the charter boat company owner at this lake was Eli. Eli was also found hacked to pieces in his charter boat. When his remains were found, there were ancient Indian symbols painted on his boat which matched ancient warning-related hieroglyphic symbols found carved into trees on the island a century or more ago. The symbols found on his boat had been painted on in his own blood. I deduced from research that wood from local trees had been used to make his boat by a local wood craftsman. Wood from the trees may have cursed the boat.

"Strangely enough, I studied more obscure reports extensively. From them, I learned that Eli had the symbol carvings, just like the ones on the island trees, carved into his flesh as well. I can't imagine one person did all that alone without concern of being caught. The boat docks attached to Baskin's are not in an out-of-the-way place. What if Baskin's had security cameras? The murder seems too contrived to me. It leads me to believe Eli had been targeted by more than one person involved in the murder." Laura made her final remarks on the matter: "I can't imagine there are multiple people out there who would have banded together to perform this act. They'd have to be a bunch of demented sickos! Imagine someone having any reason to brutally murder a young man, such as Eli was, then being able to convince others to go along with ending the life of someone."

"The area is known for satanic cult rituals as well," Caroline reminded them. "They perform sacrifices together, so it would not be out of the question that multiple psychopaths could have been working together. People have been known to do bizarre things in honor of their religion and gods."

Caroline and Cheryl looked at each other with wonder while Laura downed sips of water before continuing to speak. "I should also tell you about an old man who was Janet's neighbor by the name of Irwin. He had been found in a broken, twisted, bloodied condition of death after what was assumed to be an accidental fall down his own basement stairs. It may have been an accident," she voiced before adding her opinion. "One has to wonder with all that had gone on here last summer. If that's not enough to make you think, that's not even the end of the stories from last summer.

"At the time all this was going on, an observing police officer was posted down the street from Janet's house. He was found dead at his post. He had been injected with poison while on the job, observing and protecting Janet, her guests, and her neighbors. All things considered, Janet went through a few traumatic experiences immediately upon moving here. Despite Sheriff Dean's disturbance of the sacred island grounds during investigations, Dean is still very much alive and doing well in the arms of Janet. So much for being cursed! If I could get a house on this lake and a virile man in my arms, I'd say let's find that curse!" Laura laughed. "We should take a charter boat excursion tomorrow while we are out. The tour host may inform us of some unpublished information." She sure hoped so.

Caroline believed that there might be some truth to the stories other people might consider a bunch of hooey. "I am concerned about screwing around with that voodoo stuff," she said with great worry. "It is local legend that when an Indian is seen by someone in Antioch woods, it means you have been marked by them for judgment. They will protect the righteous and destroy their enemies. Mostly, it means dangerous times ahead for most people unlucky enough to spot them."

"You believe that crap?" Laura asked being of sound and scientific, logical mindset. "Besides, what have you done to offend them? I admit, your face has been known to offend me, but I don't think that's enough to cause their people to set their gaze upon you! Having been beaten with the ugly stick should be enough punishment for you for one lifetime." Again, Laura said that in a joking manner. "If some old Indian is sizing you up in any woods, he's sizing you up to screw your sagging ass and that's all."

"Normally, I'd not believe this legend stuff," Caroline stated in all honesty. "It's just that the Indian I saw on our hike disturbed me. I did not say anything because I knew you two would joke, but he mentally reached out to me. He placed his thoughts into my head like some sort of extrasensory communication. I was warned there would be danger. It wasn't just my intuition. It wasn't my voice. It was his voice in my head. I'm sure the voice was exactly what he would have sounded like had he been speaking words through his own mouth. He conveyed to me that I will be seeing him again, and he isn't ever very far away. I can sense him being near, even now!"

"That's your imagination, Caroline," said Cheryl. "These stories are getting the better of you. Either that, or your pregnancy is already affecting you adversely. Did the doctor say anything you have not told us? Did he put you on some medications? I admit, there has been some marijuana smoke in the air tonight. But I only just lit up a few moments ago, and I'm blowing it away from you. You sure you aren't just freaking out on us? Should we be worried?"

"It's none of that," Laura said knowing her friends would not understand. "I don't want to worry or scare either of you. Can we just agree that life here could be dangerous? We should be alert and coherent at all times."

Cheryl and Laura looked at each other, and Cheryl said, "Now I know you are just trying to spook us with your campfire stories. You are trying to scare us. Good try! Just tell your stories without all the added drama. I think we are big girls and can take care of ourselves." She then laughed, adding, "Although I'd not mind one of those bikers at the next camp taking care of me!"

At this time, the bikers were becoming drunk and rowdy. Their voices were breaking the earlier silence and were carrying in a distanced echo between the rows of towering trees. Gradually, their voices began sounding like a conglomerate of wild monkeys gathering in a tropical rainforest. It was a reminder to the women that they were not as isolated as they had begun to feel when they first sat down at their fire.

Caroline reacted negatively in tone to Cheryl's thought even if she had only said it in jest. "Is sex all you ever think of, you whore?" No matter what Caroline would say, they were never fighting words, as the friends knew such comments were always meant to be of a joking nature and never as crudely cruel.

"That's easy for you to say, li'l Ms. I Got a Bun in the Oven," Cheryl quipped as she inhaled her breath deeply to form an extended stomach. "You aren't the only one who deserves a good fuck once in a while. The pretty girls need dick too!" She smiled with a batting of her long eyelashes. "Do tell, Caroline! What about Dale made you want to jump his bones? Nothing about him in particular stood out to me."

Laughing loudly, Caroline stated, "Something of Dale's stands out all right! It stands out a whole lot! We were making out in the back seat of his car, heavy petting. You girls should remember what that is like. I got wet. I moved my leg and discovered he had an enormous erection. He had shorts on, and it poked out of the leg section. Let me say that he was not wearing short shorts. I made a joke and began petting it as if it was a fuzzy pet. Any jokes ceased, and it became serious. He got the look of a wild animal on his face. He took me. There was no way I could have fended him off even if I had rejected his advances. I swear he barely stuck it in me for a partial thrust. It was so big that I was scared I'd not be able to take his size.

"Before I knew if I'd be able to take it or not, he was in as far as he apparently needed to be and was done. I was a bit disturbed for a moment. Then he began going down on me. He said that I would be very pleased when he finished with his oral expertise. His mouth was so warm and delicate. His tongue hit all the right spots. For the first time in my life, a man made me orgasm. I was impressed. He looks at me differently—with lust in his eyes—ever since. It's as if I can see little hearts floating in the air around him while his eyes do crazy things." Caroline was suddenly smiling happily. "I know I have not known him long at all, but he makes me happy."

Laura made an observant comment. "Well, if a girl can't find a man in this town to spread her legs, she must be one nasty ho. There are men everywhere sporting nothing but skimpy swimsuits and partying out there. Just shake a baby-maker in front of a sea of testosterone, and the cocks will be jumping out of the water. If not, that poor honey be in some sad shape, bitches! I hear even the men have no trouble scoring a cumload in this village. Plenty of seamen to go around! Ah, that's a pun, girls. Water, men—get it?" Laura said, trying to be funny, while the marijuana she was smoking started taking full effect.

"We got it. Now if you sluts would be kind enough to get off your sex topics, I'd like to talk about some real stuff that's been going on around here," Caroline continued saying.

Sticking her tongue out in a playful manner, Laura reacted to Caroline's comment. "Okay. But I'm telling you, if my pussy doesn't see action by the time we leave here, I'm going to force you down there to take care of it for me, Sugar Lips," she said with a wink of her left eye.

"Don't worry about it, Laura," Caroline informed her. "We already set you up with the gate guard. He's gonna get you creaming really good. You'll love it!"

Again, Laura stuck her tongue out in response.

"Hey, look at Laura," said Caroline. "It's a lesbian with a hard-on!" All the girls laughed at the age-old reply and continued joking before quieting down to take a silent moment to breathe. "I feel kind of silly, kind of goofy. I don't think it's secondhand pot smoke from you two. Do either of you feel the way I do right now?" Caroline was wondering.

"I sure enough do, Hot Lips," Laura admitted. "We be gettin' stoned! Don't know why you should feel high with no firsthand weed and no beers, but enjoy the wild ride. We hope you are not going to miss out completely on party time on this trip because of this baby bump handicap. On that sore subject, what do you think you will do to remedy that problem situation?"

"At this time, I am going to try to remain as sober as I can," Caroline answered. "I think that is best. I'll get some birthing books and leave the pot smoking for you two for a while." It was not a cool thing to do to a developing baby."

"Seriously, Caroline? You are thinking of carrying this baby to birth?" Laura asked with amazement in her voice.

Caroline pondered a bit before answering. "Before I left, I told my mom and dad that I did not want to keep it. They said they'd support me in my decision, but they suggested I think about it a lot before I make any decision. They don't want any responsibility raising a grandchild. I don't want to be a mother. I definitely don't want to be a wife. If the baby is born, I guess I will give it up for adoption. That does not imply that I want to carry a baby inside me. So yeah, it will hinder my partying for a while—not that I ever was a stoner like the two of you." Caroline smiled. They were not really stoners. They just enjoyed an occasional good time.

Laura cheered things up by informing Caroline, "It's not like you're all fat and everything yet. But just in case some guy looks your way, can I call dibs on him if you are not looking to get knocked up again with some far-fetched two-father, fraternal-twin thing?" She was just being screwy.

"Considering all the tales around these parts, I'm likely to birth a creature from a lagoon. It would probably still be an improvement over the baby's father!" Caroline joked as a gesture that she wasn't going to allow serious topics to interfere with their trip. In fact, she would rather keep her negative thoughts to herself and not discuss them at all.

Avoiding the conversation topic of babies would be something she would need to learn how to best deal with. However, it was nice that people were concerned about it and were trying to cheer her up.

"Let's change the topic," Cheryl suggested. She knew Caroline would appreciate that. "In my research of crime scenes in this area, I could not help but feel that nothing has ever been solved. Nothing has ever been proven or laid to rest. Several campers have gone missing over the years. Not all those campers were alone. There is an open case on the books of four campers consisting of two guys and two girls who disappeared. As you know, this was their campsite. Their asses likely sat in the very spots we are seated now. All their belongings remained in place, but the individuals did not. That was the big mystery with which I permitted you two bimbos to lure me here."

"Bimbos?" Laura questioned. "Who are you referring to as bimbos?" Again, she stuck out her tongue at Caroline.

"You stick out that tongue at me one more time, I'll have you slopping up my baby birthing ooze with it, chick," Caroline disgustingly joked. Over the years, she had learned she could alter Cheryl's behavior if she topped her in grossness. It wasn't something Caroline enjoyed doing. It simply achieved a goal. This time, as expected, it worked.

Following Caroline's comment, Laura cleaned up her attitude. She was feeling a bit more stoned than she would normally get under similar party experiences and couldn't figure why. Perhaps it was the country air, which had something to do with oxygenating her blood, providing her a higher energy level, she considered. She took a deep, invigorating breath and exhaled slowly before speaking. "You know, girls, that dead old man Irwin was rumored to be a pimp. It was said that he was suspected of being tied to some prostitution ring, sex cult, or something like that. Again, they never proved anything conclusively. If they did find any such evidence, authorities never released all the details to the public. And what of that Baskin Boat Shop guy Dan? Do you think they have enough evidence to convict him properly of all the crimes if he ever were to stand trial?"

Caroline and Cheryl shrugged their shoulders. Laura took in another deep breath and thought for a moment. She noticed that the other women had become more on the quiet side and assumed they were becoming tired. Either that, or their buzzed effects had altered their moods and they had mellowed out.

Laura spoke up again. "All I know is that Dan had been making keys at the boat shop for people and was, unbeknownst to anyone, making an extra key for himself. He was then using his extra keys to access people's homes. He was up to doing no good. I also heard he had stolen the sheriff's uniform. Authorities found that in his home, according to the newspaper article I read. Imagine, if you will, someone coming and going from your home with a key you don't know they have. It's a creepy invasion and just plain weird."

Night was wearing on, and the forest became immensely dark. Human voices from the distant camp ceased. Bugs and insects became more invasive and voracious as the campfire wore down to smoldering, glowing embers of molten lava hues. But despite the blackness directly around them, the lake mysteriously glowed from the night moon's reflection of moonbeams off the slightest of ripples upon the water's surface. Time had come for the group to slumber. After dousing out any remaining fire with water, they each took their turn in their portable potty tent. Having relieved themselves, they performed a bodily inspection for parasites before entering their sleeping quarters for the night.

From outside their tent, a figure was again watching from within the seclusion of nearby trees. He was delighted to be watching—peeping and undetected. In his hand, he held a pair of underwear he had raided from Cheryl's belongings while the women were on their earlier hike. He stood in the dark shadows, rubbing his face in the soft, silky panties that he had pilfered.

As he watched each woman leave the toilet facility and enter the main tent, he alternated rubbing the undergarment over his exposed, swollen genitals and then sniffing his own stale, musky man scent off the frail fabric. How he wished they had been worn by one of the females so as to enjoy their juicy scent. No matter, his own smell would do, and his active imagination drove him wild. Once all the women were in their tent and the zipper had been securely drawn up so they were out of sight, he masturbated into the undergarment fabric until his member exploded in a powerful shot of seminal fluid release. He made certain that every drop of his man juice was preserved in the cloth for later appreciation.

Chapter 3

From strategically placed motion cameras located inside the girls' main tent, potty tent, and the trees around their campsite, viewers were able to receive moving images of every action the girls were making and could listen in on their conversations. Some cameras had been hooked up around the campsites for a long time, having caught the escapades of many campers prior. Other cameras had specifically been placed in the girls' tents during their afternoon hike away from camp. So sophisticated were the cameras that they were tiny enough to go undetected and still produce a crystal-clear, bright image. Sound sensitivity was so technologically advanced that it could pick up the buzz of a fly entering a tent.

These were no ordinary pieces of equipment a common citizen could get their hands on. One potty tent camera, in particular, had been strategically placed so that it would actually film excrement being released from Caroline, Cheryl, or Laura each time they relieved themselves. It was evident to those who had placed the cameras that these three women would not be engaging in sex acts together. That meant this camping party would be of little interest to most of the syndicate's bigger spectating money spenders, who were most often interested in viewing only candid sex acts.

Only two cameras were really needed at the girls' site to suit the syndicate during their stay since action would be limited. Both cameras would be catering to private viewers on the dark web. The one in the portable toilet was placed to cater specifically to people all over the world who were into natural bodily functions. Another placed in the main tent would eventually catch some nicer, more artistic images of any one of the girls undressing. The solid canvas of the tents made for perfect backdrops for these unknowing models, whose candid pictures would be sold to individuals and black market kink magazine publishers everywhere. Money was intended to be made by the syndicate from every market angle possible.

Along with customers paying to view the televised images, a gambling ring was raking in big bucks with all sorts of perverse bets being placed. Horny viewers placing bets on individual's bodily details and actions were willing to gamble large amounts of cash in order to win exorbitant amounts of money and prizes. Any topic was fair game to be bet upon. Who had shaved genitals? Whose carpeting matched the drapes? Who would masturbate or have sex in their tents or in the woods? Even who would have diarrhea problems were big gaming. It was a multimillion-dollar business that Caroline, Cheryl, and Laura would soon learn about.

For today, customers had delighted in the humor they reveled in as each lady experienced an invasion of privacy. Nothing was left to the imagination as far as this scheme was involved. Any which way a buck could be made, it was. Each member in the camping party had already dropped their pants to squat and had exposed every inch of their privates. They had already been viewed, their images had been transmitted over the Internet, and they had starred in motion film; and all their many images had been converted into still photographs as well. They had been bet upon by anyone worldwide who could access all the disgusting displays.

There wasn't much need to keep the cameras up after having filmed what could be of interest. Keeping them up would only increase the possibility of being found out. Some cameras were already being removed this very night while the girls slept.

Locally, a man named Armani headed the syndicate of these cam crimes. That position was bestowed upon him only recently, catapulting his income to levels higher than that which he earned as a gigolo and occasional porn model. But despite financial gain, he remained living a modest lifestyle. Perhaps that was, in part, due to his having no place in particular to go. Still living in the home he had grown up in, the home sat positioned on Lake Marie above a block water-retaining wall across the shoreline of the campsite area.

In his basement, Armani sat at a sophisticated computer setup, overseeing a delay in the images sent to him from remote coworkers. They controlled and edited which images could potentially be suitably released to the public and, subsequently, which images should not be. As the local controller, it was his responsibility to make the final decision on which of those edited images were suitable for final transmission and to which computer sites they would be sent before hitting the final transmission buttons. It was also his job to oversee all operations within the region. This was a Mob job he had inherited from a friend and neighbor upon the man's passing. That man was the old man Irwin, who had been found dead at the base of his basement stairs a year ago.

Armani had always thought of Irwin as a father figure since his own mother and father were long since deceased. Even when alive, his mother and father had never been the best parents. Irwin had often taken Armani out on the lake to fish or to play ball games when Armani's father was unavailable or was being an abusive drunk. In return, Armani had taken care of Irwin and another neighbor, Gertty, ever since he could remember. Her name was a shortened version of Gertrude, which he had always thought she had chosen to spell unusually because she wanted to be different.

While doing all that Armani did was a burden to him at times, they had done so much for him in return. In his youth, Armani had mowed their lawns and did everything a child his age could manage to do not only to please people but also to make a dollar in the process, and not just for Irwin and Irwin's next-door neighbor Gertty but for many other neighbors too. They sought his companionship and services as much as he sought theirs. Most people from his childhood had come and gone. Gertty remained living in the very same home he had always known her to have lived in. She still resided alone with only one house between Armani's and her own dwelling. The house between them belonged to and was resided in by Janet.

Janet was a young woman five years Armani's junior. He had known her since she had been born. Janet's family had owned the house Janet now solely owned for as long as his family had owned the house he now lived in. As soon as Janet became his full-time neighbor, upon her turning twenty-one years of age, a sexual affair flared up between them. But it was short-lived, as Janet had quickly learned that Armani had many secrets he had been keeping. His sexual prowess and appreciation for filmography were no secret to Janet, as she became an unwilling participant in his cinematic activities. After becoming aware somewhat of his activities, Janet abruptly ended the relationship. As far as she was still aware, Armani's lust for photography was only a personal fetish hobby. She, as did most people, had no knowledge of Armani's business or Mob dealings. Syndicates would go to any length to protect Armani's secret involvements with them.

Irwin, though, was another story. The limits to his sexual involvement and fetishes with Armani were extensive. Armani was a handsome, well-endowed Italian stallion of a stud who had no limitations where sexual boundaries were concerned. Armani recruited prostitutes for Irwin to pimp. Armani posed naked, even when he was underage, for films and photographs, which he and Irwin made a lot of money from. Armani became the male star in many of Irwin's low-budget porn productions. In addition, Armani set up cameras for Irwin to eavesdrop on and promote the private escapades of others. The industry was one Irwin had taught Armani well, and Armani had grown into a man of few morals. This was likely because of the corruption Irwin had introduced him to, which seemed to be compensation for lack of adequate parenting.

Isolated on the secluded Lake Marie, Armani resided in his modest fortress of solitude. Money and material possessions were never of importance to him, yet he had accrued a lot of it. The only thing in life that mattered to him was his own immense, insatiable desire for sexual gratification. Socially, his life rarely expanded beyond his immediate neighbors, Janet and Gertty, whom he adored as family as best he knew how. During the day, Armani often worked as a mild-mannered gardener and handyman around the Antioch community.

Most residents who employed his services were part-time vacation homeowners too busy with their own summer lake activities and local social agendas when they were in town. Places occupied more frequently were usually rental properties or were occupied by retired elderly persons. Both types of properties were in need of as much help functioning day to day as they could get. Over the years, these people had come to trust Armani to provide the household services and personal needs they required. His reputation was untarnished as being the most reliable, most knowledgeable, and most efficient person to call upon.

Except for meeting with those clients while servicing their abodes, he chiefly kept to himself. He was definitely a loner, most people would say. Many of his clients would try to hook him up on dates with young women they thought to whom he would make a suitable mate. He would always manage to decline in an appropriate manner. Knowing all the prostitutes in nearby areas, he was able to produce an attractive woman whenever he wanted or needed. Most of those women of easy virtue owed him favors and were more than willing to accommodate his needs whatever they might be, whenever he would call upon them.

Armani was not open about any details of his life with most people, except for two individuals. One was Janet, who had moved in full-time next door only about a year ago. She had long been visiting the neighborhood with her family for twenty-one years in what was the family summer home. And the other was Gertrude, who was known as Gertty by most everyone. For a woman of fiftyish, people would think her to be a woman of a much older age. The truth was that she was an alcoholic who had led a hard life. She appeared to many people to have been ridden hard and put away wet.

Armani, now with Janet's assistance, had been turning Gertty's perspective on life around. While Gertty was rarely known to leave her home, anyone who might see her most recently would be amazed by the positive transformation she had made. Her body had recently become more mobile, limber, and slender while making positive efforts to keep up her appearance. Even though she still hit the bottle of gin, she now tried to maintain some decorum. Gin had always been her drink of choice. Despite Armani helping Gertty to somewhat control her addiction and improve her life, he wasn't able to turn his own life around. His sexual passions left him feeling trapped and hopeless. His involvement with international crime syndicates often left him feeling trapped and hopeless as well. If he ever abandoned his Mob position, he would surely end up as Irwin had: dead! So as not to complicate life, Armani managed to keep his syndicate dealings a secret from his neighbors while presenting the public persona of a mild-mannered, reclusive handyman. It worked.

Having kept his life a secret, except only from those who needed to be involved, Armani had inherited Irwin's house after Irwin's unfortunate demise. Also left to him recently was Irwin's Mob position. Nobody dear to his heart knew of that, though. If they intended to live, it was best nobody ever found out. It had taken a lot for Armani to cover Irwin's dealings after Irwin had been reported dead by Janet and Gertty. Unbeknownst to anyone at that time, Armani had found Irwin first. Luckily, he had found him soon enough to remove any evidence from Irwin's home that could have blown their operation. That would have not only incriminated himself but would also have involved other locals too.

Taking pride in his own ingenuity, Armani made sure a few clues had been left hidden around Irwin's home to throw off authorities and send them on misguided investigation paths. That was how good Armani was at manipulating facts and situations to make others believe what he wanted them to believe. It was all for the best, as there were people around who would stop at nothing to cover the Mob's and other related syndicate's activities. Armani knew that and was no dummy. In general, he was also not scared of much. He might not have been book-educated, but he did have street smarts. He also had brawn and above-average, innocent-appearing good looks. Those attributes seemed to carry him well through life. They could amount to a dangerous combination.

The rest of Irwin's meager belongings had been passed on to the estate of Irwin's sister. She was in no condition to contest any legal will decisions in her old, decrepit age. She was barely alive and would have amazed anyone who might have learned that she was still living a year after Irwin had passed—not that it mattered to Armani. The woman was barely hanging on to life minute to minute. If she had known how Irwin had acquired anything he had owned in life, she likely would not have wanted any inheritance anyway. Had anyone known his belongings were obtained with Mob money, they would likely all have been seized. Armani was just happy with what he got.

As Armani sat in his chair, viewing a multitude of images of Caroline, Laura, and Cheryl, he found humor in the details of each of the three's pussy hair formations. Cheryl had been fully shaven. Laura had a full, thick blonde bush. Caroline's was the nicest, he thought, displaying a designed runway-style trimming. Caroline's bathroom procedure also interested Armani and the web viewing audience. She always took a moment to feel her pussy lips and spread the labia while in the process of sitting on the throne. Her ritual was always followed by smelling of her fingers. One camera under the toilet seat managed to catch Caroline in perfect light and position, showing every graphic detail. Another in the corner crease of the tent captured the rest of her ritual. Actually, all the females' actions in there were captured, but it was Caroline's that interested him, and the others didn't.

Some of the pictures were tasteful for candid, nude shots, and it was no wonder Armani was exciting himself viewing them. He had been known to get aroused at the drop of a hat. While contemplating masturbating, his thoughts were distracted by a ringtone from one of his multiple cellphones. He picked up the device immediately and pushed the necessary buttons to answer it.

"Her," a voice all too familiar to Armani said. "The one they call Caroline, there is a buyer for her as quickly as they can produce her." Armani acknowledged the message with approval and disconnected the caller without further discussion. The less time spent on the phone, the better in case business calls were ever being traced or eavesdropped upon. He knew the person they wanted delivered to them, and it was just another business deal as usual. It was not in Armani's job description to deliver Caroline in person. He would only need to pass on the word to those who would perform the dirty work.

Not yet, though, he thought. This trio of beauties could still provide some material suitable for the foreign web and snuff film editing. Armani didn't want to miss anything he could use. Material was money in the pocket. In time, soon enough, at least Caroline would come to know the frightening truth behind the horrible plans awaiting her and the baby she was carrying. To Armani, she was just another dollar sign making him money he didn't need in the least. It was all a game he enjoyed to fulfill time in an otherwise empty, loveless, and corrupt life.

It was in moments like this when Armani would begin to feel unease. Before Janet moved to town, bringing an appealing sensuousness with her, his activities had provided some comfort for the pent-up anger and emotional pain he continuously endured. Now Janet was so near. She was only next door to him. But she had rejected him. Each time he now thought of gaining some satisfaction from his illicit activities, those thoughts became thwarted by visions of Janet. In a perfect world, she would be only his, and they would live happily ever after. In the reality of his imperfect world, Janet only confused his twisted mind more so. She was an angel, and he was a demon in his visions.

Armani wanted to be all Janet wanted him to be. He was aware it would forever be impossible for him to regain Janet's trust and escape the life he had become trapped in. It was a life tormented by his own twisted thoughts and actions. It was a life he was forever trapped in by his conspirators. And all that while being tempted by the one desire he could not allow himself to just take—take in the same way he had taken so many other poor souls and robbed them of their innocence, in the same manner in which he felt his own innocence had once been robbed from him. In his mind now, the taking of Janet was what he desired most. She was the one woman he had grown to secretly love—that is, if he could ever know what love was.

Topping that all off, Janet was now involved with Sheriff Dean, his own childhood best friend. How he now loathed Dean. Armani despised that he had to smile and be polite each time he saw Dean. How it agonizingly tormented him each time he saw Dean and Janet embrace or show any act of affection toward each other. It was a type of affection he knew he would never gain from Janet willingly. If he could ever reveal his secrets to her or anyone in full, nobody would ever show him such affection as Janet showed

Dean, least of all the likes of an angel such as Janet was perceived to be. What a tangled web of self-torment Armani had spent his life weaving. But despite the complexity of his own life, he always seemed to think of himself as the victim or to find a way to blame others for his being the demon he had become.

Breaking his concentration from the horrors consuming his mind, Armani continued to analyze a multitude of images. He smiled an evil grin knowing any bit of activity the women provided would make for great foreign web porn and snuff films he would himself later edit for marketing. Yes, these girls would be stars in a movie they were unaware was being made. It might even be a movie they might actually survive the making of. Had they known, they obviously would not have consented. Already, so many people Armani had been in contact with during his life had died because of this business. He hoped he would never become another one of those statistics. Such a horrible, fiendish future surely awaited these young women, and they had no clue.

Armani did, however, realize that only he could be of any help in being their savior if he chose to be so. That gave him a feeling of diverse power he was unable to fully comprehend because he probably just didn't want that responsibility. Knowing he had the power was grand, but utilizing it was something different. He could be a devil to people. He could also be their only savior. The balance between good and evil was so vast in his own mind that he could not even begin to bridge that gap with comprehension. Nor did Armani ever think about how his own decisions might someday influence his own fate and well-being. It was all too confusing for him.

Chapter 4

Having slept soundly into the night, none of the campers had awakened during the blackness to even briefly observe the dark world around them. What slithered and crept from the shadows or emerged from the darkness in hazy fog was of furthest concern in any of their minds. Dreams and thoughts were only that of the pleasant sort. Meanwhile, steam arose from and appeared to dance atop the surface of Lake Marie. The water beneath the vapor created a dense, vaporous cloud and blocked any image of the surface of the water. Eerily, the damp steam wafted inland throughout the forest and created a winding tapestry of haunting beauty. Had the women awakened, it would have been nearly impossible for them to see but only a couple of feet in front of their faces in the night in the fog. But they hadn't awakened, and so it mattered not.

As the new day began, the dense fog only started to barely clear. It would take some hours into the morning sun to completely clear the vicinity of all mist and dry up any remaining residue. A haze was still carpeting the ground so heavily that anyone walking outside would not see their feet touching the dirt. It was not as thick of a fog as the night had brought at its peak, but it was still thick enough to alter vision and perception. The rising sun was helping illuminate the surroundings as the blinding shade of night diminished. Stepping outdoors in the early morning hours on this day could prove to be dangerous if one was not careful where they landed their foot.

One by one, the women awakened and attempted to work their way to their toilet facility tent. Caroline went first. Her attempt to walk the mere fifteen feet to their toilet did not go well. Just a few steps outside the tent, she tripped and fell over a sizable branch under the ground fog. She knew the wood had not been there earlier, as the area had been completely cleared clean upon their arrival. Caroline chose not to be overly analytical about it, as branches often naturally broke off and fell from trees. Her fall to the ground caused her pain, but she would be okay and would not make any fuss over it.

Caroline soon returned to the main tent with a walking stick and suggested the others use it to feel their way while outside the tent. It would be prudent even if only a few steps were being taken out there. She did not want to ruin their first full day together because of any avoidable injuries. They heeded her advice and decided that carrying sticks with them at all times in the future might not be such a bad idea while navigating the potentially rough terrain. "Beware of gopher and snake holes too," Caroline advised. "The ground can cave in easily beneath you."

Morning wore on as the fog gradually cleared. The beauty of the park was once again being exposed for the awesome, stunning, panoramic environment it was. The women sat in the screened room, sipping their choice of morning beverages while chatting. They were anxiously awaiting an appropriate time to drive to the boat shop and downtown to the village shops. They knew the boat shop diner would be serving breakfast shortly. They were famished and unanimously agreed upon the restaurant at the establishment to fill their bellies. It was wonderful, they thought, that they would be able to explore the business as they had planned and get their breakfast at the same time.

"Look at those beautiful birds," Caroline pointed out. "They are egrets and cranes drawn to the lake water." A flock of each had been gradually accumulating, floating down from the gradually brightening sky above. Most were hunting fish in the shallows of the lake, pecking out marine life from under a thin layer of remaining fog. The few Caroline and her friends were seeing had wandered into the trees within their campsite.

Once the women heard the sound of motorboats on the lake, the birds seemed to flee from the area. As activity in the world around them started to pulsate, they felt comfortable more aggressively getting a move on starting their own day ahead. Calm water became choppy. Fish stopped jumping. Animals disappeared from sight. The mist churned atop the lake water and dissipated rapidly. Noise was mounting. The early morning action was a good sign as to how busy the lake activities would become later in the day. It was bound to be a very bustling day on Lake Marie. Again, the loudest of voices were becoming audible from the nearby bikers' campsite, and then their Hogs began revving up. It was as good a time as any to leave the grounds and explore Antioch. For those who had never done that, it should become a memorable excursion.

As the women departed the park, their car seemed to be experiencing an unusually rough ride. The rough dirt and gravel roads winding through the campsite were not well-laid and were chock-full of potholes. The low-riding car seemed to bounce in and out of many pits, shaking and rattling the car in all directions. The road seemed to be in a worse condition than any of them had noticed coming in. The series of holes and dips still led them to the main gate, where their friend the gate guard made an attempt to stop them long enough to talk. Instead, the women waved and passed by without stopping. Had they known what he wanted to speak to them about, perhaps they would have been better off stopping.

The Baskin Boat Shop was their first stop for the day. Walking through the screened door and into the small market part of the establishment, a tiny brass bell tinkled, alerting any staff they had entered. It was charming inside. The aura was that of an old-time mom-and-pop market from days gone by. It was reminiscent of the early 1960s. A distinct, pleasant aroma was created by a melding of all sorts of items being sold in the shop. Fresh-cut flowers by the door were the predominant scent. A small bakery counter smelled sweet and delicious. The deli counter air was ripe with cheeses and cold cuts. Cooking food aromas wafted into the shopping area from the back kitchen.

A rather handsome young man working at the shop greeted the women as they entered. "Welcome," he said. "I haven't seen you three lovely women here before. Are you visiting?"

"Yes," Caroline replied thinking of how friendly he seemed in comparison to other establishments she was used to frequenting. "We are from over the state border. We are camping at the campgrounds at Lake Marie."

"Ah, Camp Oak. My name is Chuck," he said. "It's really Charlie, but folks just call me Chuck. Just call out my name if I can be of help."

"Thank you," Cheryl replied, dragging Caroline away from the conversation by the arm and over to a bulletin board Laura was already studying.

"Would you just look at this?" Laura suggested. It was a board on the wall containing a plethora of advertisements, business cards, and pictures of missing people. They all stared at the pictures intently. Julie's picture was still hanging there.

"Hey, Chuck!" Laura called out. "Are these the people we have been hearing about in the news? The ones who are missing from the campsite here?"

Chuck walked over to the board and discussed it in some detail. "These campers are missing people. The police are looking for them. I don't know if they are missing because they want to be or because they ran into trouble," he informed them, "except this one young lady. Her name is Julie. Julie is the friend of a resident here on the lake who went missing while visiting her local friend. Folks around these parts tend to think of her more prominently, as people here knew her. She wasn't just another unknown tourist."

"Do you know her friend?" Laura inquired.

"I'm new working here at the shop, and I don't know everyone all that well yet," Chuck admitted. "I assume you are speaking of her good friend Janet. I have met and seen Janet a few times when she came in here. She would have preferred to stay out of the news with connection to her missing friend, but you know how the media is when it comes to reporting. Between the news people, authorities, and tourists, someone is always asking questions. Locally, nobody around claims to have heard anything new or recent pertaining to any of these people. No new faces on the board either. I assume pieces of these puzzles will come to light someday when we least expect it. For now, they are just pictures on a bulletin board as far as I'm concerned."

"We are familiar with the stories as far as what we learned from the news," Laura told Chuck. "We'd like to meet Janet, if possible. Do you know her address? You see, I'm educating myself to be a criminologist and would very interested in speaking with her regarding the disappearances."

"Many people have asked about the local news stories and about Janet in particular," Chuck said, directing his voice toward Laura. "Nobody has ever asked for Janet's address, though." He pondered their request momentarily before starting to speak again. "Since she discovered the body of the Kinski woman chopped up in her basement freezer and has been dealing with the disappearance of Julie, she has tried to lie low," he said while considering their request some more. "While she may think it an invasion of her privacy, you women seem like nice women. If you promise not to tell her where you obtained her address from, I can tell you which house she lives in. I don't know the exact street address, though, but it's not hard to find, as there are only a few private homes on the lake, and they are not difficult to reach."

"That would be so kind of you to direct us," Laura said with a polite smile.

"If you know anything of criminology and can help Dan Baskin become cleared of the crimes of which he has been accused, I'm willing to be of any help," Chuck said. "Dan's family has been very distraught over the whole ordeal. Anything which can be of help would be appreciated by them, I'm sure. They've been so kind to me."

"We will do our best," Laura offered, not thinking they would ever be of any real help.

Chuck provided detailed directions to Janet's home on a small slip of cash register receipt paper with a tiny, hand-drawn map. "You'll know her house. It will be on the left, the lakeside. You'll see her garage with a coach house apartment above it. It's the only house with the garage tall enough to store a big boat and have a second-floor apartment above it. She uses the upper space as a work studio. She's a local artist. Perhaps Janet would be more apt to entertain you if she thought you were there to see her artworks."

"Thanks, Chuck! You are a sweetheart," Laura told him. "We would like to have breakfast here before we shop. Is the diner section open?"

"Sure!" Chuck said almost too overly enthusiastically. The women could tell he liked them. "We open at daybreak during the warmer seasons. Just have a seat at any of the tables outside. I'll get you settled with menus and then send someone right out to take your order."

"Thanks," the women told him as they moved toward the outside tables overlooking the lake.

Laura provided a flirtatious wink as she noticed Chuck locking eyes with her. Chuck winked back and provided a sexy smile. Laura could tell he was younger than she, but that would not stop her from picking him up sometime if the mood struck her. She thought he was very cute and he was of legal age.

Cheryl walked ahead while Caroline and Laura followed. Chuck was right behind them. Having selected what really was the best table—located at the end of a deck extending over the water—they commented upon how phenomenal the view was. Chuck pulled out Laura's chair as they seated themselves.

The other women couldn't miss the mutual attraction shared between Chuck and Laura.

Morning fog had completely lifted by this time, as the quickly warming sun had burned it all off. Larger motorboats were starting to make their appearance, as most all the smaller fishing boats had become scarce. Everything happening was of interest to the women, and they delighted in discussing every detail of the visuals.

Before long, breakfast had been served and consumed. Rising up from their seats, the three of them proceeded to tour the establishment. Capable of storing a hundred boats stacked a few high, the boat storage facility was amazing to them. Just how they hoisted the boats up in the air was an amazing sight to behold. Boats were stacked as high as five on a crane-like system. Many boats were for sale on the lot, and the luxuriousness of some there was grand. They had no idea some boat owners owned such phenomenal boats on a country lake. They looked like something someone would have on a sea or on the larger Great Lakes. Then again, Lake Marie and its connecting waters were not that small.

Inside the main shopping building, everything looked just as they had seen advertised online. Some aisles appeared as though they had remained unchanged for decades. Some products being sold were brand names the women had not thought about in years. The owner had probably been carrying those products over time and refused to keep up with current consumer product trends. It was refreshing to see in this day and age.

A small hardware section was well-stocked with basic hardware needs. Caroline was quick to point out a key-making machine behind the counter. "I'd bet that is the same machine Dan used to make keys to gain entry into the homes of his victims," she whispered while tapping her friends on their shoulders. They nodded in agreement. In fact, it was the very same machine. Their eyes were fixated upon the contraption as if it was something stupendous to behold.

There were other sections of the store viewed, but none was of as much interest to them. One section was for fishing enthusiasts. It contained various baits, poles and reels, lures, sonar equipment, nets, and anything one planning on fishing might desire. It surprised the women how advanced and impressive some of the equipment was. They never expected that fish reaching six feet in length could be swimming in the Lake Marie waters. It rather made the old legend of an eight-foot catfish swallowing small children in the lake seem more believable. Another section was set up for displaying a few camping necessities. It did seem a bit crude that there was an advertisement for a horror movie about a camp slasher posted above that merchandise. The advertisement was probably posted because the movie was actually playing at the theater in town. Perhaps they would even go to see it one night if they had nothing better to do. They would at least be able to escape the bugs and heat for a spell if it got to be too much for them.

Of most interest to the women were the gift shop and food market sections. The gift shop had all sorts of typical souvenirs and small gift items while the food market section was where they entered when they first arrived. Homemade bakery goods gained the attention of the three. Each dessert looked more scrumptious and tempting than the one they viewed before it. Chuck moved over to the counter and seemed to be continuing to flirt with Laura. It then became obvious he was flirting when he gifted her with a complimentary box of sweets. "A small gesture for something else sweet," he called them. It would not be noticed by Laura until later, but he had written his name and personal phone number inside the box cover.

Laura, Caroline, and Cheryl, each carrying many items in their clutches, followed Chuck to an old-fashioned cash register atop a glass countertop. Under the glass in the countertop, more newspaper clippings could be seen displayed. Many were vintage ads of items once sold on the premises. Others were articles on locals or visitors having previously visited the shop. Noticing attention was being paid to the articles, Chuck made an attempt to sell them a book he had written on the Antioch area. "Most all these articles are mentioned in my book," Chuck said with an additional sales pitch reminiscent of used-car salesmen. "It's much easier to buy the book and read it at your convenience than to try to take all the information in while standing at this counter. I'm not the best writer there is. My stories are considered to be informative and entertaining, though."

The women couldn't resist each adding his book to their purchases and requested Chuck sign them all. It pleased him that they asked. "Thanks for everything, Chuck," Caroline said first with the others following in gratuity. "By the way," Caroline questioned, "is that the key-cutting machine over there which Dan supposedly used to make duplicate keys on? Then he used the duplicate keys to access people's homes and such to reportedly commit crimes?"

As Chuck sadly nodded his head in a confirming motion, Laura commented, "I was trying to be sincere and not mention Dan's name, but since Caroline brought it up, I must ask. Did you personally know Dan Baskin?"

"I knew of him from school," Chuck confessed. "I am the newest employee, and I replaced him since his absence from here. I'm not exactly much of a replacement in all ways. You know, he is the son of the owners, Mrs. and Mr. Baskin. He grew up helping his mom and dad around here. He was born into this business and proficient at his work. I am just learning and a very poor substitute for Dan, I'm afraid."

"Yet you took a job working at filling his shoes?" Laura asked in amazement. "Just the murder of Dan's alleged friend Eli in the boat he kept docked here would have freaked me out."

"Those who knew Dan will find it difficult to believe that he killed Eli. I knew Eli in school too, and the two of them were really the best of buddies,"

Chuck stated factually. "I find it unreal that people as nice as the Baskin family are facing these horrors and upset."

"Which boat slip was the boat docked in when Eli was found?" Laura asked with inquisitive wonder.

"Go out the door you came in and head straight ahead down the pier. The third boat slip on the left," Chuck added.

"Thanks, Chuck. You've been very sweet."

"Don't mention it. Enjoy your visit to Antioch. Will I be seeing you three again?" he hoped.

"Since you signed my copy of your book with your phone number included, there is a good chance you might," Laura stated while winking again at Chuck. Again, he winked back with a big grin.

"If you lose the number, you can also look inside the pastry box," Chuck informed Laura with a sly dog smile.

"Come on, *Juliet*," Cheryl said, tugging Laura's arm and smiling at Chuck while he grinned ear to ear. Chuck continued smiling at them the entire time they all said goodbye. They enjoyed meeting him and hoped they would be seeing him again too.

Chuck couldn't help observing the curvature of their feminine bodies as they departed the door with the brass tinkling bell sound chiming over their heads. "Every time a bell rings, an angel gets wings," he said aloud to nobody there. "And those are three mighty fine angels."

Chapter 5

Janet sat upon an oversized beach towel, which she had sprawled across her private boat dock pier attached to the property of her house. She was relaxed and felt at one with the surrounding nature had developed in such an awe-inspiring way. Janet belonged right where she was and knew it was where her soul would always want to be. Family experiences over her lifetime at Lake Marie had compiled to create unforgettable memories she would treasure her whole life. Since moving in full-time, Janet felt as if those memories were preserved and as close to virtually being relived anytime she wanted to recall them in her mind. It was a place in body and mind in which Janet believed time almost stood still—a permanent, unchanging representation of a once happy childhood.

By her side, a dog and cat snuggled next to her and were appreciating the warmth of the sun. Her Jack Russell terrier, Mignon, was peering through the slats in the pier at something that seemed to intrigue him under the water surface. His attentiveness was entertaining Janet. Usually, it was only just the fish that attracted his attention. At other times, it was a twig or piece of litter floating around. Eventually, something else caught Mignon's attention, and he let out a small yipping bark. Mignon seemed interested in something alongside the house.

He had a short attention span, and it was difficult to ever determine what he was detecting. His attention was often directed at multiple things at once, and he was prone to hearing and seeing things nobody else seemed to. He was still juvenile in his behavior. Being just over one year old, he was an inquisitive puppy at heart. Mignon found interest and entertainment in everything. Any bird, squirrel, or animal especially piqued his curiosity. At least he stayed put by Janet's side and did not take off to chase after everything, as many dogs tended to do.

As for Janet's cat, Cleopatra, she slept most all the days through as long as she was warm and contented. Nights when people slept were when the cat was most active—usually with chasing field mice or starting up fights with other cats. Janet was not appreciative of that and tried to keep her cat indoors as much as possible when she was not being watched over.

For how cool it had been during the nights for this time of year, it was surprising how much the days would heat up into the high eighties. In the sun, where water reflected the luminous rays, it could even feel much warmer on the skin. The animals liked the heat. Janet liked it too. Sunning herself on her pier with the pets by her side was probably her favorite thing to do, but she knew the dangers of sun rays and appropriately limited her time outdoors.

From within the trees and bushes alongside the house, an old Indian man stood motionless and was watching Janet momentarily through the branches. She was oblivious of the visitor invading her privacy. At the very same time, the curtains in her four-season room window dropped back. A dark apparition, who had been staring at her, sank back into the house, away from the drapery and glass. Of that activity, Janet was also unaware. Mignon noticed, though. His head alternated directions, turning repeatedly from one object to another, as he let out more yipping sounds.

The male Indian figure eventually ventured forth onto the pier. Mignon's yips turned to a louder, more ecstatic bark. While telling the dog to quiet down, it was the vibration of footsteps on the pier that caused Janet to turn around and spot the approaching unfamiliar male figure. The sun was rather blinding Janet, and her eyes took time to focus. Somewhat alarmed by the impending trespasser, she composed herself accordingly and addressed him with decorum.

"Please don't be frightened," an old Native American man said as he drew nearer to her on the pier. "It is not my intent to startle you! I come in peace." He chuckled. It was an old Indian cliché he loved to say to people.

As he moved closer to her, Janet realized it was not the first time she had encountered this man, and she had suspected she would someday be seeing him again. But they had never formally met, not exactly.

"Who are you?" Janet loudly inquired while attempting to quiet her pup. His yapping and barking had become excessive and difficult to control.

"People in my tribe call me by my Indian name, Running Fox," he said, extending his hand for a handshake as he drew close enough to reach her. "My people were once of a noble Native American tribe in these parts of Illinois. Now my ancestors are mostly long gone from residing on these lands. Few remain," he managed to say with an abundance of dignity and pride in his voice. "But you can call me Leo."

Janet looked at his outstretched hand but declined to shake it. Her tanned hands were dripping with sun oil. "Not Fox?" she inquired.

"No," said Leo. "Fox is the name of my twin brother, who was born first and has claimed to that name. It's an honor he was given that name before I was able to receive it just because he popped his head into the world minutes before I did," Leo said laughingly as if trying to ease Janet with some light humor. "The rest of us are provided with longer honorary names. They include Running Fox, Sleeping Fox, and so on. My real name is Leo, but I am a member of the Fox family lineage. Here is my card." Leo reached into his shirt pocket and removed a business card. Stated in bold letters on the card were the words SECURITY SERVICES.

"Security services?" Janet laughed after reading the card she had been handed by a man who appeared old enough to be the grandfather of Moses. He did not fit the image of any burly security man she had ever known.

"Actually, Janet, we—meaning my brother and I—are retired. May I start from the beginning and inform you of why I am here?" Leo asked knowing Janet would be interested in listening.

Janet stood up from her towel upon the pier and escorted Leo to a picnic table on her lawn, where she could sit across him at eye level and keep an eye on him. Mignon followed while the cat continued basking on the warm wooden planks of the pier. Walking to the table, Janet noticed a bad limp the man had. He favored his left leg.

"I'd offer you a drink, but I'd rather not be friendly until I know what is going on here," Janet said to Leo. She was not at all certain she could trust the man yet.

"That's fine. I'm not in need of a libation. I think a young, attractive woman should always be on guard. It's a dangerous world," he stated.

Before Leo could say more, Janet's boyfriend, Sheriff Dean, approached from behind her. Mignon ran to greet him with his tail wagging at high speed. "Hi, Janet! Hi, Leo," said Dean. "I see the two of you have already introduced yourselves. Sorry. I was detained."

Just the sight of Dean put Janet at ease. Still, this was a confusing but intriguing introduction.

Janet did not have the fondest memories of the local Indians she had encountered, and many questions had long awaited being asked. "You two know each other?" Janet asked with surprise in her voice.

"Yes," Dean answered as he arrived at the picnic table and took a seat next to Janet. "Leo and I met today, and we had a long talk. I know you'll find what he had to say to me to be of interest, Janet. I checked him out, and he's legitimate. We can trust him."

Leo began his story to Janet by explaining that he and his brother, Fox, had never meant to frighten her in previous encounters. It all started over a year ago. "I'm going back to before you moved in, Janet. My brother and I were hired by a confidential source I can't name to look into a matter around here. It is a matter with which we now know you are somewhat familiar. Dean told us what he could, and I agreed to work with him as a consultant on his assignments as of today."

Janet was pleased to hear that Dean was getting assistance. However, she still did not know where this conversation was heading. It had been confidentially and mutually agreed upon that anything her friends and neighbors had previously been involved with was going to remain a buried secret among them and that any crimes would be left up to the courts to decide a ruling upon. She wasn't quite sure she wanted to hear what Leo would say because her intuition told her it would rock the otherwise tranquil foundation of the lifestyle she had created for herself. Any bad memories could easily resurface and upset her happy life. She had worked hard to forget about them and any ugliness in her past. Luckily, thoughts of those disturbing events rarely crossed her mind these days.

"My brother and I think you might be in danger," Leo stated with great concern. There. It was said. Those were just the words Janet did not want to hear. Just the possibility that she could be in danger would rock her otherwise peaceful existence. Leo had managed to upset her with just a few simple words.

"Please let me start from the beginning. My brother and I wish we could have resolved this sooner. We are sorry for not having done so, but understand we were not involved until it was too late for us to comprehend the complexity of that which we had permitted ourselves to become wrapped up in. Then we had no proof of anything we could substantiate," Leo stated apologetically and with disgrace. "We tried to be as discrete as possible right from the start. Then it seemed we best stay away and keep out of it."

Janet sat quietly, as she still did not know what Leo was getting at. Her family secrets had not been much to discuss with anyone at this time, and an apology did not seem to be in order. She was not about to speak until she knew what matters she was speaking of or even what topics Leo was speaking about.

After a momentary silence, Leo began to weave a tale as Janet kept an open mind. "You already know, Janet, that your neighbor two doors down died as a result of falling down his basement stairs. Irwin is the one who first hired Fox and I. That started our involvement. Dean told me today that you were aware that Irwin had been pimping out prostitutes. Well, there was more to it. There has been a human trafficking organization functioning discretely around here. It's more of a sex cult ring. Actually, they traffic people for any number of reasons, one of which is a good reason."

Janet did not know that, and her eyes widened. "Go ahead," she requested with regard to his information.

"Irwin was going to visit his sister, and he wanted us to provide additional basic exterior home security patrols. You know of the type of service—just simple work to be certain his home wasn't being broken into or there wasn't any trouble in his absence. An unoccupied home can be an easy target for crime. Before officially starting our assignment, Fox and I made a couple trips to the neighborhood to scope out his house layout and the whole area before we were to actually start working.

"We knew Irwin was supposed to be leaving town by the time we were to start our patrols. As things turned out, we ended up coming early because we learned from a source that Irwin changed his mind about ever leaving. Our staff was unable to reach Irwin by phone. We wanted to confirm if there was going to be any change in our scheduling. That's when things started happening. As you well know, Irwin never made it to his sister's place because he was found dead. I understand you were the one who found him at the bottom of his basement steps."

"Gertty, my neighbor, and I both did," Janet replied, making sure Leo knew she had not made the grizzly discovery on her own.

"Right," Leo answered. "We never were able to reach Irwin. When we found out that he was dead, we immediately thought we didn't have a job to do. Worse, we may not get paid if we continued to do the work with Irwin not alive to pay. So we stayed away briefly."

Janet was understanding the situation but still wanted to hear the rest of what Leo had to say. "So then why are you still coming around here?" she asked.

"Immediately following Irwin's death, we were hired by a different client, also one wishing to remain confidential. Confidentiality is not unusual when it comes to security, you understand. Our firm was informed that information exists in the form of a computer memory stick. It allegedly contains all the information pertaining to an organized Mob activity. It lists its members, and it also lists all the victims of their crimes and what became of missing bodies. It was believed by my client that the memory stick was hidden around your home. We were led to believe that it was Irwin who had supposedly possessed that stick at the time of his demise and kept it safely tucked away."

"Let me guess!" Janet figured. "My family was not here full-time, and my parents had given a spare key to Irwin years ago. For safekeeping, he was keeping the stick where he figured nobody would find it: here in my house."

"Before any of us jump to conclusions, let me state this," Leo said, clarifying matters. "We don't know if Irwin was the original creator of that information file or if it had fallen into his possession. Here is the kicker. When Irwin came back to get it from behind a freezer you had downstairs in your basement, it was supposedly gone. Then he immediately turned up dead from what has been considered by investigators to be an accidental tumble down his own basement stairs. There may be people aware of the existence of that information who will stop at nothing to get hold of it, Janet."

Janet looked at Dean, and Dean nodded. "I told you that I did not feel his death was accidental," he stated, reminding Janet of what he had told her during the death investigation. There was never any proof to prove it was or was not an accident.

"That explains why I felt people had been in my home. It apparently didn't all have to do with the Kinski body parts found in my downstairs freezer," Janet stated.

"Possibly not, Janet," Dean told her. "That's why I wanted Leo to meet you instead of letting this be a dormant topic swept under the rug. I don't want to worry you, but I also don't want you to be unaware that there may be more to the incidents of last year."

"I understand," Janet said. "But it has been peaceful around here for twelve months, and I've not been noticing anything suspicious." Janet thought momentarily. "But, Leo, I have had a couple of concerns about you and your brother coming around here. One time, Fox came right into my home when I wasn't home. Guests were staying here. They assumed it was okay for him to do that. When I learned of his walking right into my home uninvited, I became alarmed. What did he want?"

"He had heard about Irwin and had wished to pass on our condolences," Leo said while now giving their condolences in person for both him and his brother. "It seemed peculiar to us that Irwin was suddenly dead. Just perhaps, Fox and I suspected at the time, the death of Irwin was much more than an accidental coincidence. I mean, the old man could possibly have had other reasons for suddenly hiring us for security. Fox came here hoping to find an answer as to why Irwin died but then had second thoughts about becoming involved once he got here. It really wasn't any of our business at that point in time. We had only been hired to look after his property. We were never hired to protect him."

Leo then told Janet that Fox had mentioned having come by her home that day. "Also, when my brother came here, he discovered you had guests staying here. He did not want to bother all of you." As for walking into her home uninvited, Leo didn't know his brother had done so. "Unfortunately, my brother is not known for his manners," he added, apologizing for his brother's behavior. "My tribe is an informal and hospitable group. We tend to forget that other people are not always so accepting of our ways. For our people, it's neighborly to let oneself in an open door. For your people, it is trespassing."

"There are still many neighbors here too who consider an open door to be a neighborly invitation to come right in," Janet agreed. "I'll let your brother's actions slide this time. Your apology is accepted on his behalf," she responded, trying to be hospitable. "There's another alarming situation I wish to discuss."

Stopping her before she continued speaking, Leo mentioned, "The incident in the road?"

"Yes," Janet replied. "That incident!"

"It was I whom you had come across that day. I tried to stop you in your car. I'm afraid that didn't go over too well. When I stopped you, you became alarmed and began yelling at me," Leo said, trying to explain his side of what had happened.

"I became physically hurt somehow, and you left me there alone in the road," Janet cited with upset in her voice.

Leo continued to explain. "I didn't know for sure that you were hurt. You see, while I was speaking to you, a huge rock came flying through the air. I saw more than one person surrounding us, and I got scared. Nothing like that had ever happened to me, and I assumed they were after you. I didn't want to be surrounded by these people and caught in the middle of a rock-flinging attack. I'm just an old man. Making a hasty decision, I ran as fast as I could to get away. I got myself safely into the woods to take cover.

"As I became aware they had lost sight of me, I happened to catch sight of them—well, two of them anyway. They were dressed all in black and were carrying slingshots. They were small people in stature, and I'm a short man, so I know short. That's the only description I can give. It gave me the impression that maybe they were just kids who had made a mistake with their weapon toys and also ran when they realized we were there. They may have panicked as their stray flying rock came hurling in our direction. I tried to discretely follow them into the forest. But I soon stepped into a big hole in the ground and badly hurt my foot, ankle, and leg. Small bones were broken. They are brittle in my old age. I couldn't continue following the assailants."

"So that's why you are still limping?" Janet asked Leo.

"Yes, Miss," Leo replied. "It took me a while to make my way back to the road that day. You were gone when I got back to the road where I had initially stopped you. I assumed you were okay since you and your car were gone. After that, it took all the strength I could muster to get back to my own vehicle. I headed right over to the hospital with my injuries. While there, I kept asking if you had come in. Staff told me you had not come in. I was thinking of you the whole time I was there. By the time I left the hospital, I assumed you were okay, or you would have not driven off. Doctors had me doped up on pain medications, and I was unable to drive after that. I was picked up by my family and don't recall much more after having been medicated and taken home to recuperate."

"Why have you never returned since then to discuss the street incident?" Janet inquired. She thought he would have cared enough to do so.

"My memory of the day was a bit hazy after having been drugged at the hospital. As I recall by the way you greeted me on the road, I didn't think you'd want to see me ever again. You were yelling at me like I was some senile old coot blocking your roadway." Leo smiled. "After that, I didn't know if the rock incident was an intentional attack upon you. I didn't want to become involved in your dangerous situations. Honestly, Janet, I didn't know what to think. By the time I considered it all and made a decision to come back, police cars were lined up here. All these situations led me to believe you were a high-maintenance individual I had no business being around. Today, Dean has set my thinking straight. I'm sorry I had such a poor opinion of you."

"The squad cars lined up here must have been when we discovered the Kinski remains in my freezer," Janet figured. "The police came, and their cars were all over the road. I can see why you wanted to stay clear of me." Janet wasn't the popular type of person whom everyone wanted to make friends with. She also was not the type of person who wanted people to stay away. She was sensitive and cared about what other people thought of her.

"That was the day. I heard about it on the news," Leo informed Janet. "It just seemed as if it was never the right time to sit down and talk with you and become involved."

"So why are you involved now?" Janet wondered. "Isn't what happened a year ago over with and being forgotten about? Someone likely got their memory stick, as everything seems quiet for a year now. What's going on?"

Having already used up his free time for the day, Leo excused himself in the middle of their conversation. "Dean can fill you in. He wanted me to come by and meet you. I agreed to do that much. Now it's time I must leave," he said, excusing himself. "Fox had other business in town, and I must go get him. He's been waiting long enough," Leo commented, raising himself up from the table and starting to leave. Dean nodded with approval, and Janet said her goodbyes to the old man. She hoped he would be her new friend.

As Leo walked away, Dean leaned over and kissed Janet passionately upon her lips. Being covered with suntan oil, she pulled away quickly so as not to soil his pristine uniform. "Oil doesn't come out so easily, Dear," she informed him.

Dean smiled at her and then said with regret, "I can't make our dinner tonight, Honey."

"Why not? I was so looking forward to our time together. I could use some of your sweet loving later tonight," she said while flirting playfully. "Will you be here at all tonight?"

"I could use some comfort too," Dean assured her. "I was looking forward to pitching some woo. Unfortunately, duty calls."

"Again?" she asked. "Don't tell me that you are behind in your routine paperwork. Can't it wait? You know, tonight was to be a special night."

"There will be paperwork, which can't wait, but that is not it," Dean confided. "It's got to do with how Leo and I came to meet today." A frown crossed his face as he explained his situation. "Police are uncovering a mass grave site in shallow waters across the lake. It's over by all the cattails and reed. A tribe member Leo knows was fishing with a net and dragged up some human bones from the water. We sent scuba divers out to look, and they are likely uncovering other corpses and skeletons while we speak. Some of the remains are not yet fully deteriorated to the bone, I'm sorry to say. It implies they may be fairly recent deaths.

"The fisherman who found the bones called the police, and then he called Leo for support. One conversation led to another with Leo. He began confiding in me about last year. That's when you as a topic came up. I thought you should hear what he had to say for himself. Then I convinced Leo to come here to meet you. I have only taken a short break to be here too. I knew you'd be at home."

"Do you think Julie's bones could be there?" Janet questioned.

"No reason they might not be," Dean responded. "It will take some time before forensics can identify remains. Don't put too much thought into it. I'll make sure you are the first to know once I know anything at all. I may not be able to freely discuss all information with you, but any news pertaining to Julie's whereabouts is one detail I'd never keep from you."

After talking, Dean excused himself to go back to work. He was anxious to return to the excavation site and learn about what had transpired in the brief time since he had left there. Janet requested that she be able to join him, but Dean denied the request.

"The area is quarantined, and I can't even let you pass into it. It is a crime scene for the time being. Authorities do not want anything potentially disturbed," he informed her. "It would not do you any good to be there even if I could bring you along. If you could come along, I'd only be focusing on your beautiful face instead of business."

"When will I see you again?" Janet asked with hopes it would be soon.

"If you want, I'll come by after work, and we can see how I feel. If it gets too late, I'll just slip in and crawl into bed," he suggested. "Don't expect too much out of me, though. I might be too exhausted to care. I don't know when I will get home to you and the kids." By that, he meant Mignon and Cleopatra, their Egyptian breed of cat. It was obvious that Mignon favored Janet while Cleopatra was partial to Dean. All parties involved seemed content in knowing that.

"It's a date," Janet responded while walking Dean to his car. "I'll count the minutes we are apart—until I get tired of counting, that is," she wisecracked.

Chapter 6

As Dean got into his vehicle and began pulling away, Janet stood watching as three young women slowly pulled up in a sporty car right in front of her garage door. One of them rolled down her window and yelled out, "Hello! Are you Janet?"

"Yes," Janet replied. "Who is asking?"

The car came to a stop, and the engine quit as the three women got out. Mignon ran to the car and greeted the unfamiliar visitors with excitement.

"We hope our being here isn't an inconvenience," Laura said. "I'm Laura. These are my friends Caroline and Cheryl. May we talk to you for a few minutes—that is, if you aren't too busy?"

"Talk? What about?" Janet first wanted to know some details.

"A few things," said Laura, "such as your art and the history of the area. Honestly, though, I'm continuing my education to be a criminologist. We are on summer vacation and chose this location to visit because of the things that had occurred around here—particularly those things that happened last year. It would be a lie if we said we are only here about your art. We want to know things." Laura hoped her honesty and sincerity would appeal to Janet.

"Was that the sheriff leaving?" Cheryl asked before Janet could answer Laura.

"It was—Sheriff Dean," Janet said with a reply directed toward Cheryl. "As for anything else you may be wanting to discuss with me, I don't know what I possibly have to say to you," she continued saying.

Cheryl reached into her purse and pulled out the lighter she had found. "This has a name engraved on it. Do you know the person it belongs to?"

Janet did recognize it. It was the same lighter Julie had used to light up her smokes when she was visiting Janet's house before her disappearance. Janet even once held it in her hand when Julie had passed it to her. "Where did you get it?" Janet inquired.

"At the campsite where we are staying across the lake," Cheryl stated. "I found it on the ground when I was cleaning up to assemble a campfire pit. I understand that Julie was a guest at your home. We didn't know how it had ended up being found by me at the campsite."

"Come on in for a moment," Janet said, extending a courteous invite to them.

Leading the women in her door and through her home, Janet guided the women into the kitchen and served up each a glass of lemonade. It was by pure coincidence that Armani, who had been performing handyman tasks in the basement, emerged from the basement doorway in the hallway at that moment. Armani immediately spotted the women in the house.

From his vantage point, he could clearly see Cheryl, Caroline, and Laura with Janet in the kitchen. They did not turn to see him. If they had, no mention was made as to his presence. Even Mignon was too busy investigating the three guests to pay any mind to Armani, a man Mignon was already all too well-acquainted with. It was mind-boggling to Armani that these particular women, whom he had viewed on his camera monitors, were in the same home that he was in. In some respects, that rather disturbed him. *What reason could they have for being here?* he pondered.

Within a brief minute after serving drinks, Janet directed the women through the house and out the back door, toward the lake. She explained on her way out the door, "I don't want my suntan lotion on my furniture, and I'm covered in it. Lotion is a way of life here when spending time in the sun. There is a picnic table by the water where we all can sit together. I hope that is fine with all of you."

Armani hid behind the curtain of the window nearest the picnic table the women sat at. He concealed his large, manly frame behind curtains and in the shadows. Pressing his ear as close to the window screen as he could, he listened in on the conversation the women were engaging in. Fortunately, their voices echoed loudly enough for him to hear almost everything with all the windows in the room being ajar.

The women said nothing Armani had not already known. Janet mainly filled them in on evidence collected by investigators that linked Dan Baskin to Antioch crimes. The evidence had many convinced that Dan was definitely the responsible party. They assumed that if he had not been the sole perpetrator of the crimes, he had managed to play a big part in them. But despite the incriminating evidence, still many people found it difficult to believe that the Dan they had known and befriended for years had been capable of such heinous actions. Especially, they did not believe Dan had been capable of murdering his own lifelong best friend Eli. Strangers who did not know Dan and Eli were definitely sexually straight might have even confused them with being a gay couple. Such an accusation was often falsely rumored. Two men could not have been closer, but they were close only in a loving, brotherly way. Still, rumors of all sorts were spread, as people loved to gossip when the talk was cheap.

While Cheryl again mentioned having found Julie's cigarette lighter, there wasn't much more to say on that subject. Janet thought it interesting that it had been found at the camp. Showing up at the camp or anywhere else should not have been impossible. There would be no saying how it had ended up there. Julie might have been at the campsite before her disappearance for all anyone knew. Julie was a free spirit nobody ever kept tabs on. Another possibility was that someone had found it and had taken it to the campgrounds, where it was lost. Janet's brain was thinking. She knew it was an odd find but couldn't think of what the find could imply. Not wanting to make anything of it, she shrugged it off. Janet asked Cheryl if she could have it to keep. It did mean something to Janet, and she thought it would be a nice memento, if nothing else. Cheryl obliged, handing over the lighter as a gift.

Noticing that the guests were preparing to stand up and depart, Armani backed away from the window. He could no longer clearly make heads or tails of most of the words being spoken. He had been in the basement when the women arrived, and they initially spoke of the lighter. Now this part of the conversation pertaining to a lighter was impossible for him to comprehend. Little did he know that the lighter could play an intricate part in linking old crimes to the camp, those very same crimes to which he could easily be linked and someday be held accountable for.

Polite conversation continued for a brief period, and Janet began to feel a strong bond to her guests. Somehow, she felt as if this would not be the last time they would communicate. Something sinister seemed to be brewing, but she couldn't put her finger on what it could be, and she hoped she was wrong. While Janet had worked at being friendly with the Antioch locals, she never quite knew how other people felt about her. Past history could paint her and her family in a dark light. But these women were genuinely nice and caring. They were not locals.

They hadn't judged her. They had found her life and conversation to be fascinating. It seemed to Janet that they had wanted to learn as much as they could about her and her friends without passing judgment. It was refreshing to let her guard down and not feel as if she was part of a witch hunt.

Janet talked for a longer time at their car until she had to politely request that her guests depart. She was expecting company to arrive for a visit and could not spare any more casual conversation time at the moment. Perhaps someday, they would meet up in life and talk again. They all would like to think they would have that opportunity.

Somewhere midconversation, Armani gave up listening in entirely. Their conversation had become too mundane, and he had lost interest. All he could think of was, *What a bunch of cackling hens.* He had already wasted enough of his time eavesdropping and knew he should return to his repair tasks. Had he stayed to listen in longer, he would not have gained anything.

Janet and Mignon bid their guests farewell, but not before exchanging phone numbers and Janet thanking Laura again for the much-appreciated gift. As the car drove away, Janet could not help but think of how the trio reminded her so much of her relationship with her missing friend, Julie, and their best friend Gloria. She looked down at her watch and realized it would only be an hour before Gloria would be arriving from Prospect Heights for a few days' stay. It was a visit Janet was very much looking forward to.

Chapter 7

Noisily, the screen door to her house creaked as Janet entered. Armani heard her coming in and abruptly stopped his work to head up the stairs from the basement to greet her. Janet could hear Armani's footsteps approaching up the old wooden stairs, and she waited in place for a moment for him to reach her.

"Who were those beautiful women?" Armani questioned. "I haven't met them before." He hid his past awareness of them well from Janet. "Any chance they are locals I can become familiar with? Grrr!"

Janet replied, "I had never met them before either. They were just some young thrill seekers. They wanted to question me about Lake Marie folklore. Tourists! They are gone now. But they reminded me so much of Julie, Gloria, and myself that I enjoyed taking a few moments of my time to speak with them. It brought back memories. They were lovely and delightful, I'd say."

Armani nodded and informed Janet he had accomplished all he could in her basement until another day when he would pick up some needed hardware in town. Janet made one additional request: that Armani fix the screen door creak before leaving if he could. Armani agreed to oil the hinges for now and see if that would resolve the problem for her.

"I'm going to go clean myself up before Gloria arrives," Janet explained. "Could you be so kind as to lock the door behind you on your way out?" she asked.

"May I just stay and watch?" Armani joked.

Janet didn't take kindly to Armani's joke. She never quite got over the fact that Armani had installed cameras prior to her moving in. It was no secret he had been monitoring her at that time. The cameras had been installed at the request of her father as a security precaution back when her parents still owned the property. She was unaware he had installed them. Despite them having been installed, he had no business using them to spy on her. While Armani had knowingly taken advantage of that situation, so many other undesirable things had transpired between him and Janet. Upon initial discussion of that topic, the incidents were agreed upon to be forgiven and forgotten. They never really were totally forgotten, though. This was the first time since then that Armani had made any sexual comment in her presence. His words made her feel uncomfortable. Many memories came to mind—bad memories. While it was in the past, it was not a topic to jest about.

"Armani, I—" Janet started to say.

Before being able to complete her full sentence, Armani interjected. "I know. You don't need to say anything. It was just a bad joke. I can tell by the expression on your face that it wasn't appreciated. It's just my personality. I wasn't thinking. Forgive me," he said apologetically. He bowed his head with a pouting look.

Even Janet thought this reaction was a bit irresistible. He certainly knew when to manipulate women, or so he thinks. Janet nodded and bowed her own head down before walking away without another word being said. She found it difficult to look him in the eye after that, having admitted to herself that she still found some of his personality traits and features to be irresistible.

Armani had hoped Janet had truly forgiven him for his past behavior. Obviously, she had not. In his twisted mind, he could not process how much his past actions had truly hurt her. He loved her so dearly that he would have forgiven her for everything and anything she could have possibly ever done to him. He hoped she could reciprocate that forgiveness and think of him the same way, but one of the many problems with that was that she had never wronged him and had nothing to be forgiven for. That was a big difference.

As the water in the bathroom shower began running, Armani finished up oiling the screen door. Before he could exit and lock the door behind him, Gloria arrived, having pulled up with honking of her car horn. Armani knew Gloria as being Janet's dear friend for many years. He was happy to see her come to town again. Her face lit up as she saw him. She, too, was equally as happy to see him. He walked the sidewalk path to greet her partway, and they exchanged hugs as they met. He kissed her on her forehead knowing that a new boyfriend in her life might not approve of a big wet one planted directly on her lips. Gloria did not find the action to require any thought. She would have accepted a kiss anywhere Armani might have desired to kiss her.

"You are looking fine as always, Stud!" Gloria said flirtatiously as she grabbed Armani's firm biceps. Looking down and around his side, she checked out his solid buttocks. "Yep, mighty fine."

"As are you," Armani said, returning the compliment while grabbing her butt cheeks. "You still seeing that guy?" he wondered. He had heard she was, but things had been known to change in life. It was ironic how he thought twice about desiring to kiss her on the lips, yet he saw no problem with grabbing her ass. It was, again, just how his mind worked. He could not help himself when it came to some actions.

"I am. No ring on my finger, not yet!" Gloria stated while pointing to her naked ring finger. "You still have a chance with me, but I'll not wait forever."

Armani laughed knowing their comments were only that of a playful nature. Even if he wanted Gloria that way, he believed his lifestyle would not accommodate such a relationship. Putting her or any other woman in his life in any danger would not be what he would want. "Janet is inside, taking a shower," he informed Gloria. "She will be so happy to see you. It seems like ages since you've come around here."

"None of us get together as often as we should," Gloria professed in a somber tone. "I thought we'd see each other often when Janet moved here. I knew she wanted her space getting situated here, and I gave it to her. After that, Janet seemed to be tied up with Dean, then winter came. People got sick during the pandemic. My life then became busy and complicated with my beau. I've seen Janet in Prospect Heights when she visited her folks. We talk on the phone almost daily. It's been the next best thing to actually being here, but I'm here now!"

Armani jokingly responded with some truth: "I feel left out. You never call. You never write."

"I didn't know you cared," Gloria answered equally as jokingly as he walked her to the house door. They walked side by side with their arms at each other's waist as their flirtatious banter continued along the few extra steps.

Janet had just finished primping following her shower and heard Gloria and Armani talking at the screen door. Only Gloria entered the house, as Armani thought it was best he leave. Janet would have expected him to already have left, and his last attempt at humor with her pertaining to lingering around had ended on a sour note. He did not want Janet to think his loitering had been intentional.

"Gloria!" Janet yelled audibly enough to be heard through the entire home. She rushed to the center of the home to greet her friend as Gloria made her way deeper into the house.

"Janet!" Gloria yelled as she rushed to embrace Janet in a comforting embrace. "It's been too long. Is Dean here to greet me, or is he working again?"

"He's working on something big!" Janet could not wait to tell Gloria all about it. "It's possible they found Julie's remains. A mass grave has been discovered on the far side of the lake. Dean is there right now as we are standing here. It's ironic you should show up at this time. I've been so lost in thought over Julie and can use your support. Your being here means so much."

"I don't know what to say, Janet," Gloria said, looking dumbfounded. "It would be nice to know Julie's whereabouts and have some closure. God, I hope she isn't dead. How ghastly. I'd be terribly devastated. I always think she will just show up out of the blue and let us know she is fine."

"Julie simply must be there. I'd be surprised if she isn't," Janet believed. "I haven't told you on the phone, but I'm having visions again. Weird things are happening, just like last summer."

"What else has been happening?" Gloria asked, wanting to hear all about it. She sat herself down on the sofa. Patting the seat next to her with her hand, she indicated that she wanted Janet to come sit down beside her and tell all.

"I've been seeing things," Janet expressed again, "Julie in particular. At other times, I've seen a dark, humanly shaped shadow inside my windows when I am outside and looking back at the house."

"Julie?" Gloria asked with a gasp. "You are certain it is her?"

"Yes," Janet confirmed. "But not in full body form at all times. She's sometimes ghostly transparent as I view her out my window. She stands poised, dripping wet, by the lake, pointing at the water. By the time I run out of the house to meet her, she's gone. I know I am seeing something because Mignon often directs my attention to the apparition." Mignon had never met Gloria and was finally settling down since Gloria's entrance into the house. "That's Mignon, by the way," Janet stated as a formal introduction. "He likes you." Mignon was begging for Gloria's attention.

"I figured as much," Gloria said while petting the pooch now perched on her lap. It hadn't taken him long to accept her as a friend. One of Mignon's best qualities was that he always liked everyone. He was probably the friendliest dog one could meet. Cowardly at times too. Gloria attempted to find some other explanation for what Janet was telling her. "Are you still taking your medications? Does this happen at night when you may have been dreaming?"

"It happens day and night," Janet said without any hesitation. "Usually, she has a strange green glow around her when it's dark outside. The darker it is outside, the more intensely her shape glows. Lately, the glow has become a shade of purple. I can tell it's got to be her ghost. I can feel it in my heart that she is dead. She must be in the water. That is why she points to it. That's why I believe Dean will find her in a watery grave."

"I believe you believe," Gloria said while pulling Janet close to her. "It's not out of the question that they could find her there. As for spooks, it could be your imagination, medications, or any number of things. While I do believe what you say, you really should be speaking to your psychiatrist and Dean about these visions. They are not normal. I wish I had not had to cancel my previous visits here due to all that has transpired over the last year. I so wanted to be right here for you."

"I missed you being here as well, but no," Janet stated adamantly. "Sightings of Julie have been too infrequent to worry about medication side effects, and my medications have been working perfectly otherwise. They are doing just what they are intended to do for me. While we both know hallucinations can be potential side effects of the drugs I take, I know that isn't the case here. Mignon sees whatever I think I have been seeing too. I am certain the sightings are not due to hallucinations. They are too real.

"By the way, I've not even mentioned any of this to Dean. That may be because I am in denial over the possible death of Julie. If it is her ghost I see, she would be dead. I also don't want Dean to worry about me and silly things. He's always so stressed over his job. I don't want to be a bother. Whatever I believe is or isn't going on around here, I do believe in what I am telling you, and I haven't been able to comprehend any of it. This is all so different from any past experiences you know I've had. Those experiences made me question myself and my sanity. I wasn't ever sure of what I was seeing. These sightings are real without question. I know the apparitions are really there. If they are not otherworldly, someone is gaslighting me!"

"I believe all that," Gloria said in a supportive tone. "I'm sure it all means something. I just want to make sure you are okay. You know that." She continued, "I've not worried at all about you because I knew Dean has been here. If you aren't always being totally honest with him, I'm going to start worrying. You can't keep these kinds of secrets. It's dangerous."

"With you here by my side, I'm sure we will get to the bottom of some concerns," Janet explained. "Let's get you settled in and start enjoying our time together. I heard you and Armani outside. I'm glad you saw him. Gertty wants you to stop by next door and see her too. I figure we'll venture out after getting you situated and see her on our way out to eat. I'm hungry! I didn't shop for groceries yet because I wanted to ask you how much dining out we'd be doing and what food you want me to keep in the house."

Janet's thoughts ran from one topic to another, as they so often did but to a lesser extent these days now that her newer medications had been working effectively. "Somewhere around here is the cat, Cleopatra. Don't mind her. She comes and goes as she pleases and does her own thing. She never wanders far. She'll greet you when she's ready in her own time. I try to keep her in when possible. Should she make a run for it out the door, don't be concerned. She'll come back when she is ready."

"All that sounds perfect, Janet," Gloria stated, wanting to be a perfect guest in the home. "As for food, anything is fine, just as long as you don't serve me venison out of your freezer." That was a private joke, but it was not said in good taste. It was in reference to Kim Kinski's hacked-up corpse being found in Janet's freezer, mixed in with packages of wild deer roadkill.

"Everyone wants to be a comedian these days," Janet replied. "Armani made an off-color joke before you got here about wanting to watch me in the shower. It's just like the old days all over again. While I'm thinking of it, you'll be happy to know the appliances in the house have been replaced. There have not been any dead hookers stashed in them—unless Dean is keeping something from me." Janet smiled.

"Now who is making off-color jokes, Janet?" Gloria said with a big smile. "I'm glad you've been able to put some of the past behind you and loosen up. Many people would not even continue to live in this home after what you went through. Have you told anyone that the deer meat you'd been serving guests may have been Kim's flesh accidentally prepared? That is the most bizarre thing anyone I've ever known may have done."

"That is a secret you and I will take to our graves. If you ever mention it again, I'll be serving you up at the next dinner party," said Janet, entertaining Gloria with an evil grin. "As for your other comment, it's just a house," she pointed out. "The fond memories over generations have far exceeded any bad ones from last summer. It would take more than one summer of bad experiences to scare me out of here. You know I love this place. It is a part of me. I'd no sooner give it up than I would cut off my arm. Besides, Dean and I have managed to create many wonderful new memories since last year. Those alone are priceless."

"I'll bet the two of you have! Has Dean moved in full-time yet?" Gloria questioned.

"He is here most of the time," Janet seemed happy to announce. "He still has his place. It's the place he was living in when we met. He'll not have that for much longer. There are just some details for him to wrap up before he's completely out of there for good. He now only tends to go there if he just wants to catch a quick nap from work or has something he is tied up with, in town. In fact, he was debating if he should stay there while you are visiting so as not to interfere with our girl time. He must think we sit around applying mud masks on our faces and playing with dolls or something like that."

Gloria had mixed feelings about his being away from the house. "I hope he doesn't feel put out that I am here. I just assumed he would be staying here with us, at least some of the time. I so wanted one-on-one time to get to know him better. You know, I still haven't given the two of you my blessing. I've known you my whole life and would know if he is the right man for you."

Gloria was never to be taken too seriously. She enjoyed toying with Janet, and Janet enjoyed toying with her. But this time, there was some truth to what Gloria was saying. She had known Janet her whole life. She knew Janet better than anyone over the years. They always shared secrets and never disclosed them to outsiders. In most circumstances, Gloria did know what was best for Janet, even when Janet didn't know herself.

"We'll leave it to him to decide," Janet suggested. "I try to give him his space and not tell him what to do. Knowing him and his job, recent discoveries at the mass grave will have him tied up during your visit. He did not plan that. You understand, I know. His duty calls."

Yes, Gloria understood the importance of his career.

Chapter 8

After helping Gloria unpack and become situated at the house, Gloria and Janet strolled next door to see Gertty, just as Gertty had earlier requested. Gloria had no personal friendship with Gertty, but Gertty and Gloria felt as if they knew each other very well because of frequent conversations with Janet. For an aging alcoholic who had always refused any form of professional treatment, Gertty was doing quite fine on her own these days. Thanks to Janet's support, Gertty was doing better than she had in years. Any friend of Janet's was a friend of Gertty's as far as Gertty was concerned.

"Hi, you two," Gertty said as she greeted them at her door. She stepped outside to chat and take in the marvelous weather. The sun was shining. The temperature could not have been better for such a summer day. Gertty embraced the two women in a quick group hug, speaking only briefly. "I know you just arrived, Gloria, but I wanted to see you. I wasn't even sure if I'd even recognize you and wanted to put a face to the name, but I do recognize you. Seeing you has reminded me."

"That's all right, Gertty," Gloria replied. "It's nice to see you too. Janet has told me so much about you since you two have become such close friends. I feel as if I've been here with you two all along. I speak to Janet almost daily by phone, and she fills me in on many of your day-to-day conversations. I'm glad you are doing well. Janet said that you've really been making self-improvement efforts. That's great!"

"I know just what you mean, Child. Janet is like an angel to me. I don't know what I'd do without her," Gertty said, then said nothing more. There was an awkward silence for a few moments as the three stood there just looking around at nothing in particular.

"We were just on our way to town to do some shopping and grab a bite to eat. May I bring you something from town?" Janet politely offered, breaking the silence.

"Maybe just a bottle of gin, if it's not too much trouble. I'll have some baked goods for you girls when you get back. I'm just putting the finishing touches on my baking from this morning. I have breads, cupcakes, and cookies. If you pass by the bakery while in town, resist the urge to stop in. I'll stock you up with the good stuff when you return. Then Gloria can see what a real baker is capable of creating. That bakery in town has got nothing on me!" Gertty announced.

"We'll see you as soon as we get back," Janet said. She and Gloria waved, turned around, and headed away simultaneously with their bodies perfectly matching in every motion.

Once Gloria saw that Gertty had gone back inside, Gloria confided in Janet. "That sure was awkward. I mean, it was nice to see Gertty, but I really don't have anything in common to discuss with her. I froze and didn't know what to say at one point. And what is up with the request for booze? I thought she gave up the bottle."

"You'd really like Gertty if you had the chance to know her better," Janet commented. "If we have time, we can invite her over while you are here. She makes for an entertaining dinner guest. While she has cut way back on her drinking, she has not quit entirely. She claims it helps relieve some of her pain at bedtime. It helps her rest more soundly. It probably does. She's always trying out home remedies for whatever is ailing her since she can't always afford a doctor. Too many different pains are always giving her woe. Gin seems to always be her answer for most whatever is ailing her. Got pain? Drink booze. Can't sleep? Drink booze. Got a hangover—"

"Drink more booze!" Janet and Gloria said at once in harmony. They laughed as they held hands and walked home to Janet's place.

"Coincidentally, Janet, I heard from your brother. He was in Minnesota at a famous medical hospital. I thought it was strange he contacted me for the first time in a year. He just called me out of the blue. It was very nice hearing from him. I was hoping he's all right," Gloria said with a doubting question in her voice.

"I heard from him too," Janet responded. "I told him you would be visiting me. He said how nice it would be if he could come by while you are in town. He suspected his medical appointments were going to interfere with his scheduling. He was to let me know should his plans change and permit him to visit. Since that conversation with him, I have not heard back. You know how flighty he can be. My conversation with him probably gave him the idea to call you. He seems to be exceptionally lonely these days. I don't believe things have been going well for him and his significant other in Palm Springs.

"I have noticed that he beats around the bush if I ask any personal relationship questions. At first, I thought he perhaps wasn't comfortable telling me details about their lifestyle. Over time, I've come to think it is because things are not going well between them. It's just my intuition. It's hard to tell with him because you know how secretive he's always been. I guess we should consider ourselves lucky to have received any phone calls from him at all." Janet thought for a moment and then rescinded her comment. "I shouldn't say that. He's been pretty good about calling my family since his visit here last year. You might be surprised to know that he and Dean speak more often than I get a chance to speak with him. I sometimes think Dean knows my brother better than I do."

"Wow! He told me you informed him I'd be coming to town. You are probably correct in assuming that prompted him to call me. Absence makes the heart grow fonder," Gloria assumed.

"I'm sure that's it. I know he misses us. His health has not improved much over the last year. Lyme disease has complicated his other ailments. I know some of his ailments have improved while other new ailments have arisen. He said that he's a diabetic now. I would never have imagined he'd be a diabetic. I've since learned a lot about the disease and now know it's a hereditary condition running in our family. His regular diet of fast food and junk food probably hasn't helped him."

Gloria thought she felt a tap on her shoulder. Turning quickly to look, there was nothing there. Then she felt as if eyes were gazing upon her, eyes piercing into her soul. Looking around, still she saw nothing.

"What's up, Gloria?" Janet couldn't help but notice that Gloria seemed ill at ease.

"I don't know. I felt something. It was just my imagination," Gloria stated with a quivering verbal stutter of confusion. It was a feeling she had never experienced in her life. "Something touched me. I felt we were not alone." Gloria was trying to brush the awkward feeling off.

"You are probably experiencing what I experience from time to time," Janet explained. "Maybe you'll start to understand what I've been trying to tell you. I get weird feelings, as you described. They've become second nature to me, and I often don't even give them a second thought. They'd make me crazy if I did."

The two walked and talked until they reached Janet's garage. Janet decided that it was best she let Mignon out before they departed. It was better to be safe than to come home to a mess. Not knowing how long they might be gone, she didn't want to take any unnecessary chances. Mignon was not used to being left alone much. He tended to do naughty things out of spite when on his own.

Gloria understood how much attention animals could require. Outside the gate to Janet's home, she commented that she could see Armani working in his garden. She would pass time speaking with him until Janet was ready to depart. Even when Armani's conversation wasn't very enjoyable, he still made for good eye candy.

In his garden, Armani worked shirtless and in a pair of cutoffs. Sweat glistened on his rippled muscles, which could be seen from a distance as Gloria began her approach. He sensed her presence and looked up. Watching as she made her way through his gate and across his lawn, he stood to greet her. Cutting sheers fell from the grip of his hands to the ground. Gloria's pace hastened as she saw Armani's reaction. His upper physique had improved greatly since she had last seen him shirtless. His body was impressive. If not for knowing how Armani had treated Janet, Gloria would have tried harder to secure him for herself.

In many ways, he appealed to her more than the man she had been seeing, but there was still that side of him she knew she could not tolerate: His sexual appetite was that of an alley cat. He was not one to ever be monogamous or trusted, she imagined. From what her friends Janet and Julie had told her, he was hugely endowed between his legs and could be a rough ride. Gloria's taste sided more toward the sensitive and gentle. She knew any fantasy of being with a man like Armani would be better than the actual act of physically being with him.

"Would you just look at that body tone?" Gloria blurted out to him. "And that hairy chest. You're giving me hot flashes, Mister!"

Armani was vain and knew his body was impressive. He loved to show it off every chance he could. Making an effort to tease Gloria, he began flexing his pecs, causing his erect nipples to bob up and down. Gloria reached out with her right hand and rubbed his chest while making a fanning motion with her left hand. "Ooh la la!" she exclaimed.

Armani actually blushed for what was probably the first time in his life. "I'm at a loss," he told her. He wanted to grab her in his arms, but he knew his sweat would not be appreciated on her clothing. He also wanted to cup her breasts in reciprocation for her having felt up his chest, but he knew that would be uncouth. It was not like Armani to be at a loss for words or actions at any time. This made him think. Appropriate words to say just would not come to his mind.

"Janet is just letting Mignon out before we go to town. I saw you out here and thought I'd visit with you for a few moments while I wait for her," Gloria said as justification for visiting. She found a lot to say. She informed him of the mass grave Dean was checking out. That news surprised him. "They may find Julie there."

Armani had not known of the existence or the finding of such a site. He hoped they would find Julie, just not in a grave of any sort. He hoped she was alive and well. He remained silent on the subject and tried not to speak much about that which he knew nothing of. He felt more at ease keeping the conversation limited to Gloria's words.

"You are most welcome to visit anytime you see me about, Gloria." Armani didn't mind company as long as nobody had to bother him while he was inside his home. "I don't like to be bothered when I'm inside my home because I could be sleeping at any hour and keeping to myself. If you ever see me outside, feel free to come over. I'm usually just puttering in the garden or the garage."

Gloria giggled. "I know what kind of puttering you do in the garage," she informed him. "Julie and Janet told me all about their experiences with you in there. In Julie's case, Dan too! Turn off the cameras and I might take you up on your offer to visit you in your garage sometime," Gloria flirtatiously said with a wink of the eye.

Armani nodded. "I'm sure I'd be happy to be of service," his voice said in a deep tone while he smirked slyly.

Gloria had not intended to glance down at Armani's crotch, but she caught herself fixating her eyes there. She wondered if it was really as large as she had heard it was. Armani noticed her gazing, and he felt his bulge quickly growing. Neither of them had a chance to speak another word before Janet yelled over the fence, "Mignon is done with his business. He was quick about it. I'm ready to depart."

Gloria and Armani smiled at each other, and she said, "Until later."

He replied, "Until later, Dear."

Chapter 9

It was a lovely day in town. The shops were busy, and the weather was fine. Janet and Gloria strolled the markets and stocked up on everything they desired. Janet pointed out everything of importance along the way and talked obsessively. "There is the pet shop I purchased Mignon and his cat friend at. There's the bakery I buy all my treats from when Gertty or I haven't baked. And there is the market I'll buy Gertty's gin at while we shop for some food. We should stock up my bar too."

Janet was never at a loss for words. She delighted in going to town and was even more excited this time that Gloria was with her. Gloria was not unfamiliar with the town. She had been there many times before when visiting Janet over the years. Except for a couple of newer shops, little of what Janet was saying was informative to Gloria. Gloria didn't mind. She let Janet repeat the same old stories without protest. It pleased Gloria to see Janet so happy, and conversation continued through their lunch at their favorite pizza place.

Following lunch, Janet and Gloria concluded their shopping trip with stopping at the grocery market. They had intentionally saved that stop for last because of the refrigerated products they would be buying. "I'll let you pick out the food, Gloria," Janet suggested. "Just get what you want for us. I only need a few other items for Dean and to stock cupboards. I don't mind preparing or eating whatever you want." The aisles were strolled casually and without rush. The shopping experience was part of their adventure out. They always tried to make everything an adventure.

Gloria had hoped they would dine out or order in most meals. With Gertty supplying baked goods, many junk food would not be necessary. Of course, they would not forget Gertty's gin and some additional adult beverages for themselves. In the liquor aisle, Janet spotted her new acquaintances. Laura, Cheryl, and Caroline were shopping as well. "Gloria, there are the three tourists I recently met. Let me introduce you to them," Janet requested with enthusiasm in her voice. Gloria thought that she hadn't seen Janet act so excited in many years, probably not ever since their high school days. Village life seemed to bring out the best in Janet.

Laura, Cheryl, and Caroline noticed Janet as quickly as she noticed them. "Twice meeting in one day," Caroline verbally noted. Gloria took an instant liking to them, and all were speaking over one another with so much to say. Janet noticed how well they were all interacting and asked if they would be interested in coming over for an impromptu cocktail party in just a few hours. That was an offer that they did not refuse.

Janet was so engaged in their conversation and wallowing in her happiness that she gave no thought as to how Dean would react to having party guests over. He would likely be tired after work and might not be appreciative of such a gathering. Knowing Gloria was in town, Dean would know to expect the unexpected, though. In that moment, Janet's thoughts were scattered. Her mind was on planning a party. She would invite Gertty and Armani too. She would serve cocktails and hors d'oeuvres. It would be the first time she entertained this many people in her own home. Janet was finally having a party like she had been wanting to host ever since moving to town. Even on short notice, she would do her best to make it a wonderful shindig.

"Just one thing," Cheryl asked. "The showers at the camp are really gross. Could I impose upon you to permit me to take a shower at your place? It would be so nice to see the inside of a normal bathroom." Janet didn't mind at all and invited them to stop by all the earlier to clean themselves up.

Before heading homeward, Janet suggested she and Gloria swing by Dean's office to see if he was there. He was. Janet was thrilled. While Dean was extremely busy, he spared a moment to speak. He already looked weary, and Janet explained her evening plans quickly in the time he could spare. Dean could make no promises but said he would at least stop by the party if he could. Being that he needed his rest, they would not be spending the night together, as previously decided upon, though. There was simply too much going on for both of them. Dean was feeling overwhelmed. Of course, Janet fully understood and sympathized with Dean's burden.

While work was progressing at the mass grave site, no news could be provided to Janet. Dean was about to head back there, as daylight hours were rapidly dwindling. "Oh my! It is getting later than I thought," Janet commented. Dean gave her a passionate kiss, and the staff in the department cheered him on until Janet left. On her way out, Janet strutted her stuff as a playful joke to break the stressed tension in the workplace. Those on duty saw the humor in her actions and applauded. Dean's cheeks turned a blushed-rose color.

There were a couple of quick stops Janet and Gloria made along the way. First, they stopped at Armani's house while passing by. "I'd like to extend an invitation for you to stop by this evening for a cocktail party," Janet offered. That sounded fantastic to Armani at first until he learned that Janet was inviting the tourists. Having learned that, his invitation acceptance quickly changed to a decline. He considered it might not be wise for him to have contact with those on whom the Mob was focusing.

Besides, he would rather not take the time to get to know the tourists personally. It would complicate his job if he involved emotional feelings after getting to know them intimately. All considered, he commented that he had forgotten about a prior obligation and quickly rescinded his acceptance to attend the gathering. Janet found his sudden change of enthusiasm to be awkward. She noticed that something was concerning when Armani seemed to be excited about coming over one moment and then quickly changing his mind.

From Armani's place, Janet and Gloria went to visit with Gertty. It was a quick visit, during which Gertty was handed her bottle and invited to the party. Gertty happily accepted both without hesitation.

Chapter 10

Evening came as the sky dimmed to a darker shade. A gentle summer breeze began to blow, creating a pleasant feel in the air. Nighttime critters stirred outside as party guests began coming up the walkway to Janet's home. Laura, Cheryl, and Caroline met Gloria at the door with a couple of bottles of wine and flowers. They were early and eager to clean themselves up in the bathrooms.

Passing through the kitchen, the women saw that Janet was putting the finishing touches on an appetizer platter. She cordially greeted her guests and led everyone to the bar in the living room. Cheryl and Laura declined drinks for the time being, as they elected to be first in the bathrooms to shower. They would wait until they were cleaned up so their drinks would not become too watered down. Caroline accepted a sparkling water.

"We'll save toasting until we are all together and Gertty has arrived," Janet said approvingly. Having said that, Gertty entered the house.

"I'm here!" Gertty yelled loudly through the house. "Let the party begin and the drinks flow!" She was never one to keep guests waiting long at any party.

Janet explained to Gertty about the other guests and about how they were early to utilize the showers. Gertty apologized for being early. She was sure she had been told to be there an hour later than the time was, but she became confused over the time and decided to rush over upon seeing the other guests arriving. It did not matter that Gertty came early. She was always welcome in Janet's home, even had there not been a party taking place.

The celebration was eventually in full swing and being enjoyed by all. Gertty was the life of the party, as usual. That was typical anywhere when Gertty was present with a drink in hand. She could talk in the loudest tone Janet had ever heard and bellow her voice across a room better than anyone. Janet noticed how Gertty's personal tales had changed from when Janet had first moved to the countryside. Gertty once had a negative twist on everything she said. These days, everything was positive and joyous. It was a shame Janet and Gertty had to share nasty events in the past to reach this point in their friendship. It would have been nice had they shared only the good times.

All things considered, this was now what Janet had imagined life would be like at Lake Marie. Friends, parties, and good times created a comfortable life for her, making her feel appreciative to be alive and glad to be living at the lake. With that in mind,

Janet lifted her glass of wine. "To friends and life," she toasted. As the words flowed from her lips, Janet thought of Julie. Julie wasn't there, and an instantaneous sadness filled her thoughts. Gloria picked up on it and could almost read Janet's thoughts. "As I was saying, to friends and life," Janet continued. "May we not forget the friends who could not be with us today and hope they are happy and at peace wherever they are. Here is to new friends as well. May we share many happy times together as we grow old." Everyone thought that was adequately stated.

It was as though everyone thought of Julie at once. The toast opened up conversation about the past. One by one, the guests began asking personal questions about the previous summer. Janet explained all she could think of, sharing intimate details, but never did she disclose any secretive information. Gertty and Gloria knew most all the secrets and did well at pretending there weren't any at all. In the telling of the disturbing story of last summer, there was little being told now that the visitors had not already known. Nonetheless, the story seemed more intriguing with Janet telling it from firsthand experience in chronological story form.

As for other Antioch yarns, they had not all known about some of the more obscure tales surrounding Lake Marie and Antioch. There were all sorts of tales. Occult practices within the woods around the lake always made listeners uneasy. Ghost sightings were frequently reported. Janet told of her more recent sightings of Julie, Julie's spirit, or whatever she had been witnessing. Everyone had their own opinions when it came to ghosts. Nobody made fun of Janet despite this person thinking it was a joke or that person disbelieving. Others believed that Janet really was seeing Julie's ghost.

Caroline was listening earnestly, as the paranormal was of interest to her. Then there were all the tales of murder and missing people throughout time. Janet realized she had not talked about these events in such detail since a year ago. It surprised her that she was able to speak so easily about them now. "This evening has been so much more enjoyable than I could have imagined. It's probably going to be the highlight of our trip," Caroline said. The women thanked Janet profusely and raised their glasses to toast her. While the party had been a snap to pull together, it was turning into a hit with her guests. Janet was happier than a pig in slop.

While the women partied hard, Caroline's cellphone rang. She excused herself from the party with an announcement that Dale was calling. "Who is Dale?" Janet questioned. Cheryl told Caroline and Janet that she would answer that question while Caroline was away. Caroline left the party group in search of a quiet place in which to speak.

Cheryl explained Caroline's relationship with Dale despite there not being much to say. It was a dull story for this evening when compared to those Janet, Gloria, and Gertty had told. But contrary to Cheryl feeling as if she was trying her hardest to make a dull story sound interesting, Janet, Gloria, and Gertty were just happy to be learning something personal about the visitors. It was a change of pace from the horror and gore discussions. As women, they could all relate to what Caroline must be feeling. "She is lucky to have friends at this time," Janet concluded.

Caroline exited the house and strolled the grounds casually as she spoke with Dale on the phone. At times, the discussion seemed heated. Caroline and Dale were not in agreement. Their relationship and the eventual future of a baby were in question. Caroline paced in the outside darkness, which had now peaked, except for what was illuminated by the glow of a full moon. Crickets chirped. Frogs and toads croaked. Insects buzzed. From within the house, laughter and chatter from the women echoed across the property and beyond. Sounds seemed to echo farther in these wide-open country spaces.

When the phone call ended, Caroline felt unsettled. The happiness she had experienced inside at the party had completely diminished. Leaning with her back against an oak by a clump of large trees and brush, she thought about her situation, only her thoughts were muddled and confused. She sighed heavily and exhaled. From around the tree, a gloved hand containing a rag saturated with chloroform and concentrated with other chemicals covered her face. Before she could react, a strap wrapped around her waist and held her tightly to the tree. She passed out quickly with minimal struggle.

Time passed with the women not even taking notice of the moving hands upon the clock. None cared about the time and only thought of the fun they were having and the cocktails that were pouring freely. Around 10:30 p.m., Dean entered the home. It was then during introductions that the women noticed that Caroline had not returned. She should already have, but nobody could tell how long she had been gone to be certain. Janet explained to Dean how she had come to know these tourists better and asked if he had seen Caroline around outside when he arrived. "Nobody was outside that I noticed, but I wasn't exactly looking for anyone," he replied.

"I'm going to go look for her," Laura stated. "She may be sulking over her phone conversation. She's a bit bewildered over Dale and her pregnancy." Laura shrugged her shoulders as she turned away.

Laura combed the vicinity well. She called for Caroline repeatedly, but never did she receive any answer. As she turned the corner to the last side of the house yet to be searched, a huge figure dressed all in black grabbed hold of her tightly and covered her face with a rag doused in a chloroform chemical mixture. A second figure dressed all in black was there to assist. He, too, made sure any scream she might have made was muffled and she was held securely. Laura dropped to the ground with merely a gasp escaping from her lips. As soon as she dropped, the figures in black carried her off into the night.

Dean apologized for having to leave the party so soon after arriving. Everyone understood the pressure he was under at work and why he couldn't stay. He planned to go to his place in town and get some sleep while he had some time to do so. He bid his adieus. Outside the house, he yelled, directed to those who might be outside, "Goodbye. Nice to have met you!" He was so tired that any formality or details were avoided. Uncertain if he had met everyone, he didn't care if anyone answered back. Dean just wanted to get to his bed safely and go to sleep. His departing words were wasted. Nobody was near enough to hear.

"What do we do now?" Cheryl asked. Time had lapsed, and Laura and Caroline still had not returned. Janet suggested that Gloria and Cheryl could go look for them together while she walked Gertty home. Gertty wasn't able to walk well to begin with. Considering her ailments, walking at night outdoors alone and while drunk, it all could easily add up to a recipe for disaster. They all agreed.

Upon Janet's return to the house, Cheryl announced to her that the other women were not found. "At first, I thought Caroline may have run off with Dale. She has been known to be a bit irresponsible that way. When Dale called, I thought he might be in the area," Cheryl explained. "But that would not explain where Laura went."

Janet tensed up, as she knew this was not sounding like a normal situation they should be facing. "I should call Dean, but he's so exhausted," she expressed. "Let's just call the police station and have them send an officer here. I don't want to jump to any conclusions. I also don't want to waste time if something is askew." Janet picked up her phone and dialed.

Chapter 11

Dean showed up in an unmarked car and was followed by an officer in a separate squad vehicle. Multicolored gumball lights from the squad car accompanying Dean flashed all about. Dean and the officer began searching the yard with their flashlights, creating even more luminescent glares in the dark. From within the house, the women could easily see that help had arrived. Red and blue lights entered the house through windows and produced strobe light effects onto the interior walls of various rooms.

"Dean, I didn't expect you to come. I know how busy you are," Janet expressed to him. "I'm glad you came, though. The longer we sat here waiting, the more alarmed I became. Oh, Dean!" she said as she grabbed Dean and hugged him tightly. "Laura and Caroline went outside some time ago and never returned. I'm worried!"

Cheryl stepped in and started from the beginning with all the details she could provide Dean and the officer with. After listening to her, Dean gave the women the nicest reprimand he could verbalize. Grabbing Janet's face tenderly in his cupped hands, he planted a kiss upon her forehead. "Janet, I would have expected you to call me first. You know you can always call on me no matter what is happening. I want to always be here for you. Don't worry." He hugged her closely. Then he assured the other women that they should not be panicking at this time.

"There could be any number of explanations," Dean addressed. "We have not had any reports of foul play in this area since Dan was arrested last summer. There is no reason to believe there has been any foul play now," he said, comforting everyone. "I'll get officers on it right away. Of course, let us know if you can think of anything you may have forgotten to tell me," he added. "We will do what we can for now. It is too soon to jump to any irrational conclusions being that they are adults, you know."

Janet nodded silently. She knew as much. "How are things going at the grave?" She was anxious to hear any details.

"They have stopped excavating now that it is dark. They seem to have recovered all that was visible and easily accessible on the bottom of the lake. Most everything left is buried under sediment. Some important things may have even washed away from the shoreline area and may never be discovered. For now, we are taking our time to carefully recover anything and everything we can locate.

"There are many nonrelated items being recovered. A lot is litter. We need to take care, excavating every square inch carefully. Since it is dark out now, authorities are taking a close look at what we removed from the lake today. Diving will resume bright and early tomorrow," Dean assured them. "Now I have to get back to work and then try to get some sleep tonight. I'll tell what staff they can spare to get started on the whereabouts of your friends immediately," he stated during his departure out the door.

The party group could hear the other officer say, "Should I remain in the area tonight and patrol this side of the lake?" Dean agreed that would be a good idea. "I'll keep an eye on your friends for you, Dean."

"At least until Caroline and Laura return," Dean instructed. "I want someone here on duty at all times until you are instructed otherwise. Let's hope they show up with a logical explanation. You know all the crazy things tourists do. They could have gone off somewhere for a midnight swim, or they could be entertaining the Casanova living next door. Armani has been known to lure young women to his lair. You may want to ring his doorbell and ask if he has seen them about."

"What do I do now?" Cheryl inquired of Janet and Gloria. "I am not comfortable with this. It would be terrifying for me to go back to the campsite by myself. I don't live too far away. I guess I could drive myself home."

"We would not hear of such a thing. You'll stay the night here with us. We insist. There is an extra guest bedroom, and you being here will not be an imposition. Besides, Dean had mentioned to me that we should stick together and not leave the house until he has some time to check things out," Janet insisted, stating her idea would be best.

"Thank you! It's kind of you to let me stay—not that I will sleep a wink," Cheryl said with certainty.

"I'm sure we will all have a difficult night sleeping. If you feel the need, help yourself to the bar and drink yourself silly until you pass out." That was one suggestion Janet had. "If that isn't your style, I have prescription sleeping pills if you'd like to take one." That was another suggestion Janet made. "If that still isn't your style, Cheryl, I can burn you a joint to help you relax." She was trying to be helpful. "Feel at ease to make yourself at home while you are here. Help yourself if you need anything. If you so desire, you can crash right here on the sofa. Many people have managed to do that, even when there has been a loud party going on. It's very comfortable to sleep on." Janet wanted to be accommodating.

Conversation began to dwindle, and Cheryl asked about the house. Janet explained the uneventful history of the home up until her purchase of it. Most older history of the home had only been preserved in writings on paper. Janet didn't seem to recall much about that which she had read. Her brain simply had not retained those details of names and dates. She had few memories of stories going back to when her grandparents had owned the home. She had grown up with her parents, Peg and Wes, having owned the property, and those memories were more plentiful.

Upon eventually retiring to bed, nobody slept well. Janet felt that Dean's words of attempted comfort had been of no comfort. His words were only what he was expected to tell family and friends in such concerning situations. What was happening was an all-too-familiar scenario that Janet had experienced with the disappearance of Julie. Julie had been on her property a year ago and disappeared without a trace. Janet had no reason to believe the disappearances of Caroline and Laura would turn out any differently. Sure, Dan had been arrested. However, Janet was one of the skeptics who believed he was framed. He just could not have committed all the horrible crimes he had been accused of. Janet had always known him to be such a kind, accommodating soul.

Tonight, even Janet's prescription pills were not helping her sleep well. When she managed to doze for a few short minutes, she awakened in sweat from a brief, indescribable nightmare. All she could recall of the dream was that it was a conglomerate of unrelated, wicked images. Satan and his demons played a part in it, dancing all around her home and garden. She reached over to stroke the fur of Mignon and immediately felt comfort.

In the next bedroom, Cheryl gently wept. She wasn't particularly scared. She was confused and did not know what to do. Trying hard to think of ways to help her friends, she was unknowing if they were in any need. Despite her confusion, Cheryl received satisfaction in knowing that Janet and Gloria were there with her. Even Janet's home and the bedroom she was resting in was comforting. It was homey and welcoming. It was well-appointed too.

The sound of nature outside the window replicated those she would fall asleep to in her own country living bedroom at home. It was soothing. Even the wall color was almost the same as the tone on her own bedroom walls. Cheryl was trying to think of anything she could to relax her mind. Cleopatra jumped up on the bed and snuggled beside her. The cat purred with contentment as Cheryl began massaging her ears. The cat's relaxed nature made Cheryl smile.

At the other end of the house, Gloria was staying in a bedroom separated from the others. The events of the evening had disturbed her more than she cared to admit. She had loved Julie dearly despite their conflicts at times. Her sudden disappearance had been hard to bear. Attempting to sleep was futile. Reaching into her purse on the nightstand, she withdrew a joint and headed out of her room to go for tokes.

Down a hallway and through rooms, Gloria quietly shuffled her feet through the house until she entered the four-season room on the lakeside part of the house. Sitting in a tufted chair, she hiked up her feet onto an ottoman, closed her eyes, threw her head back, and took a deep breath. She sighed upon exhaling. Lighting her joint, she was careful not to inhale too deeply. Too much harsh smoke inhaled at once always made her choke, and she didn't want to disturb her friends with a coughing fit. Not much could be seen outside the window except the dark and what little bit the moonlight illuminated. Then something caught her eye near the lake. It was a morbidly purple glow.

Walking apprehensively to the window for a closer look, Gloria could not believe her eyes. She could clearly identify that it was a vision of Julie. It was Julie, just as Janet had stated having seen on rare nights. Julie was glowing and pointing toward the lake, just as Janet had described her. But it couldn't be. These things just did not happen, or so Gloria believed. But it was unmistakable, and it wasn't the pot and alcohol playing tricks with her mind. Gloria made her way to the door. Opening the door to outside, Gloria's sight was blocked only momentarily by the swinging wooden rectangle. That momentary obstruction was just long enough for her to lose sight of the apparition. The glowing spectacle was completely gone.

Gloria contemplated if it was all a hallucination brought on by Janet's description—some sort of mass hysteria perhaps? Maybe it was a movie projection prank played by some heartless individuals. It had Gloria so wound up that she felt she just had to go to Janet's room and see if Janet was still awake. She was.

"Janet, I was in the four-season room. I know I have been drinking, and I'll admit to having just toked a few hits of a joint. Upon looking outside, I saw the apparition of Julie you mentioned," Gloria admitted. "It was shrouded in a purple glow."

"I'm so glad," Janet said with excitement as she pulled Gloria close for a hug. "I know there has been something out there at times. Nobody ever believed me."

Cheryl then appeared in the open door to Janet's room and attempted making a joke. "Is there a lesbian lovefest going on in here? Count me in!" On another night, Cheryl might have seriously considered joining in on an all-girl ménage à trois, but not tonight. Janet explained that Gloria had just informed her that she had borne witness to an apparition of Julie, the same apparition that Janet had earlier explained to Cheryl that she had been seeing herself. It was appreciated and reassuring that someone was confirming that she wasn't completely delusional.

"Really, a ghost sighting? Caroline would be in her glory to witness that. That sort of stuff is what she lives for," Cheryl said with a bit of excitement in her voice. Somehow, this conversation with Janet and Gloria was comforting her. It was no different from a conversation she might have had with Caroline and Laura. But they weren't Caroline and Laura. That thought brought sadness again. "Girls, what if I never see my friends again? What if something bad happened to them? I don't know what I'd do."

"Oh, Honey, don't think that way. What are the chances they have disappeared permanently? Our friends, including Julie specifically, would come and go at will all the time," Janet explained. "Haven't your friends ever gone off on their own on an excursion without you knowing about it?"

"Yes, I guess so. We even had a pact when we arrived here that any one of us running off with a guy and abandoning the others would need to kiss and grope the guard at the camp gate. He kind of freaked us out. While we may go off on our own at times, we never reneged on a bet," Cheryl said with a gentle smile. "Maybe I am jumping to conclusions too soon."

Gloria questioned something Cheryl said. "Your friends pursue guys? I'm only asking because it's not uncommon for guys around here to pick up girls anywhere. If they were out back and Armani had seen them from next door, he might be banging them right now at his place. There was a time even Janet couldn't resist his physique and charms," Gloria said slyly with a wink directed at Janet. "He stole her virginity."

"That much is true," Janet admitted. "Women can't resist his charms. But it is late, and I can't imagine they are still with him, if they ever were. He is not known for having tricks inside his home. They usually are entertained in his garage in a wham-bam manner." Janet thought for a moment before suggesting they try to get a bit of shut-eye. "We can all look into the concerns of tonight in the morning when it's light out and we are somewhat rested. It's bad enough we will have hangovers tomorrow, I'm sure. We may see things differently after some rest."

Gloria and Cheryl disagreed with Janet's desire to sleep. They began playfully pulling her by her arms to get her out of her bed. There would be no sleep until they went outside to where the apparition had been seen. If there was a clue to be discovered, they were determined to find it before the clue was gone. Janet knew that nothing would be discovered because she had already looked after all her previous sightings. She went along outside begrudgingly.

They stayed close so as not to separate. Each shining a flashlight, they searched every crevice and treetop in that section of the yard. As had always been, an inspection provided no clues. "Ghosts don't leave clues," Janet concluded. The others didn't know if they were yet convinced ghosts existed in the first place. And even if they did exist, they were not convinced this had been a ghost sighting.

Chapter 12

Inside an aged basement dug out beneath a vacant utility barn, three large prison pens were occupied. Caroline was in one of them; Laura in another. In the third, a Native American girl stood at the iron bars, calling out to Caroline and Laura. "Hello! Hello! Won't you wake up? I need help," the young girl said loudly while sobbing.

Caroline awakened gradually. She had obliviously been drugged and felt horrible. Her wrists and ankles were bound in heavy shackles. Her dizzying state caused her vision to vibrate. Everything she could see appeared contorted. Caroline shook her head, trying to clear her eyesight. The girl spoke to her, but the words seemed rather inaudible. Shaking her head and looking to her side, Caroline could see Laura in a separate prison cell next to her. She, too, was shackled. Laura was wrapped in a blanket and still unconscious on the dirt floor.

"Please look at me. Speak to me," the girl pleaded. "I've been kidnapped, and I don't understand why. Can you please tell me what I'm doing here? Where are we?" The girl was very scared.

"Hell if I know," Caroline replied honestly. "My name is Caroline. That's my friend Laura." Caroline coughed a dry cough while feeling like crap. "I was at a party and went outside to take a call from my boyfriend. I was attacked and passed out. They used some kind of chemicals on me. I can still smell the horrible scent up my nostrils. I have never smelled anything like it."

"Is your boyfriend the father of your baby?" The young girl was to the point with her line of questioning. She seemed very mature and educated for the age she appeared to be.

"How did you know I am pregnant?" Caroline was extremely curious how the young stranger could have known such a personal fact.

"The men who bring people here mentioned it when they brought you in. They were extra gentle with you because they didn't want your baby put in any danger." That was really all the youth knew of the matter.

Caroline grabbed her head and pressed hard with her fingers. "Laura! Laura! Wake up!" she called out with desperation.

Laura began to moan and come to. Eventually, she began to speak. "I was looking for you at the party. You seemed to be gone a long time. It was dark outside, and I don't know what hit me. I feel as if I have the worst hangover in history; just look at me. It seems I am—or was—bleeding from my head.

Perhaps I fell and hit my head. I just don't know. All I remember is a blunt pain on top of my head and another at the base of my neck hitting me simultaneously. It felt like karate chops hitting me in multiple places. What is going on here? Where are we? Why am I naked and chained up?" Her questions and clear speech indicated that she was not too out of it.

Caroline was in a bit less discomfort and had been alert for a few moments longer than Laura had been. Caroline had not been drinking alcohol earlier because of her pregnancy. Hence, she had no hangover to contend with. Caroline had only been knocked out with the chloroform-infused solution and then later drugged to keep her sedated. She had not been knocked out with a force and chemicals too in the way Laura had been. That was intentional on the part of her abductors, as they had not wanted to risk injuring the fetus. They had taken extra care of her.

Laura looked toward Caroline and questioned, "Why are we naked and chained up?" Caroline was still not thinking clearly and had not even thought of their nudity. Her mind wasn't fully focusing yet. "I'm not well, Caroline." Laura abruptly spewed vomit down her front side. Whatever she had endured wasn't reacting well with the booze in her system, and whatever had hit her had caused a nauseating migraine.

"Nobody has determined the answers to any questions," Caroline stated as she tried to ponder their situation in greater detail. "Perhaps this was a setup. Have you considered that Dean and Janet may be responsible for our being here, that their little party was part of the plan to kidnap us?" Anything was possible.

"Who are you?" Laura asked the girl. "How did you get here, and how long have you been here?"

"My name is Diana. I'm part of the local indigenous tribe," the young Indian girl responded.

"Part of the Fox family tribe?" Laura asked.

"You know of my family?" Diana answered Laura's question with surprise in her voice. "I am known as Sun Fox. I was born at sunrise. My father tells people I am the sunshine in his life."

"Caroline and I know of your family," Laura stated with conciseness. "In fact, the woman giving the party told us of your Fox-named family shortly before we were taken from the party. A coincidence? You may know the woman hosting the party: Janet. Her home was the center of a crime investigation last year."

"I do know of her," Diana admitted. "Well, I have heard my family speak of her. Some of my family are private investigators, and they have had some sort of business dealings involving Dean and Janet. That's about all I know, except for any details I may have heard in the news. But I don't specifically recall any off the top of my head. I don't watch the news much."

"How old are you?" Caroline questioned, joining in on the conversation.

"I'm fifteen," Diana replied. "I'll be sixteen next week." She looked even younger than that. One might have guessed she was thirteen at most.

"You are only a couple of years younger than we are," Laura informed Diana. "You look so much younger than you are, so much younger than us. I'm only making an observation."

"So we are teenaged females. What would you think we are doing here?" Caroline asked rhetorically.

"Human trafficking?" Laura answered.

Diana began crying. "What will they expect of us and where will they take us?" Her innocent youth was exposing itself.

"Don't cry. Please!" Laura requested. "Caroline and I are just trying to figure this out logically. Obviously, those who have taken us target young females. No sign of any men captives down here with us. They want us to feel vulnerable. That's why we are naked and chained up. From the looks of these cells, they are not new and were not built on our account alone. What is happening to us has happened to other people. It's probably going to keep happening. The kidnappers are not novices. They also did not put us down here to die. Someone will be coming shortly, and we will be taken elsewhere. I'm certain of it. It surprises me that you are a local, Diana. Caroline and I are just tourists. Local people will express more concern for you."

The moment Laura finished speaking, a disguised voice came over a concealed speaker. "Bravo! You've managed to state the obvious," the stranger said. "We will be down shortly with some food and water. A medical expert will also look each of you over. I want you all to know that I am just one of many people involved in your abductions. Nobody you will see here was responsible for selecting you. I personally will never again lay eyes upon you once you are removed from the premises. Please try not to give anyone too much trouble during your stay here. We are only trying to help in doing as we have been instructed to do. I'd strongly advise you to do as you are instructed to do."

"You think that makes you any less responsible for what is happening here? You, too, have hurt us. You scare us. Well, admit it. You are a horrible excuse for a human being. May you burn in hell, and we can rejoice for you then." Laura was furious as she shouted at the unidentified, disembodied voice. "I'd kill you if I had the chance. You are a sorry excuse, you piece of shit!"

"I don't expect you to like me or for you to understand. No matter what you think of me or say, I shall speak to you cordially and keep you informed as to what you may expect next," the unfamiliar voice said kindly as if he and the young women were well-acquainted friends. "I'd suggest you follow my instructions. The others more so responsible for your abduction will not take any bullshit from you. They are serious and are killers. They will not hesitate to waste you or those you love if you give them even the slightest bit of trouble. They know all about you and your families. There is nobody here who will save you from your fates. You will be transferred out of here likely before anyone could figure out where you now are. That was a brilliant deduction Laura had made earlier. This place was not constructed for you. It has been here a long time and has never been discovered. So don't have too high hopes that you'll be the first ones to be rescued here."

Chapter 13

Cheryl was first to come out of her room. She peeked in on Janet, who was slowly awakening. Janet heard her open the door to her room, and she looked at Cheryl from her bed. "I'm sorry for not knocking first," Cheryl said apologetically. "I didn't want to awaken you if you were asleep. I know it's early. I just can't sit still any longer. The sun is coming up, and I am going to take a more extensive look around outside."

Gloria was awakened by the opening of another door. Dean arrived and tried to enter quietly through the back door. Gloria yelled out to Dean from her bed as she jumped up. Dean slapped his knuckle against the bedroom door, and Gloria requested he enter. As the bedroom door swung ajar, she finished applying her robe and slippers.

"I was just getting ready to get out of bed," Gloria announced. "You aren't disturbing me. It's time I start the day."

"Did your friends show up last night?" Dean needed to know. "Nobody contacted me last night to say that they had heard from them. Our patrol reported things were quiet all night since he started patrolling. Normally, no news is good news, but I am not so sure in this instance."

"I did eventually fall asleep. I am not aware if Laura and Caroline have returned. I'd think I'd have known if they had," Gloria said to Dean. "There is something I want to say to you but don't want Janet hearing," she said as she walked over and closed her bedroom door for privacy. "Janet has been seeing things, unusual things. She hasn't wanted to say anything to you because she hasn't wanted to involve or worry you. She knows how busy you are.

"In particular, she has been seeing ghostly apparitions of Julie. Now after being here, I have seen the same apparition. I don't know if someone is playing some sick game, but I'm determined to get to the bottom of this. It may even be her ghost, if you could believe such a thing. I think you should be around here as much as you can, Dean. I know how important your job is, but Janet is important too. After all that has transpired last night, I think you'll agree there is reason to start expressing a greater concern for her safety and well-being."

"Wow! She hasn't said anything to me," Dean replied. "Did you tell Janet you saw Julie?"

"Yes. She felt comforted knowing I'm here to help," Gloria was happy to say. "She needs some looking after. I'll do all I can. I'm no substitute for a strong, virile man. She needs you—not that she has said that herself. It's only my opinion."

"I'm not disagreeing that Janet can use some looking after," Dean agreed. "I am just not certain you should be supporting any far-out delusions she may be seeing and thinking. I believe you saw something. It certainly could be some sick joke involving Julie. But I don't want you supporting some far-out theory of ghosts. Promise me you'll take her to her psychiatrist's office and attend a session with her. See for yourself what her doctor has to say. Obviously, I am unable to count on her sharing information with me. I'll try to speak to her about that without telling her you and I spoke behind her back."

Dean was actually happy Gloria had shared these words with him. He had been busy and always regretted not being able to share the amount of quality time with Janet he would have liked to. Until the discovery of the bodies, he had not been too busy. It bothered him that Janet had not discussed Julie with him at an earlier time, when he might have been able to be of more help.

Gloria followed Dean into the kitchen, where they met up with Cheryl. "Look who I found," Gloria was happy to announce. They each exchanged a pleasant greeting in passing while Dean progressed to his and Janet's bedroom to see his love.

Janet was thrilled to see her man. "Darling!" she shrieked joyously when he approached. "I'm just getting up this morning. It was a rather sleepless night around here for all of us."

"And you look positively radiant," Dean said to Janet, as he did each morning without fail. "I hope to be staying here as much as I can through this investigation. I just hope I can sleep with a houseful of your friends letting loose." It pleased Janet to hear that. "One more thing. You have always understood that my job requires me keeping professional secrets. I understand that you too may not always share everything going on around here with me. Considering what is happening, I need you to be very open with me now. It is not the time for you to consider keeping secrets from me. Lives may be at stake." Janet understood and told Dean all she had been keeping from him pertaining to Julie.

"I'm sure you're fine," he said. "You are a strong woman. But just to be on the safe side, I want you to take Gloria to see your psychiatrist. I spoke to her, and she wants to go. She needs to speak to him about some things, and you can ask his opinions while you are there. Make sure your medications are doing right by you." He hoped that comment would take some of the pressure off Janet. She could think they were going for Gloria's good too. He then kissed her passionately. "I don't want to have to worry about anything with you or Gloria."

Janet slipped out of her nightshirt to dress for the day, and Dean realized that it had been a few days since they had intense physical contact. Swinging her around, he grabbed her lustfully and cupped her breasts in his hand while preparing his mouth to kiss her deeply. Janet made a brief motion to protest, citing that they were not alone in the house. Dean did not care. The thought of people being around excited him more. They usually had the house to themselves but had never performed with others near. His cock swelled rapidly, and he knew he would finish quickly. Swinging Janet around, he threw her on the bed and yanked her lacy pink panties down below her firm buttocks. Spitting in his hand, he rubbed his lubricating fluid onto his swollen cock. Janet cooperated willingly and wanted him as much he wanted her.

Gently, he mounted her. His thrusts were slow at first. It was pleasing as her pussy began creaming. The warm feeling inside her escalated his desire. Her clit shifted back and forth with each thrust. His penis never felt so good inside her. Janet realized this was the first time their sexual experience wasn't involving foreplay and would not involve cuddle time after. It would be just a raw sexual experience with no frills. Dean had never treated her in that manner before, and there was something primal in the experience. It excited her, and it excited him too. She began to moan louder and louder, and she covered her mouth to suppress her screams of passion.

He fought his own desire to moan loudly, as was his way, not wanting to alert the others in the house to their fornication. Trying not to make a sound seemed to affect his breathing, and oxygen seemed restrained while climaxing. To his surprise, Janet was thrusting and creaming as he had never known her to do before. It was always special when they came in unison. Completing the act, Dean collapsed on

Janet's back before rolling over off to her side. They looked each other in the eyes, and each was reminded of the special, loving bond they shared. They beamed as they panted heavily.

"Look at what you've done now," Janet jokingly complained. "Now I will need to take a shower before I start my day."

"No," Dean requested. "I don't want you to. I want you to carry our love around with you today. I want you to feel I am with you all day. Will you do that for me? I want to think about you doing that as a favor for me today. Life is stressful right now, and I need that distraction. I'll be thinking of you whenever I can."

"Even if it will make me feel dirty, I'll do that for you," Janet agreed. "That means you don't wash off either. I want to see that dry cum flaking off your cock when I see you next, you nasty, dirty white boy!" Somehow, it sounded sexier to him when he made the request of her. But turnabout was fair play, and he would do anything for Janet even if it meant donning his spunk for the entire day. It amazed him how they could share a conversation and intimacy in a matter of minutes and that it could make the world's woes seem to lessen.

"Let's not be selfish any longer," Dean suggested. "The women are still missing. I think we can assume something is definitely askew. The department would say that not enough time has elapsed since they were last seen to put much effort into finding them. Still, I think I need to step up to a more aggressive investigation. I was hoping the missing women would be sitting at your kitchen table this morning when I came in. I could envision you all sitting around, sipping coffee or tea. You all would be laughing as though nothing was wrong. I wish I knew why this horror is starting up again."

"Do you think perhaps Dan wasn't the guilty party in all this?" Janet expressed her feelings. Dean already knew what she thought on the subject. Nobody who knew Dan wanted to think Dan was capable of all the crimes. However, assuming Dan had been guilty and was now safely put away had made the world seem like a safer place. If Dan wasn't to blame, there was no way of knowing how much trouble the community would be facing.

"I have never imagined Dan had committed the crimes all on his own. Now that we have found the watery graves, we can assume that the wrong man is locked up. Some of the corpses we've recovered are of those who've died rather recently. Dan could not have been responsible for their deaths from where he is. Yet it's peculiar we've not had any reports of missing persons locally over this last year since Dan was put away." Janet had no words.

Dean said his goodbyes to Gloria and Cheryl in the kitchen on his way out of the house. Janet sat down at the table with her friends, who were discussing the day ahead. She suggested they take her motorboat to Baskin's for breakfast. They could finish planning their daily agenda there. Janet thought the fresh air and nourishment would do them good.

But first, she wanted to go talk to Armani and Gertty. Armani might know something, and Gertty would want to know anything.

While Cheryl and Gloria combed Janet's property and its surroundings for clues, Janet strolled next door to Armani's home. Armani was not at home, but that was no coincidence. He had intentionally planned to be away during the abductions and had stayed away from the town all night. He made certain he would have an alibi. He had his routines down pat.

Gertty was at home and was sorry to hear that their friends were still missing. It bothered her that she had met the women and that they had disappeared from a party she, too, was in attendance. "I worry so much about you young women in the world. Nobody would bother with an old hag like me. You young women need to watch your backs. It's a dangerous world out there." These words of warning Gertty shared were the exact words she had shared with Janet on multiple occasions since they met. "I want to help find your friends. I'm not much good at much of anything, but I can try to help," Gertty sincerely offered.

"Any help is appreciated. If you can think of anything, you'll let us know, won't you?" Janet asked. "If you see Armani, could you fill him in?" Gertty nodded. "We'll be at Baskin's for breakfast. I'll check back with you later today."

Walking back to her house, Janet's phone rang. It was her mother and father checking up on her. She had not talked with them since before Gloria arrived. There was no way she would worry them with talk of Laura and Caroline. Knowing Gloria was to be visiting, Janet's parents would not expect to stay on the call with Janet for long. They would know she was busy entertaining. Being that they were calling, it was evident they were just being polite and making certain Gloria had arrived and settled in safely. They had known Gloria as long as Janet did, and they thought of her fondly.

"Hello!" Janet greeted her mom on the phone. "Gloria arrived and is settled in. We are just about to go for breakfast." Janet's mom said she didn't want to be a disturbance. Janet knew that wasn't true. Her mother had always been a nosy busybody, and her words stating otherwise never disguised that fact. The conversation was brief, and Janet wanted to keep it that way—short and sweet. "I will, Mom. I'll be sure to tell Gloria to enjoy herself and take care. I'll tell her you called. I'll call you after she goes home and tells you all about her stay. Yes, Mom. Bye, Mom!" Janet disconnected the call and was glad to be off the phone. If her mother knew there was trouble, she and Janet's father would be showing up in no time. Janet would never involve them. If there was danger, putting them in danger too would not be wise. It wasn't always easy to keep things from her parents. They could smell trouble with family all the way from their hometown, Prospect Heights.

Chapter 14

Janet's boat was an older model, but it ran magnificently. It still looked beautiful and was becoming a classic. Her family had taken great care of it over the years. The vessel also had a great engine with a lot of power. Suitable for seating several people, there was a front deck designed for sunbathing and a small back deck for diving. The colors were aqua and white, which once matched her home of white with aqua trim. The family car had also once matched the house and boat. One could estimate the age of the boat if they considered how long ago such a color scheme had been in style.

She had often deliberated in her mind replacing the boat with a newer model. Just as she got excited over the concept, all the fond memories she had shared on the watercraft with her friends and family would cause her to reconsider. The boat was a possession she held dear to her heart. That meant a lot to Janet, as she wasn't usually the type to covet possessions.

The women cruised the lake on their way to the channel leading to Baskin's. The weather was perfect and could not have been nicer. Great weather during peak seasons caused the lake to be occupied by an exceptionally large number of water enthusiasts. Today was no exception. Entering the channel leading to their destination, their boat slowed to the posted speed limit. Men on piers and boat after boat of studs clad in skimpy swim trunks catcalled the lovely trio as they passed by. Whistles, shouts, and comments of a sexual nature were coming from all directions. In this environment, it was to be expected. These women were pretty, and they would not go by unnoticed. Gloria and Laura were enjoying the attention.

Pulling up to Baskin's, the scene was more serene. People were coming and going in a more businesslike atmosphere. They docked their boat and made their way into the establishment. Mr. Baskin was there and greeted Janet cordially. He had known her since she was born but had not had the chance to see her often or get to know her until Janet had moved to the lake on her own. Janet felt awkward whenever he was at the establishment. Baskin knew that Janet wished Dan the best, but that did not offset the fact that Dean had been the one to help put Dan away.

Janet felt that there must be some extent of underlying bitterness Baskin had for her although he had never said so. Janet once had a long talk with the man in hopes that he would understand she had no ill feelings toward Dan. She even informed Baskin that she was occasionally in contact with Dan and wished to support him in any way she could. While Mr. Baskin thought Janet's words were kind, Janet never felt better for having had the discussion. Mr. Baskin had only listened to her and stated he thought she was sweet. He had never disclosed how he personally felt.

Janet wanted some pacification to feel that there had been some closure. She wanted Baskin to tell her that she needed not blame herself. She wanted to hear that he did not blame her and that there were no hard feelings. Mr. Baskin had never made any such comments. There was no reason he would be clearing the air today.

As would be expected, he sat them at a dining table on a deck overlooking the water and mentioned a few of the daily specials. Chuck was busy working at the boat shop too. He was happy to see Janet and Cheryl and be their server. His responsibilities at the moment only allowed him brief, interrupted moments to talk about any personal matters. Other customers were calling upon him to provide service, and he was trying his best to accommodate all of them. He recognized Cheryl and knew he had been the one who had originally led her to meeting Janet by providing Cheryl and her friends with the address of Janet.

Janet introduced Chuck to Gloria today. While taking their drink order, Chuck asked about Laura. Cheryl stated that Laura had left and that they didn't know where she had gone to at this time. Chuck thought that sounded ominous, but being too busy, he accepted their answer for what it was. Perhaps, he thought, he had been too personal and that it was none of his business. The women noticed that he seemed letdown that Cheryl wasn't with them. It struck Janet as being very peculiar, but she did not know how Chuck and Laura had acted together when they met. There had been a definite mutual attraction. Cheryl thought nothing of it and considered the inquiry Chuck made to be darling.

As they settled at the table and Chuck left, the women began to discuss the day ahead. "I need to get back to my camp," Cheryl mentioned. "Our things are there. My friends might be too. Also, I really should notify our families that there is a problem. They are probably going to be mad at me that I have not already called them. I'm going to emphasize that Dean suggested we not jump to any conclusions, and I'll place the blame on him."

"After breakfast, why don't we take you back to my place? You can call everyone you need to from there," Janet offered. "Mignon will need to go out. It will give me chance to tend to his other needs." Cheryl liked that suggestion. "But I do not think we should go to the campsite for your things until we speak to Dean. I was thinking we should swing by the graves and check things out for ourselves. He should be there by now. We can't interfere, but we should get a grasp on what is happening over there. Dean may want to have investigators look around your campsite before we disturb it. After all, many people go missing from the exact site you are staying at. It may have some connection to Caroline and Laura's sudden disappearance. Perhaps investigators will see something we wouldn't know to look for."

"Good thinking," Gloria said while applauding Janet with a quiet clapping of her hands. "You and Dean are probably starting to think alike. I like that."

"That's what I've learned from observing Dean at work for so long," Janet replied. "Any other thoughts as to how we should proceed?" At that moment, Janet's phone vibrated atop the table. She reached for it and picked it up. There was an Amber Alert. The police department had posted a notice stating that Diana was reported missing. Details were plentiful enough for Janet to comprehend that the missing youth was part of the Indian tribe nearby. It was the same reservation the Fox family was affiliated with.

"I think my question has just been answered," Janet stated while explaining the alert. "We should visit the Fox family and find out what they know— show our support, at the very least. I don't want to interfere with Dean's work, so we will first ask him if it would be all right if we do that."

"It sounds as if we have a busy day ahead of us. This visit is once again not turning into the relaxing vacation I was expecting—not that I mind. There is never any excitement and adventure in Prospect Heights. I'm just glad I came alone this time," Gloria commented with a smile. "I could just imagine what my boyfriend would be thinking if he had come along with me."

"Thanks for standing by me and helping," Cheryl replied. "Both of you are so kind. I know you don't need to involve yourselves in this, and it means a lot to have your support at this time."

"When one is involved with Dean, shit happens. The need to help people has sort of rubbed off on me," Janet said. "Meanwhile, don't mention it. We will all do what we can, I'm sure. But as Gertty said to me earlier, I don't know if what we can do will be enough."

"Let's hurry up here and get on our way. The sooner, the better," Gloria suggested as they finished dining, and Chuck brought the bill to their table.

On their way into the store, passing through on their way out of the restaurant area, Janet had a vision. She wasn't certain from the angle from which she had entered from the far dining end, but someone resembling Julie seemed to be in the store with them. It simply could not be. The store area was not very large. Further inspection of the area proved that nobody else was around, except for Mr. Baskin behind one of the counters.

"Can I help you ladies with anything else today?" Mr. Baskin cordially offered.

"I don't think so, Mr. Baskin. We'll just be browsing for but a moment," Janet answered.

Mr. Baskin exited the counter area and walked toward the dining room door before planning to go outside to the deck dining area. "I'm going to quickly survey the dining area. If you need anything, I'll be back at the counter in just a moment," he said from the doorway. "If not, kindly let yourselves out," he added. "I can trust you and your friends alone in here for just a minute, Janet. If I find there was any trouble when I get back, I know where you live and how to get ahold of Dean." He laughed.

"We will let ourselves out, Mr. Baskin," Janet replied. "I don't think we will be needing anything else. We just intend to browse for a moment."

"Well, I'll be back in just a moment," he assured them.

"What are you browsing for, Janet?" Gloria questioned. "I thought we wanted to get on our way."

Janet explained what she thought she had seen, but it could not have been as she thought because nobody else was inside the shop. Had there been and they had gone toward the dining area, that person would have noticeably passed by them. Had that person gone out of the store through the main door, a brass bell hanging above the exit would have made a loud tinkling sound. There was no indication that anyone at all had been there where Janet had seen Julie standing.

"Where exactly do you think you saw her?" Gloria questioned.

"Right where we are standing. She was looking at the bulletin board of missing persons here on the wall," Janet said while pointing to it with her index finger extended. "It must have some meaning." As she stepped close to the board, she felt dizziness overcome her. Reaching out to steady herself, she placed the palm of her hand onto the wall hanging. As she did that, speckles of bright lights filled her eyeballs, and she was blinded for a brief moment. She lost her balance but caught herself before fully collapsing, but not before the pressure of her hand sliding against the message board caused the item to come loose from the wall.

Cheryl reached out to assist in helping keep it from falling to the ground. The board had slid quite a bit from the original position and exposed a small cutout in the wall. Inside the cutout was a book. Gloria quickly reached for it, pulling it out of its hiding spot. Cheryl positioned the bulletin board back into its original position on the wall. Janet composed herself and suddenly felt fine again. Her dizziness passed just as suddenly as the episode had struck.

"Are you all right, Janet?" Gloria asked with great concern. "What happened?"

"Just a momentary dizzy spell came over me. I've had them before—not often. The doctor hasn't been concerned because they never seem to occur around the time I have medical appointments. He said we'd look into it further if they become bothersome. They only happen once every few months. Perhaps it is just my body processing sugar from the meal," Janet figured, trying to offer her friends an acceptable explanation.

"Look at this old book, though," Gloria said with an inquisitive look upon her face. She opened the book, and they glanced inside.

"Where did you get that?" Janet wanted to know.

"From inside the wall. I pulled it from a concealed spot when the board tilted and exposed it inside of a hole cut into the wall," Gloria informed Janet.

"Quick. Let's get out of here before anyone sees us with it," Janet instructed.

"Are we going to steal it? It's not our book," Cheryl clearly stated.

"I'll explain after we are away from here. This is important, very important. Please hurry, and let's get out with the book now while we can!" Janet's voice became even harsher and demanding. It surprised Gloria, who had never heard her speak in that tone.

As their boat parted the dock, Janet tried to explain the book. "I will not know more until I have time to study it, but this book may be very important. A memory stick is rumored to exist which lists a lot of very important information. It is said that it contains a list of everyone who is missing and what became of them. It mentions the names of Mob members. It's something of local legend. I think this is a handwritten version of that computer data. I'll need to take a longer look at it to be certain."

Once through the channel and back on Lake Marie, Janet stalled the engine. They examined the book. What Janet suspected was exactly what it looked to be. Events seemed to be documented in chronological time order. Julie's name was not mentioned. Neither were those of Caroline, Laura, or the girl mentioned in the Amber Alert. It could have been that the most recent missing persons had not yet been entered.

"Let's get this over to Dean right away," Janet requested. "He should be at the grave site, and that is just right over there," she indicated while pointing to a lot of activity on the nearby lake edge. It would be hard for anyone not to identify the location due to all the equipment and activity. There were emergency vehicles, news crews, and construction trucks for digging that cluttered the landscape. "I'll only be able to get so close. I'll dock the boat at the nearest pier, and we will need to walk there along the lake."

Having walked the distance, the women approached a taped-off area. A guard recognized Janet and greeted her. "We need to speak to Dean right away," she requested.

"He's here," the guard spoke as he reached to his waist for radio to contact Dean with. "Janet is here to see you. She said it's important." Dean responded by saying he would be right over. It didn't take him long to meet Janet and her friends.

"What brings you by? It's nice to see you."

"We've something in our possession which we think is very important. I need to speak to you in private right away," Janet stated with desperate concern in her voice.

Pulling Dean aside and away from prying eyes and ears, Janet discussed how they had found the book at Baskin's. It was the strangest thing, Janet mentioned about the shifting of the board. Having thought she had seen Julie and then locating the book in that location was too weird. One could think that Julie had led her to it.

"You stole this from Baskin's?" Dean asked.

"Dean, you know we need to cover up the facts about how you and I came to obtain it. Yes, it was actually obtained illegally, but I wasn't about to risk letting it out of our sight. It's not as if we haven't had secrets before. People committing these crimes are playing dirty, and I know that sometimes, even the law needs to play dirty to combat them. Get over the technicalities. You know as well as I do how important this book is. There are a number of people who would stop at nothing to get ahold of this. You know that," Janet emphasized. "But there's something else. While I've not had time to completely study the book, there is no mention of Julie, Caroline, or Laura in it where entries are expected to be. No mention of the child in the Amber Alert either. I do not know if the child is linked to this or if that is a separate case. I brought it right over to you as soon as possible without reading it all." Janet was glad to assist.

"You're going to need to make sure your friends back you on your story. The last thing we need is for any evidence to be dismissed because of technicalities. I'm going to say an unidentified woman approached me and handed the book to me. That's all I can say," Dean concocted. "Most of all, I want to be certain you are okay. I don't like that you were feeling dizzy again. Please speak to your doctor sometime soon." Janet nodded reassuringly.

Dean continued, "Just to be certain, I am going to check with Mr. Baskin and ask about his security cameras. I've seen his system last year during investigations. It's been a whole year, though. If he put in new cameras or adjusted those he had, he may have seen you girls take this book. If he knew of this book and saw you, you and your friends will be in great danger." Dean and Janet began to realize just how much danger. "I want you to take Gloria home, and I am going to send a guard home with you. Leave Cheryl here. I'm going to send a couple of specialists to her campsite to investigate there. If all appears to be in order, we will pack up her camp and deliver her to the house. I want her with us in case any questions arise."

Dean had everything planned out, and Janet admired how he could think up things so quickly and make decisive decisions. She was not like that at all. Her thoughts always seemed to be so random and jump from one topic to another until she became very confused. Thank goodness for doctors and medications.

"I'm okay with that for now, except Cheryl needs to call her loved ones. She's concerned about doing that right away," Janet said on Cheryl's behalf. "We also thought about visiting the Fox family. We have seen the Amber Alert and wanted to show our support. As you suggested, though, Gloria and I will go home and relax until you bring Cheryl."

"We'll see to it that Cheryl's loved ones are contacted appropriately. I'll try to instruct her on what to say and what not to. It's best authorities help take care of any calls. Let's go back to your friends and discuss our plans, and let's hope your friends will fully cooperate. The slightest slipups could be catastrophic. The safety of people and the protection of evidence are imperative. I need not remind you of that. As far as you and your friends are concerned for now, none of you knows anything about this book," Dean stressed.

"I get it, Dean. Let's go talk to Cheryl and Gloria."

Gloria and Cheryl agreed to fully cooperate. Being deceitful didn't bother their conscience as long as it meant helping people. The excitement gave them each an unusual thrill. What had been transpiring was a hope that their friends would be safely rescued. That hope was terrific! Their usually uneventful lives suddenly became interesting.

They all followed plans respectfully. Cheryl remained behind as a couple of armed private security escorts rode to Janet's home with her and Gloria in Janet's boat. The passengers all remained quiet during the duration of the ride. Janet and Gloria were afraid to say anything that could be used against them. The women would wait to get to Janet's home before speaking privately.

Chapter 15

It was late afternoon when Dean pulled up to Janet's home with Cheryl and the camping gear. Janet and Gloria ran from the television set to greet them. "Thank goodness you are here. It's been so uneasy with security men around. We've been counting the minutes until your return," Gloria complained. "I'm here on vacation, not for confinement. No matter which guard was speaking to us, they talked like the Gestapo."

"Good news, then. Things are progressing nicely," Dean was happy to announce. "I'm delivering Cheryl to you with her gear. She is going to stay with us—for a few days, at least. I think it's best for her safety that we keep an eye on her."

Everyone assisted in carrying the heavy gear into the house and down into the basement, where it would remain out of the way.

Dean continued. "As for the security cameras at Baskin's, I'm certain there is nothing to worry about. We checked the place out and looked at surveillance tapes. Nothing to see. We told Mr. Baskin that we were looking for some pedestrians and thought they may have been at his place at some point in recent time. Baskin suspected nothing out of the ordinary was afoot and cooperated fully. I've known him my whole life and think I could have determined if he suspected anything unusual." Janet, Gloria, and Cheryl were relieved to hear that. "At this moment, we believe the book had been placed there by Dan Baskin, and his father probably knew nothing of it being in existence."

"That implicates Dan even further." Janet was in disbelief.

"It seems so," Dean said in a disheartened manner. He knew many people would not be happy to hear that. Those who believed in Dan's innocence had been wrong all along. "Oh, and the grave excavation has come to an end. It's believed they have recovered all they can. Those bodies recovered are definitely linked to the Mob. Meanwhile, I'm sure there are missing pieces to the puzzle still in that lake. It wasn't my decision to end the recovery mission. The higher-ups felt they had recovered all they reasonably could. It's not worth their time and taxpayer money to sift through the lake bottom sediment to come up with litter having nothing to do with their investigation."

"Most of that sounds like good news," Gloria exclaimed. "Does all this mean we can ditch the Gestapo now?"

"I'll be taking them with me and stationing a single police officer outside the house. Mignon will protect you too," Dean said while laughing because of Mignon's cowardliness. Mignon was only capable of possibly loving someone to death. Generally speaking, the pup was afraid of his own shadow. The cat had more nerve. "The bad news is that I will not be staying here for a while. This is a big case, and I do not want my involvement to interfere with home life. I need to be sure any sign of danger has passed."

That depressed Janet. It was strange to think that the same man able to protect her could be the one to draw harm to her. Dean and the security guards left the inside of the house, and the women were finally alone.

"We aren't going to just sit around this house doing nothing, are we?" Gloria asked.

"Recent developments aside, we'd have been staying in tonight anyway," Janet reminded Gloria. "We will order pizza and watch horror movies. I've got some new ones. Do you like horror movies, Cheryl?" Cheryl liked them and very much liked the plan for the sedate evening. "Let's clean ourselves up and start cocktail hour."

"We can do our hair and nails," Gloria suggested. "I've got some new polish colors I've been wanting to try." The women liked her idea. "Then we can apply mud masks and play with dolls!" Gloria thought she would add that as an inside joke about what Dean thought women did on an evening together.

It wasn't long before the women reconvened in the living room. Janet turned on trendy music and poured drinks. The doorbell rang. It was Gertty.

"Can you smell an open bottle of liquor from next door?" Janet greeted Gertty verbally upon letting her in. "We just poured the cocktails."

"Oh, don't mind if I do," Gertty said, pushing her way past Janet without officially being asked to join them. "Howdy, y'all!" she bellowed, walking into the living room and right up to the bar. "It's only Gertty! I saw an officer patrolling outside and wondered what the hell is going on."

The women filled Gertty in as they all drank and chatted. Janet's phone rang, and she ran to the other room to take the call. It was Dean with a question.

"You have a knack for knowing things, Janet," Dean said before leading to a question he was searching for the answer to. "Having looked over the book I received earlier; it appears to be a private journal belonging to an individual. It's not a full copy of what the infamous memory stick might contain. It is possibly a written documentation of Dan Baskin's sole involvement. It is still a very valuable piece of evidence.

"The reason I am calling is, there is reference to a holding house. It is a secret lair where they take those kidnapped for holding. There is no exact reference as to where that may be, except the journal mentions it is somewhere in Antioch. There is only a reference to a pipe with running water. Then it states to go to the two nearest buildings. Nobody here can determine where that could possibly be. The pipe and two buildings could refer to any pipe in this village. If you can think of any specific, remote place this journal is referencing, let me know please."

"That is vague. I'll ponder it," Janet promised.

"By the way, don't call me with any information," Dean requested. "I don't want to discuss this book any longer by phone. Remember, you know nothing about this book. You've never seen it. Even if you are being tortured, you have never seen it. One other thing I wanted to mention. I spoke with Armani and mentioned your friends were missing from your yard. He was not in town at the time in question. He was away all night. His story checked out. He could not have witnessed anything," he mentioned. Then after expressing his love, he ended the call.

Janet joined her guests and apologized for running out of the room on them. She explained why Dean had called. Gertty could be trusted with any information and had been known for keeping secrets. Gloria and Cheryl sat quietly while Gloria painted Cheryl's nails and they sipped their libations. Janet wanted to hear from Cheryl about how the phone call to the families had gone. Cheryl had only called her family while officers called the families of Caroline and Laura. She spoke of the call until the doorbell rang.

Will these interruptions ever cease? Janet wondered. At the door stood her brother, Steven. "Steven! What in the world are you doing here? I'm so happy to see you!"

"I tried to get here sooner but was tied up at a medical clinic in Minnesota. I knew Gloria was coming and thought I'd stop in before going back home to Palm Springs." Steven was equally as happy to see his sister. "What's up with the officer outside? He's a cute one! Even my flirting couldn't get me in to see you. He wouldn't let me near the house until he spoke with Dean and got permission to let me onto the property."

"There has been trouble again, Steven. After you put your belongings in my studio in the carriage house above the garage, I'll explain everything to you. I can really hardly wait to explain the story all over again to yet another person." Janet sighed facetiously. "But I insist you stay here. I already have guests in the main house, and you'll need to stay above the garage," she said, filling Steven in on that much for the time being.

"Ladies, attention, please! My brother is here. He'll be in shortly after he puts his belongings above the garage," Janet announced while hardly able to contain her excitement over the surprise. Everyone present with the exception of Cheryl had known Steven since he was a young boy. They were all ecstatic he was there. Even Cheryl was very happy to be meeting him.

Joining the group's festivities again, Janet filled Cheryl in on her brother. Steven wasn't an unfamiliar name to Cheryl. Stories about him had been brought up since she started associating with this group, and his name had been in the news last year. Janet talked about Steven until Steven entered the room, at which point he took over talking about himself. His health wasn't good. Besides that, all else seemed to be copacetic, per his words. Upon Steven running out of conversation about himself, Janet filled him in on all that had been happening. Janet and Steven also did not keep secrets from each other anymore. He got the full story, secrets and all.

Hearing the story as Janet explained it, Cheryl had a thought. Something in the way that Janet mentioned a pipe brought back memories. She considered the rusty pipe in the shower at the campsite. Being that people disappeared from the camp and there was a pipe there, it seemed to be meaningful. Having discussed it, Janet felt that Dean should know immediately. Trying to reach him at the department, she was informed he was away from the office. He also wasn't answering his own cell phone.

She left messages stating she must see him as soon as possible knowing he would not want her discussing any matters by phone. There was no way of knowing how long it would take for him to get back to her. The more she contemplated reaching Dean via an emergency call, the more she decided that Cheryl's idea could just be a mistaken theory. Dean only accepted emergency calls in actual emergencies. Cheryl felt otherwise and told Janet so when she got off the phone.

"We can't wait all night for Dean to return your call," Cheryl informed Janet. "Besides, he will probably need to get search warrants and whatever other technicalities his profession requires. I have my car here and the campground gate pass. I'll just go check it out and see if I can discover anything. I can't just sit here, having good times, while my friends might be in trouble. Every minute could prove to be valuable."

"It will not be that easy with the patrol guard outside," Janet responded, considering potential plans. "We'll first need a plan to get you out of here."

And so a plan was devised by the group. Once conceived, Janet spelled it all out while being careful not to overlook any details. The plan seemed flawless after everyone contributed their thoughts and ideas. Janet would take Mignon outside and inform the patrolman that she had seen something on the lakeside of the house. That would distract the guard and give Gertty, Cheryl, and Gloria a chance to sneak out the street side of the house to get to Gertty's garage.

The three could go to the camp in Gertty's car, which was parked in Gertty's garage. Janet and Steven would remain behind in case Dean or the patrolman called or rang the bell. "But get back as soon as possible. I don't like the idea of us splitting up. It could be dangerous. I don't feel comfortable and will be much happier when you are all back here safely," Janet stated with Steven being in agreement of the plan.

Their plan worked beautifully. Janet was able to keep the patrolman busy long enough to distract him while the women made their escape from the home. She also misled the guy into believing her cat had sneaked out the door when she exited with Mignon.

Cleopatra was actually peacefully asleep, sprawled under the guest bedroom bed. The guard insisted he help look for the feline. When Janet decided she had enough of the bogus search, she took Mignon back into the house. Even then, the officer continued the search in order to be most helpful. Distracted by the search for the cat, the guard passed quite a bit of time. It gave him something to do during an otherwise boring shift. During Janet's absence, Steven did a fantastic job making the party sound as if it was still going on full swing inside.

Perhaps it was a well-thought-out plan, but there was a problem nobody had counted on. While the patrolman stuck his head into bushes and was preoccupied looking up and down trees for the non-existent cat, someone was able to sneak onto the property unnoticed. Dressed from head to toe in black with his head covered in a hood, the uninvited visitor blended in perfectly with the ominous shadows of the night. As the patrolman searched high and low, he eventually fell into the spider's web. The man in black came up from behind without a sound and jammed a long, thick needle into the muscular neck of his prey.

There had been enough poison within the syringe to kill an elephant, and the victim dropped quickly before he ever knew what had caused the sting. This creeper wasn't going to take any chances. He had a plan, and his plan had to be foolproof, or his own life and the lives of those he loved would end. Even if the patrolman had been doing his job to the best of his ability, there would have been no way for him cover all four sides of the house at once. The invader would have succeeded in gaining access to the property one way or another. As a bonus opportunity, the assailant appreciated obtaining the patrolman's uniform for himself.

Across the lake, the women were already approaching the campground area. There wasn't a gate guard posted at this time. There never was this late at night and in the dark. That was the reason for guests being provided a gate access card—to open the automated gate by themselves. Cheryl's card did work, and the women progressed inward to the camp showers. Coming to a halt, Gertty ducked down and remained in her seat behind the wheel, keeping an eye out for any sign of trouble. The women went and inspected the shower, which disgusted Gloria.

"No wonder you ladies wanted to shower at Janet's. The board of health should condemn this place!" Gloria commented while making a gagging motion with a finger in her mouth.

"Let's look outside," Cheryl said, leading the way. "I don't know what we are looking for, but I would bet we'll find it. I guess we should be looking for the two nearest buildings."

A short distance away, Cheryl and Gloria came upon a small cabin all boarded up. Little did they know that they had stumbled upon a major find. Unfortunately, they were unable to find a way to enter. The only door was locked and would not budge at all. For now, they would need to bypass the cabin and move onward. A short distance from that, they came upon another building. It was a wooden structure in the shape of a small barn made of wood about to decay. Windows had been boarded up. It, too, had been seemingly abandoned. Cheryl and Gloria wanted to explore further with Cheryl taking the right side of the building and Gloria going left.

Upon separating, Cheryl heard a noise and turned, finding herself face-to-face with the creepy gate guard, whom she recognized all too well. He had been holding three food trays in his hands with a stack of dishes on top of them. It was dark, but Cheryl could not avoid being seen right in front of him. He dropped the contents of his hands, which made loud clanging noises as the pieces hit the ground. "What are you doing here?" he yelled, recognizing who she was.

Cheryl was caught off guard and stumbled over her words unconvincingly. "I'm a guest here. You checked my friends and me in. I was just strolling the grounds, and I became lost. I've not wandered into any restricted area or anything, have I?"

The creepy man did not believe her story for a moment. He had been at the gate when authorities took her away with her gear. While her campsite was still paid for and registered to her and her friends, he knew she wasn't staying there any longer. He wasted no time in pulling a pistol from the black holster belt around his waist. Cheryl raised her hands into the air and tried explaining that she was really just lost, not considering that he would not fall for her lies. She tried in desperation to think of what else she could say.

Gloria had come from around the corner of the building and quietly sneaked up behind the man. She could see that Cheryl was in trouble. While she did not know exactly what was occurring, she knew Cheryl was definitely involved in an inappropriate conflict. Grabbing a small log from off the ground, Gloria smacked the man atop his head, causing him to collapse unconscionably on the dirt beneath him. Several snapping and cracking sounds could be heard. Cheryl admitted she did not know what his deal was, but she knew his pulling a gun on her was out of line.

The door he had come out of was still unlocked, and Gloria suggested they drag him inside. There wasn't much inside the structure, except for a chair by a table with a lit lantern upon it and an amateur radio next to a landline phone from what they could see. It was dirty and creepy. While a cart existed, it had not yet been seen because it was in the darker reaches of the dwelling. It was covered with fire-wood logs and blended in with the wooden walls. Hoisting the guard onto the chair, they realized that the strike had left him severely injured. It was regrettable. Never had it been intended to wound him so severely. Decidedly, they would lie if need be to cover the results of their actions. A dry tree branch from a tree hanging over their heads falling from above and striking him where he stood seemed to be a logical explanation.

"The man really needs help, Gloria," her friend indicated as she examined him carefully.

"Yeah, well, that man could have blown our heads off. And why do you think he felt a need to draw a gun? There must be something here. I can just feel it. Let's just take a moment to compose ourselves. We need to look around while we are in here." Gloria continued talking while picking up the phone receiver. There was a dial tone. "It is working. We can call for help from here on our way out and leave an anonymous tip that a man has been injured by a falling tree limb. I find it peculiar that this old, abandoned building contains a working phone. We should think about that for a moment."

Taking the lantern in her hand, Cheryl made a quick visual sweep of the barn. "Look at the floor," she noted. "This entire place is caked with ages of thick dust. Both from the desk and from the door, dust has been disturbed in a pattern on the floor leading over to that cart over there." Her finger pointed to a cart on wheels well-stacked with firewood. "It is odd they would keep firewood in here when there is no fireplace," Cheryl commented. Noticing the cart was on wheels and there were wheel tracks in the dust, she rolled the cart off to the side. "Gloria, there is a trapdoor in the floor under this cart."

Gloria walked over to Cheryl and squatted down close to the floor. Cheryl lifted the hinged lid to the opening. The pendulous lantern in Gloria's hand was swinging over the newly exposed opening as they peered down into a dark, deep pit. A metal ladder could be seen attached to the wall below. The two discussed which of them should be the one to climb down. Cheryl was elected and began her descent with the lantern she took from Gloria's hand. Meanwhile, Gloria used her cellphone flashlight to provide additional light. Gradually, the glow from the lantern disappeared into the cavernous depths below and then even farther down into a hallway.

From the floor above, Gloria refrained from yelling out to Cheryl. She desired verbal communication, but the thought of making any noise at all made her nervous. She did not know if they were alone. It was not her intent to alert anyone to their presence. Had she not been so nervous when Cheryl went down in the pit, she might have thought of suggesting that Cheryl remain in contact by cellphone. Gloria did not know if Cheryl did have one on her person and did not have a number to call her at.

Below, Cheryl had come upon a door. Despite being afraid to open it, she mustered up all her courage and swung the door open quickly. To her surprise, she observed a frightening scene. Cheryl returned to the base of the ladder. She shouted for Gloria to inspect the guard for any keys and then come down with any found keys as fast as she could. Attached to the guard's belt on the side of his waist was a set of keys on a ring. Blood had dripped off his head onto them and was starting to broadly saturate his clothes. The bleeding looked extensive. She did what had been asked of her and joined Cheryl below with the keys speedily.

Nobody could believe their eyes down in the dungeon pit. Cheryl could not believe her eyes when she was reunited with Laura. Even more so, Laura could not believe Cheryl was actually there.

"I thought I'd never see you again. I was so scared," Laura expressed. "That's Diana there. She is hurt. Men have been brutally raping her. She stopped speaking to me as soon as the last of the monsters left shortly before you arrived." Diana was huddled in a corner, shaking uncontrollably.

"Caroline went missing too. Have you seen Caroline?" Cheryl questioned as she used the keys to free Laura before throwing the keys to Gloria to free Diana.

"She was here. They have already taken her away. I don't know where they have taken her. They kidnap people for various reasons and take them off to various places. The Mob was selling Caroline to some second-party syndicate for breeding and black market babies. They were shipping her off to a place where they could continue breeding her after she gives birth. She is young, pretty, fertile, and was already with child. That's why they specifically targeted her.

"I was wanted for overseas sex trafficking. They planned to send me to China. Diana was kidnapped for some kind of retaliation against the Fox family. Their private investigation dealings had sent someone up the river, and kidnapping Diana was meant to be payback." Laura was speaking so rapidly, and her teeth were chattering, but her words got across loud and clear.

Gloria removed her blouse and helped the child slip into it. It was adequate covering for the petite youth. Cheryl wasn't wearing a bra and apologized for not having any clothes to offer Laura. Laura didn't care. She only wanted to get out of there and as far away as they could get her. As the four exited the prison door, they were confronted by a grimacing face. "Well, what have we here?" The man spoke in a deeply sinister tone. He, with a gun in hand, ordered the women to step back into the room and go into one of the cells.

Before anyone could react, Gertty came up behind the man and headbutted him with the blunt butt of her own shotgun. He dropped where he stood. The women stripped him down and dragged him into the cell, where they shackled him. Laura applied his shirt to her body and instantly felt less exposed. Unfortunately, the pants were too large for her to utilize, or she would have taken them as well.

During the fluster of activity, Gertty continued speaking. "I saw this man arrive and decided to follow him. That was not easy for a woman in my condition. I'm not young, you know. I could barely make it through the woods. Getting down that ladder was something I thought I would never manage to do. At first, I was just following the man because I hoped I could warn you he was in the area. Then I knew there was trouble.

"He had stopped at a small cabin along the way. As he entered it, I saw a setup of surveillance video monitors and recording equipment. He must have seen what was happening here in this pit. He high-tailed it out of there as fast as he could and darted this way. I couldn't keep up. I recognize him. He's the ranger in charge of these campgrounds. I don't know him personally but know of him. It's a small village, you know. People know people."

"So that's what that small cabin is being used for. They are video monitoring things from there. We'll need to get over there and destroy any record-ings. We must not permit anyone to see we have been here," Gloria stated, wanting to be sure of that. They needed to cover their tracks, all of them. "No evi-dence of our being here tonight must be left for the finding."

"What are we going to do about these men?" Cheryl questioned. The scenario seemed too surreal for her to think about or to make any rational deci-sion on her own.

"We need to get the other guy down here from upstairs and put him in this other cell," Gloria sug-gested. "But how can we do that? We can't carry him."

"There is a dumbwaiter here. It's how the men bring their captives up and down. It's over there. Didn't you notice it in the wall upstairs?" Diana asked inquisitively.

They had not noticed. They had not noticed because the opening was on the outside of the build-ing with removable boards and a lock on it. It wasn't something they had noticed in the dark of night. Having been distracted by the guard pulling a gun on Cheryl, they hadn't had enough time to find it.

Upon venturing upstairs, Gloria asked Gertty to cover Diana's eyes. She nodded toward the guard at the desk and wanted to protect Diana from seeing him. Diana was in a state of shock anyway and might not have reacted had she seen him. She was walking in a daze, which was all the better for the women. They would not need to explain to Diana how the guard had gotten there in his condition. Checking the man over, his death was confirmed. Being that he was no longer a threat in his deceased condition, they just left him propped at the desk where he had perished.

"Gertty, please get Diana out of here and to your car," Gloria requested of the older woman. "Cheryl, Laura, and I will be right behind you as quickly as we can get a few things taken care of. Barefooted, it may be difficult for Diana to walk quickly on rocks and twigs. Tread gently. Beware of any traps on the ground. I can't imagine there would be any. Just be completely aware of your surroundings. We don't need more men sneaking up on any of us."

Gertty left instantly with Diana holding her hand. Diana's slow shuffle mimicked that of a zombie. Gertty wanted to cry just thinking of the condition the poor child was in. The pain and trauma Diana was experiencing were undeniably great.

"We will just band together and say that the organization was responsible for the death of these men," Laura suggested. "It could likely be Mob retaliation for allowing their captives to escape. While law enforcement might understand self-defense if we told the truth, think of what the Mob would do to us if they knew we were responsible for this chaos tonight," she mentioned, putting all sorts of terrible thoughts into Gloria's head.

"We've got to get moving, though. I've already got blood on my hands tonight," Gloria said, considering the facts involving the gate guard. "You two get over to the cabin. I'll stay here and take care of things," she offered. Cheryl and Laura knew what that meant and what had to be done.

"I'll stay here and take care of the ranger downstairs," Laura said. "You've done enough for me. I can't expect you to take care of that dirty deed too, Gloria. Besides, he deserves what is coming to him, and I am just the person to give it to him. You two just go ahead, and I'll be along shortly. We'll meet in the car. Just point me in the direction of it."

Laura headed down to the basement with a log and a long, sharp, pointed stick. Looking down at the ranger spread-eagle on the floor, she kicked him hard in the groin. He moaned but was not fully alert. "You son of a bitch, I wish I had more time to make you suffer. Be thankful this will be over quickly," she spoke with anger. Taking the sharp stick, she rammed it up to his anus. Blood ran out from between his hairy butt cheeks and spewed across the dirt floor. His body began to squirm as he exhaled his final breath from his respiratory system. His eyelids flipped open as tears flowed from his green eyes.

"Get a good look at me," she said to him. "Too bad you will not be able to shed nearly the amount of tears I will over this hell you've put me through," Laura said as she bent down over his face and stroked his dark curls. "Poor little baby boy. Not such a big man now, are you?" Laura took the log and smashed it down upon his head over and over until his head looked like the collapsed, crushed head of a bloodied red cabbage. His face was no longer recognizable.

Laura laughed at what she had done—not softly, though. She laughed maniacally loud. It was almost like temporary insanity, she figured. She needed to do that as a release. There would be another time for all the tears she would shed over this experience. For now, she focused and cleared her mind before heading to the car. Her mind was so clear that it was as if she had never done what she had just done. Laura turned to leave the room, never to look back. As she left the basement, she felt as if she was awakening from a bad dream—a dream she would hopefully forget all about once it was over.

While departing the building during Laura's venture down to the basement, Cheryl and Gloria proceeded with their plans. Cheryl was disgusted to see that rats had already invaded the corpse of the gate guard in the chair where he was propped. As repulsive as everything that evening had evolved into, she smiled at the sight. Her smile turned to a chuckle. Then it developed into a wild laugh. Gloria was repulsed, but she seemed to understand why Cheryl reacted as such.

As quickly as the laugh had begun, Cheryl stopped her chuckling. Cheryl had a thought, and it was as if one could literally see a light bulb turn on above her head. "Gloria, I'll meet up with you at the cabin," she stated authoritatively. "I'm going to head to the back of the building and check on that dumbwaiter contraption. I want to see if I can get the elevator open. We may need it as part of our alibi sometime."

Gloria thought that sounded ingenious. She did not know exactly how that might play a part in the story, but she knew it could possibly. Nobody knew what was going to be said yet regarding this night. There might be some more fibbing involved, and it would help to have a few aces up their sleeves to confuse any outsiders with questions. "I'll catch up with you at the surveillance cabin," Cheryl said, concluding their conversation.

Gloria left to follow through with her mission. At the cabin, she removed the few recordings and would take them with her. For extra measure, she smashed every bit of equipment she saw while making sure not to leave behind any fingerprints or evidence. On her way out of the cabin, she turned off the wall switches, and the room went dark before she made sure the door was locked behind her. It wasn't as large of a task as she thought to get the recordings. She had handled it magnificently all on her own. Gloria had never annihilated anything in such a destructive manner before in her life and found the behavior invigorating. It helped her release much pent-up anger.

Convinced she had performed her objective adequately, she departed with the recordings in hand and waited only momentarily for Cheryl, who was coming up a pathway and into view. At the car, the others were waiting anxiously to depart the woodlands.

Chapter 16

While the women were gone from Janet's house, the scene had been drastically changing there. Janet and Steven had been sitting casually at the kitchen table, talking and catching up on life. Janet's doorbell rang, and she went to the door to answer it. Outside, a man in the guard's uniform stood with his back to the door. She yelled to inform Steven it was the patrolman. Mignon, who was by Janet's side, jumped about anxiously while barking at the visitor. He was usually excitable, but this was extreme behavior, even for him.

Upon cracking the door partly open, the impostor in the dead patrolman's uniform slammed into the door with such force that it knocked Janet over. Janet screamed loudly, falling backward over Mignon. She bounced off a wall and fell down on the floor on her back. As she attempted to compose herself, she saw it was Mr. Baskin with a gun in his hand.

She knew what he wanted and why he was there. It was doubtful that he would be leaving her alive that night even if he got ahold of what he had come for. While he didn't know for certain that the women had taken the book or that Janet had it in her possession, he had already convinced himself they had taken it. There had been no other patrons left unsupervised in the shop that day. Since he did not know where else to find the other women, Janet's home was the only place he could think of heading. It was as good a place as any to start.

Mignon reacted aggressively over the intrusion and bit down on the pant leg of Mr. Baskin. Baskin kicked his leg, and Mignon released his grip before going sailing across the room. Janet was infuriated. Nobody came into her home and treated her dog that way and got away with it. Baskin pointed the weapon at Janet's head and ordered her to stay quiet, or he would not hesitate to shoot. He hoped it would not come to that, as only Janet could help him recover his missing property. He reminded Janet he had known her since she was born and didn't want to see her life end as a result of his hand.

"Who else is here with you tonight?" Mr. Baskin demanded.

"Nobody! Nobody! I swear it. It's just me here," Janet fibbed. She assumed he would not know otherwise, but earlier, he had heard the party noise and found that difficult to believe. "Nobody else is home, except for my dog here. Just my dog. Just my dog." She kept repeating that as she crawled like a crab on all fours with her back facing the floor. Her eyes remained glued to his gun. Mignon had been so startled by the treatment he had received from the unwelcome guest that he had run off to find solace with Steven.

Steven had clearly heard the commotion in the other room and grabbed a couple of knives out of the kitchen cabinet drawer. He was relieved to find that Janet had still stored them in the same location his family had kept them for generations. Everything was happening so abruptly that he felt he didn't have enough time to think and react adequately. Obtaining the nearest weapons was all he could think to do.

"Get up," Baskin ordered Janet. The two of them were moving across the floor with Baskin repeatedly stepping over Janet. He reached out his hand and yanked her off the floor like a ragdoll containing only the weight of sawdust. His strength was phenomenal. His grip held on to her wrist tightly as he shouted various questions and statements. Janet's mind was trying to focus while she panted loudly. She was scared and wasn't sure if she was possibly hyperventilating. Her heart was pounding. She feared his gun and what was going to happen. All she could think of was that she had to react quickly and that it would need to be a drastic measure she had to make. Everything was so surreal and upsetting to her that she could not even comprehend the questions Baskin was asking her.

Passing the open door threshold to the basement stairs, Janet grabbed his wrist with her free hand and flung both of their bodies down the steep wooden steps. They both fell down, tumbling all the way in slow motion. Step by step they traveled, one hard stair step at a time. Steven arrived at the threshold and witnessed them reaching the halfway point of the stairwell. Baskin's gun fired at random into the air, making a deafening noise. For a brief moment, Steven felt as if time was standing still. Janet could smell the aroma the gunfire had left behind.

The fired ammunition traveled swiftly and found its way to Steven's gut. Steven flew back. His blood flowed and sprayed from the entry wound. He hit the floor at the same time Janet and Baskin rolled slowly to a stop at the bottom of the stairs. Everyone in the house was motionless. Steven was on the ground, unconscious, in the hallway near the top of the stairs. Baskin's head had struck the cement wall at the base of the stairs and had cracked his cranium wide open. His body was contorted with a couple of arm bones protruding from his flesh. Janet was positioned under him and not moving either. She was bathed in Baskin's crimson blood. Mignon ran down the steps to Janet's side and whimpered while gently licking her face. He remained by her side.

Chapter 17

The group of women was arriving safely at Gertty's garage and noticed that the patrolman wasn't in his vehicle outside Janet's garage while they were passing by. They also noticed that Janet's back door was open. Gloria realized she had never called Janet to inform her they were returning. The women had been so busy making sure their stories explaining their actions that evening were coinciding that they had forgotten to notify Janet they were returning. The story they had concocted was not so far from the truth. It contained all the necessary details their stories would need to cover when asked. Gloria now made a call to Janet as they drove past the house. Given the scenario inside the house, Janet obviously wasn't picking up the call.

As Gertty parked her car in her own garage, she thought it wise that she went to Janet's first alone. The guard had already been provided permission for Gertty to visit, and she had never been told she could not go back and forth between her own home and

Janet's if she desired to. So it was best that she went first, and then Janet could call Gloria's phone when the coast was clear for everyone else to come.

Gertty noticed that the patrolman was still not in his car as she walked past going to Janet's gate. She wondered where he might be. It would not have made sense for Janet to invite him inside since nobody else was really to leave the house. If the patrolman had gone inside, Janet would have risked his finding out that people had left the premises without approval or security. Yet he didn't appear to be outside any-where—unless he was on the lakeside of the house, where she would not have been able to see him.

As Gertty made her way up the steps to the doorway, she could see through the screen door. Steven was on the floor inside with blood splatters surrounding him. It was a horrible sight for Gertty to behold. Bravely, she entered the home. Gertty didn't call the women to come over. Instead, she returned to her garage and met with them in person. "I'm in shock. I don't know what to do. I went inside, and Steven is on the floor, surrounded in blood. Janet is at the bottom of the stairs under the patrolman. We need to get emergency vehicles here. We need help right away. We need to come up with another good story. Dean will know we left Janet's house tonight. It's bad enough we needed to concoct stories explaining how we found Diana and Laura and about how we don't know anything about dead men when they eventually get around to asking us."

* * *

Emergency vehicles arrived quickly and emitted a variety of colored, flashing lights up and down the street. Armani saw the first set of lights arriving and immediately dashed over to see what all the trouble was about. Officers and paramedics swarmed onto the property like a locust invasion in a horror movie. Dean arrived rather quickly, but only after others got there first.

None of the friends knew how the questioning would transpire. The whole evening had become such a mess, and there were so many details to consider. Fortunately, they were able to huddle quickly and finish discussing what they would say. They would tell the truth that they left against the wishes of Dean. The only part of the evening they would not admit to was knowing anything about the camp staff. They hadn't seen anybody at the campgrounds as far as they were concerned. Keys were unattended on the desk of the barn building, and they used them to free the captives. The keys were left back upstairs on the desk when they departed with Diana and Laura. It was plain and simple.

If Laura wanted to discuss her abduction and time in captivity before her saviors arrived, that was up to her. Diana was in no condition to discuss anything with anyone. She was in too much shock to be taken seriously even if she tried. Sure, Diana had been rescued, but she never really knew any details involved in the rescue mission anyway. If Diana thought she knew anything, the women would attribute it to her delirium and not accurately clear thinking. Dean would be very upset they had left Janet's, but he would have to get over it. There was no law that would have kept them there. Missing people had been located. That was some good news tonight.

Dean arrived, and stories were provided to him. Gertty did a lot of the talking while Mignon sat frightened in her lap. Dean had a better rapport with Gertty and had known her longer than the other women. She was elected spokesperson. The women felt that Dean would find her to be more believable and give her less cross-examining. He wasn't happy. He wasn't sure he accepted the explanations. But in his heart, he was glad the women had been rescued and Baskin revealed.

Everyone was assured by paramedics that Janet and Steven would likely be okay if proper treatment was received immediately. Dean was contemplating. Had the girls not taken off, there might have been safety in numbers at Janet's house. On the other hand, the girls might have been hurt, along with Steven and Janet, had they remained at the house, as he had requested. Additionally, Diana and Laura might never have been found. Worse, Baskin could have escaped. There were bright sides to all the bad sides.

While considering scenarios, Dean said what he had to say to each of his friends. Laura got the biggest lecture. "Get an attorney before you say anything," he advised her. "You are in the worst position here. The whole situation is no good. You may think you were freed when you were rescued. You are not free at all. Authorities have studied how the Mob works, and they will likely retaliate against you for your escape. We don't know what pressure the Mob is under to deliver you to whomever you were to be delivered. If they don't deliver you, they will likely have a price to pay. That's not a debt anyone will likely forget about. Laura, please cooperate with authorities."

His conversation did not make Laura feel at ease when she was feeling tense enough. She was scared and now even more confused, but she would try to cooperate to the best of her ability. Dean made sure nobody was too overburdened with questioning at this time. Laura, Diana, Janet, and Steven were immediately rushed to the hospital. Dean radioed for officers to get over to the woods and get that area secured until a full investigation could take place there. The grounds needed to be searched before any evidence could be disturbed or destroyed. Being a public campground, any scene could easily be tampered with. Any number of people would be anxious to cover up the events.

Armani lingered close to Dean, listening to every word exchanged. He was concerned his world could come crumbling down around him. *What did anyone know?* He had to figure that out quickly. Part of him wanted to flee town. He knew that would be no way to live. If things went to pot, neither the authorities nor the Mob and related organizations would ever give up searching for him. He would spend his life perpetually on the run and looking over his shoulder.

As of this moment, he noticed that nobody seemed to be linking him to any crime at all. He began to somewhat relax. Dean eventually got around to addressing Armani and told him that he would need to leave. "This is a crime scene now, and I can't have you wandering around here," Dean informed him. Armani smiled, nodded, and left quietly knowing that authorities were not onto him. That was apparent by the way Dean and the others were speaking.

It was during this time that the patrolman's nude body was found floating under Janet's boat dock pier. With Baskin dead in the patrolman's uniform inside the house, those present and investigating the occurrence at the scene found it easy to conclude that Baskin had been up to no good. Not everyone might have known why, but Dean did. It was apparent that Baskin had come for the journal, which implied that it had been Baskin's and had not belonged to someone else, as was previously concluded. It wasn't Dan's either. While Baskin might have shared it with his son, it was clear that the handwriting contained within the leather-bound covers had been that of only one person. Handwriting analysis would later prove it to be the writings of Mr. Baskin's hand.

Dean knew that last year's crimes were believed to involve a missing memory stick. If this journal

Baskin kept had been able to bring about this much discord in one evening in his home, Dean could only imagine how much trouble a very descriptive memory stick involving many Mob members could bring. The journal the authorities now possessed contained valuable information, but it was only a small part of the Mob's dealings—a very tiny part considering that Antioch was just a dot on a map of worldwide dealings.

Dean had to wonder who else might have known of the journal and what, if any, information said persons concluded this journal might contain. Speculation alone of potentially incriminating information having been documented by Baskin in a journal, even if only assumed, could be enough to create chaos. Dean hoped that nobody on the opposing side of the law knew of the journal and that any information about its existence would not be leaked at this time. Despite the department treating this as a top-secret information file, all Dean could do was to have faith in his associates and the system.

There were other things Dean knew as well. He had not had the chance to discuss those things with Janet and wasn't sure if he should give any chance. Some official business was simply not to be released to anyone. What Dean had wanted to tell Janet was that the son of Mr. Baskin, Dan, had been questioned again. He was informed that authorities had evidence incriminating people, the grave had been located, and there was a lot more happening of which they were now aware. They wanted to give Dan a chance to tell the truth this time.

Dean knew that not everyone would ever cooperate because they feared the Mob, the authorities, or both of them. But Dean hoped that Dan would cooperate with the side of the law and provide authorities with beneficial information. That was a tedious expectation of Dan. It would mean that Dan would have to admit that he had not been telling the truth and that he was not mentally incompetent after all.

Dan was feeling defeated upon learning of the developments and had already helped fill in the blanks with spoken truths pertaining to the incidents of last year—truths as he knew them to be. With the assistance of the authorities and Dan, many missing pieces of last year's events began to make sense. Dan had made duplicate keys at the shop when locals came in for the service. The idea had come to him when his father instructed him to discretely make an extra copy of certain keys customers were bringing in. Dan's father had told him he was not to ever ask why but to just do as he was told and never speak of it.

Dan eventually came up with the idea that he could do the same for himself and make some side money robbing homes. He would sell the stolen goods and pocket the money for drugs mostly. That was his only intent. Unfortunately, he unwittingly went into homes other crimes had been taking place in. Circumstantial evidence ended up linking him to all the crimes. He felt it was easier to be a fall guy, taking all the blame, and go along with a plea of insanity. Mostly, he wanted to protect his father, and there was no need to do that any longer.

Dan really had not known the particulars of his father's dealings. These were not the types of activities his parents had discussed around the dinner table. Over time, Dan had an inkling that his father was something more than just a local shopkeeper. Enough had been heard by Dan about his father and their business when he should not have been listening at all. Dan had learned from an early age that his father was capable of aggressively beating him if he made it known he had been eavesdropping or spying on his father's activities, even when something not comprehended by Dan had been accidentally overheard or learned.

Over time, no matter what Dan had heard or seen, he kept it to himself and tried to forget. That was exactly how he handled conversations with authorities when he had been arrested. Now he had received psychological care in the institution and thought differently. He had made a promise to himself that he would tell the truth should the opportunity present itself and that it would make a difference. Plainly stated, that time was upon him.

Dan's best friend, Eli, had known too much of old man Baskin's dealings. Eli wanted to share information that should never be shared with anyone. Dan attempted convincing Eli to stay quiet and forget all about what he knew, but the talk didn't help convince him. Eli was adamant that he would be going to the police. An argument ensued, and some people thought it had been a gay lovers' quarrel that had led to Dan killing Eli.

The justice system believed that Dan had killed Eli and tried to blame it on the Indian tribe due to insanity. Dan stated that he had been possessed by an evil manitou, a North American Indian spirit known in folklore. In actuality, Dan's father had Eli killed to keep him quiet. That wasn't an easy thing for Mr. Baskin to do. Eli had been like a son to him and had always been treated like one of the family. But Mr. Baskin could not take any chances. The Mob sure wasn't going to. Dan wasn't aware that his father had ordered the killing. It had been gruesome mutilation that even Dan would not have approved of.

Authorities now knew that Mr. Baskin was one of the Mob's local kidnappers, along with the camp gate guard and forest ranger. What Eli had known had followed him to his grave. *Too bad,* Dean thought, as Eli might have been able to put a stop to a lot of this long ago had he gone to the authorities. Likely, he was trying to protect the Baskin family, and it had cost him his life and now Mr. Baskin's life too while tarnishing Dan's. Dean hoped there would be some retribution and eventual peace. *And what of Mrs. Baskin?* Dean worried. *Could she be involved in any way? If not, the woman has endured so much grief.*

Over the course of documenting crime scene details at Janet's, a couple of divers entered the water. Bright lights had been submerged under the surface and shone as far down as the bottom of the lake, which was only about six feet deep at the far end of the pier. The naked patrolman's body was easily retrieved, exposing a look of solidified horror upon his distorted face. His mouth was wide open, and his eyes were bulging. He had been a respected member of the force and was fondly admired by his peers. Seeing their comrade in this state of affair was disturbing.

As the divers continued to investigate the water, another grizzly find was stumbled upon. Chained to the pier were the skeletal remains of Julie, Janet and Gloria's friend. To whom they belonged was not known to anyone at this time, but the female skeleton bones belonged to her. It would take time to officially confirm, but dental records and other tests would eventually verify the identity. Dean was certain it was Julie just by seeing the skeletal formation and indicating factors of aged deterioration. If he imagined flesh on the bones, he could envision her once lovely face. This finding in this location was simply too coincidental to possibly imagine the bones belonging to anyone else.

This night would forever be known by many as the night all hell broke loose. Dean knew that more details coming to light would only create more unanswered questions. Not all crimes were ever solved. Some crimes were even solved incorrectly, and some crimes were only partially solved to the point that people were satisfied with the answers. That was a proven fact when Dean considered that Dan had been arrested for crimes without all the facts. It happened all the time. Dean's gut feeling told him that would be all he could ever expect from these types of local cases. The Mob would keep people from divulging too much information.

With more and more people turning up dead, it would be difficult to ever determine what stories the dead had taken with them to their own graves. Dean would never stop searching for answers and truths. It was without question that nobody would likely ever piece together how all this crime had started within this jurisdiction. He only hoped that someday, there could be an end to it all. In his mind, these thoughts were trying to conclude something ingenious.

Dean began thinking that each event was like a frame in a movie story unfolding before his eyes. Each event was contributing to the entirety of the movie, a movie that had begun randomly in one place and created a never-ending conglomerate of backstories. His eyes were the camera taking in the cinematic wonder. There was something more to that thought, he considered, but he would need to contemplate it someday at a quieter moment, if he remembered to do so. Why terms such as *movie* or *camera* were coming into his mind were of concern to him. There seemed to be some connection his thinking process was trying to make. He just couldn't come up with any link now.

Chapter 18

An eventful night had fully passed, and the glowing orb of the orange sun was rising above Antioch. Nowhere in Antioch did the sunrise seem to ever look as beautiful as it did over Lake Marie. Gertty sat in her garden and viewed the beauteous wonder. Dean walked outside onto his walkway and saw Gertty in her yard. She had not known about all the details of the late evening. He filled her in. She was heartbroken to learn of the skeletal remains found.

"Julie?" she asked.

"I think so. Who else? I am going to see Janet, Steven, Diana, and Laura at the hospital. Care to go along with me for the visit?" He knew she would appreciate getting out of the house for a while.

"I'd love to. I can be ready to go when you are."

* * *

Within Armani's bedroom, Armani was awake and pacing. He had spent almost the entire night

213

doing just that. He had thought of everything he could, including if there might be any Mob repercussions. He had not failed, he figured. "Baskin and his cronies had failed," he told himself almost convincingly. Even if he believed that wholeheartedly, the actions of the syndicate could never be assumed by anyone. People had been disciplined for less.

Armani's phone rang. It was his Mob contact number showing on the display screen. Presuming they were calling about Baskin and the freed women, his hand shook as he reached for the phone. There was no casual conversation on the line. They got right down to business. People were not happy with him. Sadly, this was when Armani learned of the camp crew being found dead. While he had been aware the women had escaped, he had not known his crew had been murdered. His bosses were looking for answers, and he was speechless. Even though they understood that he was not directly to blame, they still had to take into consideration that he was in charge of his area. His men had failed them.

In all fairness, they were the men who were involved with the territory before he was in power. Responsibility for them had been bestowed upon him no matter if he had wanted that responsibility or not. That was something else in his favor. After a long discussion, Armani knew he was not in any personal danger. Mob business in his territory would be halted for the time being pending investigations. Lake Marie had now become a hotbed of activity, swarming with law enforcement and investigators.

That was enough to keep the Mob quieted down for a while. However, Armani knew that he would some-day be called upon to seek vengeance upon others or rebuild the local business—if they let him live, that is. He was now sure he didn't want to continue in the business. "Is it possible to make a clean break at this point?" he wondered. The Mob would never allow anyone to do such a thing. He knew that. But he could hope.

* * *

Dean and Gertty arrived at the hospital and were led by a nurse to Janet's room. She seemed to be feeling okay, and the nurse stated that Janet was just remaining admitted for observation.

"I got quite a lump on my head," Janet said, pointing to a large bump on her noggin. "I am just here for observation the doctor and nurse have told me. I seem to be okay otherwise. It's so nice to see you two."

"I'm so sorry about last night. I just feel terri-ble," Gertty replied with sorrow in her voice.

"Do you recall last night?" Dean questioned Janet.

"I do, and I don't. It's like I had a dream I have awakened from—bits and pieces," Janet thought to tell him. "I recall Mr. Baskin forcing his way into the door while dressed in uniform. He kicked Mignon, and that upset me. He wanted some kind of book. I told him I didn't have such a book. I really don't have such a book. He became physically rough with me, and I fought back. We fell through the basement doorway. It was like entering a dark hole. That's the last I recall. What book was he talking about?" Janet pretended to be ignorant. She released a moan from her lips while grabbing her head.

"Forget about the book. Baskin would have liked to get his hands on the legendary memory stick if he could have. As for the book he wanted, forget all about it." Dean thought that was best.

Janet winked, giving indication that she knew it best too and would be acting as though she knew nothing at all. Changing the subject, Dean mentioned Steven's presence in the hospital. They had admitted him to another ward.

"The gunshot required surgery. He'll be fine, though. He took a bullet for the team. And Mignon is fine too. I had him taken for a checkup last night at the emergency vet clinic. Cheryl and Gloria are at the house and said they will be picking him up from the vet office shortly. They will take him right home, our home—that is, if you are ready for me to be there full-time. I should be near you at all times to keep you safe. You are the most important thing to me, and I don't want any harm coming to you," Dean lovingly emphasized.

"I'd like that," Janet said with a smile. "Our home—it has a nice ring to it."

"On a sad note, Janet, I have something to tell you which I think you are well enough to hear. A skeleton was recovered last night in the lake. It was chained to our pier. I have a strong feeling it is Julie's." Janet covered her mouth with the back of her fist, turned her head away, and gasped while her eyes began to well up with tears.

"Gloria is staying at your place as long as you need her to," Gertty informed Janet, hoping to distract her concentration. "She's in no hurry to get home and can help you during your recovery time. And I'll be around too whenever you need me to be. You just rest well here and get better soon. You'll be needing more rest once they release you. No strenuous activities or stress for you."

Gertty stayed talking with Janet while Dean went to visit Laura. Dean again addressed Laura's situation with her, just as he had done last night. He mostly reiterated what he had already told her but in more detail. She would be protected if she agreed to cooperate with authorities. It would likely require entering a witness relocation program. It was being handled above a local level, and Dean could not be of additional help. He suggested that she speak to an attorney no matter what. The only help he could offer was to help her obtain an attorney should she not be happy with any the state might appoint to her at any given time. He knew all the best legal counsel in the state.

"I simply think, in my opinion, that what you have experienced has put you in danger. I'm suggesting expert help," Dean stressed.

"What if I did kill those forest men?"

"Then definitely speak with an attorney," he professionally advised. "I'd find it hard to believe a delicate flower such as yourself could have done such a thing. I should not be sharing this with you, but the guard upstairs in that building died of a rather common injury. It was a simple and clean kill. The ranger was found elsewhere. He had obviously been intentionally and savagely murdered. I'd be surprised if you had been capable of such brutality. If you had killed them, the Mob would likely be coming after you for killing their men."

"And what if I didn't harm them? You said they'd still be after me."

"Laura, you are in trouble no matter what you do," Dean considered. "These local bums were virtually nobodies in the minds of the executive Mob bosses. The upper brass may not have even known who they were by name. They were henchmen in the field doing the dirty work, but they were their henchmen, and now they are dead. Someone will want to seek revenge and retribution for their deaths." He continued after a moment of silence. "Look, Laura, various organizations have been known to exist for generations. Letting you escape and be rescued is the first mistake any who has ever been known by authorities has made. That's because they are cunning and shrewd.

"No matter how you got away, they likely will not allow you to just walk free. I would bet that people you can't imagine are going to continue paying for this botched-up mess they have on their hands.

Some innocent people may even get harmed along the way. Nobody gets in the way of any syndicate business and lives to tell about it, I'd assume. I have no doubt that no matter how you answer questions, you'll end up in a witness protection program, as will likely your family. If the Mob is looking for you, I'd assume they will go to your family first. Please talk to a lawyer very soon and cooperate with authorities. They are your first step to salvation."

Laura nodded, understanding his suggestions. She would carefully take them into consideration.

"Of course, you can't be forced to cooperate or speak right now."

"I understand. I'll ponder it while I'm here. If I choose to make any statements, I'll consult a lawyer."

Dean and Laura conversed at some length. Personal talk about their lives created a quick trust and understanding. Dean expressed that he wished they had time to become better friends. He assured her that Janet already liked her and spoke fondly of her. His personal words comforted her in her time of need. Their conversation reached a point in which he felt comfortable asking Laura a question outright. Off the record and in confidentiality, he asked, "Did you kill those men?"

Laura answered truthfully and told him all she could in a whisper inaudible to any potential outside listeners. Dean wanted to be certain Janet was not in danger. She was not that Laura knew of. Then he asked about Gloria and Gertty. She had no reason to think so either, but she explained their involvement at the camp that night. She told Dean of how they had annihilated the security system to cover their tracks. They had cleaned the floors to make sure no footprints had been left in the floor dust. Things that had been touched had been cleaned for fingerprints. As for the murders of the forest staff, she only told Dean what she had been involved in firsthand.

"I don't know anything about the gate guard found at the desk upstairs. He was dead when I first saw him." She spoke the truth in that. "The guy downstairs? I did him in. He had it coming. He had a gun and threatened all of us when he discovered us there. Gertty accidentally knocked him out. After that, I wasn't about to leave that Mob monster alive to bear witness. After the others left, I went back and killed him with a log to the head. They had no idea.

"I would plead temporary insanity if I am brought up on charges. You have no idea what that horrible man had done to us and people before us. I wasn't about to ever let him do that to another female again. Like Diana, some were just children. We could not leave him to bear witness to our escape. Between us, I knew I would have cut him up into little pieces had I the time and a knife. You may not understand the pain we endured!"

She began crying very hard. Dean took her in his arms and rocked her until she calmed down. He could only guess how she must have felt and did not blame her for her feelings. He was not a judge or jury. Considering her as a friend first, he was even willing to put his job position aside. That was something he did with people from time to time.

Laura was able to tell Dean a few other facts. She knew for certain that Caroline was wanted for her unborn baby. Other women had been kidnapped for the same reason in previous times. Caroline had been treated well while in the cell, from what Laura had observed because their abductors had orders not to hurt the fetus.

"Keep me posted if you need anything or can think of anything," Dean requested. Laura nodded with approval. Dean stood up to leave. "You'll be all right if you get help," he said reassuringly. Dean then stopped in to see Diana in yet another ward. The Fox family was there, and Dean was sorry to see them under such circumstances.

"Don't be silly, Dean. We are glad you are here. We are all just happy to have our Diana back and will not leave her side ever again," Leo said with a tear in his eye.

"May I see her?"

"Yes. She still is not very responsive. Physically, she is healing. Mentally, she doesn't say anything. She's in shock. She may require years of mental therapy," Leo answered, leading him into the hospital room.

"Hi, Honey!" Dean said to the girl. "I want you to know how happy I am that you are safe now. It's been rough, I'm sure. When you feel better, I hope we get a chance to talk someday. You know, a woman—Caroline—was not as lucky as you to be rescued. We are still looking for her. She's in danger and not getting the help she needs. Maybe you can help her now. I need information from you to help me find her as soon as you are well enough to speak to me. Okay? So you get better soon."

Diana finally responded with her first actions since being brought into the hospital. She turned and threw her arms around Leo, who was now sitting by her side on the edge of her bed. She screamed loudly while crying hysterically. "They took her! The men who brought us there took her away. They gave her a sedative and put her in the dumbwaiter. They took her. They said she was going to another county. I don't know where. I hate those men. They hurt me. They were disgusting! I hate them!" she screamed and began crying even harder.

"I think you should leave now, Dean," Leo said. "I'm glad she is reacting. Let's not overdo it. It's too soon."

Dean left and went to see Steven in his hospital room. He was alert and complaining that the drugs administered were not helping his pain any. Steven reiterated his story about the home intrusion. That much was truthful, and all matched up with the other stories Dean had heard.

"While we are talking, I know Gertty and the girls left Janet's last night," Dean informed Steven. "No need to say more than that to anyone. Their actions shouldn't concern or involve you. You were not with them. They told you nothing about where they were going. Got that?" he suggested.

Steven got the point. "The less said, the better."

Dean concluded their conversation by inform-ing Steven about the skeletal find in the lake. He dreaded telling people about Julie's possible demise, not knowing how hard some people might take the news. Steven had been close to Julie ever since they were children. In this case, the news was hard to take. A secret few people knew and kept was that Steven was the last person known to have seen Julie alive. She had gone up to the carriage house where he had been staying and visited with him late on the night of her disappearance. He was not a murderer, and their friends saw no need to inform other people of his time with Julie.

Returning to Janet's room, Gertty and Janet sat waiting. "Everyone seems to be fine," Dean reported.

"What now?" Janet asked.

"There is not much I can do now," Dean admit-ted. "I'm going to continue looking for Caroline, but Diana is talking and mentioned Caroline may have been taken to another country. That would be out of my local jurisdiction. If the kidnappers have managed to smuggle her out of this country, that is a tough situation to manage. You know I'll always do what I can. Meanwhile, Diana isn't saying much about anything. She doesn't know much."

"What about Diana and Laura? What will become of them?" Gertty interjected.

"It's questionable," Dean said, admitting to not knowing. "They have not committed any crimes authorities are yet aware of. You are all victims at this point. Diana and Laura will likely be asked to answer in-depth questions about their abductions, any deaths, and other related topics as well. Hopefully, they will seek legal counsel before answering. They can't be forced to talk. Depending on how Diana and Laura respond to questioning, authorities will make decisions as to how best to help them. If Diana and Laura don't cooperate, there probably won't be much anyone can do. I believe they would be put in a witness protection program if they say anything.

"For now, we will not know what to expect. It's like a game of checkers. Nobody knows what the next move played will be until another move is made. Authorities will want to question all of you as soon as possible. I'm not certain Diana is up to questioning anytime soon, as she is still very unstable. Steven confirmed the story pertaining to Baskin having been at our house. That's all he knows about Baskin and any of these matters.

"Gloria and Cheryl have asked to speak with an attorney. Nobody is being charged with anything at this time. Still, Cheryl and Gloria will only agree to speak to authorities if their attorney tells them to. I've urged everyone to only talk about what they witnessed and not embellish on any other topics—no hearsay. It's best they stick only to facts, try to answer with a basic yes or no response when possible. The less said, the better. That goes for the two of you as well. Got it? You know I'm not an attorney. This is just friendly advice."

"A statement?" Gertty repeated. She had a bewildered look upon her face.

"Gloria's story is simple. She is stating that you all were discussing a pipe I asked about. You, Cheryl, and Gloria arrived in your car at the woods to check up on a hunch Cheryl had. You searched the area and found an open, barnlike structure. Inside, you found a trapdoor, and there had been keys on a table. You all unexpectedly found your way to Diana and Laura, whereupon you set them free with the keys. Cheryl was first to see them. Gloria next in formation. And, Gertty, you followed down into the basement behind Cheryl. You all left in Gertty's car together. No more details needed," Dean advised. His words were spoken with the intent that Gertty and Janet would know to stick to one story.

They knew what his intent was. Janet had not been in the woods. All she could do was confirm that her guests had left her house to check out the pipe theory. "That was what happened, no? A shorter version with missing details, it was almost as it happened. Until someone goes on record telling the truth about the dead forest crew, I am not going to speculate." Janet and Gertty both confirmed with Dean that they had not killed anyone. That was all that mattered in this conversation. "Nobody saw any people at all at the woods that night, right?"

"I'd not know that. I wasn't at the woods," Janet explained.

"I have this covered, Dean. I know the story," Gertty stated, agreeing to go along with everyone.

Chapter 19

Days went by, and important changes gradually occurred. The skeletal remains of Julie had finally been confirmed. The body had been so badly decomposed that no exact cause of death could be documented on her death certificate. Her death by strangulation would go unknown by anyone except the killer, if he was still alive. Her remains would be the property of her family to be put to rest. Janet and her friends felt saddened by that. Julie's family had never cared much about anything, including what was best for Julie.

Julie had one living parent, and that was her father. He had long been an alcoholic and never cared much for what his adult children did in their lives. Sure, he would be saddened to learn of the death of his daughter, but Janet knew that she and Gloria were having a harder time dealing with the reported death than he would ever have. Janet wished she and Gloria could have laid Julie to rest instead of her family. Given how Julie had died, Julie's father seemed to blame Janet and Gloria for allowing this to happen to his child. He made it clear that the funeral would be private, for family only, and Gloria and Janet were not to attend.

That request was not taken well by Janet's and Gloria's families. They had known and loved Julie during her growing years. They would have liked to attend her official funeral as well. In honor of Julie, Janet would hold a celebration of life ceremony for Julie at the lake as soon as things settled down. Janet wondered if Julie's spirit remained behind or if it had been freed upon the discovery of her remains. Perhaps Julie could attend the celebration in spirit, Janet and Gloria had discussed.

In a surprising turn of events, Laura had disappeared. She was to show up at the station for questioning one day and never reported. Dean had some brief conversations with her since he last visited with her in person at the hospital and before her release from the facility. It seemed she had been reporting ailments so her stay could be extended there. It frightened her to leave. Dean supposed there was a chance she was a flight risk and would take it on the run. However, he had hoped she would not do that.

Her disappearance created a lot of talk around Antioch. People thought the Mob had nabbed her again upon her hospital release. In fact, as far as anyone knew, it could be a real possibility they had. It was also a possibility that she was a corpse now and had replaced Julie's skeleton under the pier in a watery grave. Nobody would be the wiser, at least not for the time being. Nobody could help her now if she would not let them. Dean wasn't a religious man by nature, but he found himself praying often for her safety. He liked her and felt sorry for her. An innocent trip with friends had permanently changed her life. It did not seem fair.

Janet had been released from the hospital, and her brother would soon be as well. Janet was happy to be home. There was no place she would rather be. Her joy was refreshing as she entered her home upon her return from the hospital. Greeting Mignon was her top priority. There weren't words to express how happy he was to see her and she to see him! Dean had moved all his belongings in during her absence. It was very nice even though many items seemed out of place for her taste. She convinced herself that she didn't mind. It would take time to adjust. Except for a couple of ugly art pieces and one old, tattered recliner, she would live with them for now.

Gloria had remained at Janet's home. She had kept her promise and saw to it that things ran smoothly around the place during Janet's absence. She had even scoured all the bloodstains off every- thing until the surfaces shone more clearly than ever. Gloria could not have been happier to see Janet come home. She sat with Janet outside, overlooking Lake Marie. They reminisced about Julie.

"I wonder if visions of Julie will cease now that she has been found," Janet said.

"Time will tell," Gloria responded. "Strange how Julie was right here under our noses the entire time. I may even miss her more now that I know she'll never be coming back to us."

"We'll need to find another way to ease your loneliness," Janet said to Gloria.

"I've already found it, Janet." Gloria wanted to explain when the right moment came along. "You like Cheryl, don't you?"

Janet nodded. She did indeed. "You think she is capable of taking Julie's place in our friendship?" she asked, wondering if Cheryl could. At times, Julie could be a big problem. They had known Julie since they were small children, and Cheryl did not seem to be anything like her. That was probably a good thing when all was considered.

"Not friendship exactly, Janet. You have Dean, and I now have Cheryl," Gloria divulged. "We've been hitting it off well—very well, if you know what I mean. She's decided to stay, and so have I. My boyfriend never really was the right fit for me. He was a nice guy and all, but it wasn't love. Janet, I fell in love with Cheryl."

"I'm fly with that. Isn't that what people say these days? But stay? Here at this house?"

"No, you silly chick, not exactly." Gloria tried to explain as clearly as she could. "You know Armani inherited Irwin's old home. He's done remodeling it. Cheryl and I spoke to Armani about renting. Armani thought that would be a great idea. Dean and Gertty know, and both think it might be good for you to have us near. Of course, we want your blessing. We don't want to interfere in your world if you will not have us."

"Of course you are welcome to be my neighbors," Janet said, giving her blessing and wishing for their happiness. "You have my blessing with your relationship with Cheryl too." Honestly, though, the news was a shock to Janet. "What about all the boyfriends you've had? I didn't know you liked women in that way. You never made a pass at me. I don't know if I should be happy about that or insulted. You never made a pass at me! I know when I've been insulted! I know when I've been insulted!" Janet joked loudly.

"You are not my type. You're not pretty enough." Gloria and Janet chuckled. "You know this lesbian relationship will be a new concept for me. It's new to Cheryl too. It just happened. We fell in love, and I can't explain it, but we think it's wonderful," Gloria attested.

"What about jobs and affordability?" Janet wondered. She knew how expensive lakefront property could be, even just to rent.

"Being that Armani knows us, he offered us a great deal. It's not like he had to pay for the inherited house, I guess. In the meantime, we have bigger plans. Cheryl did take a job in town as a waitress at the village alehouse. I actually landed a pretty good job here. I've been interviewing with a local attorney since before I came to visit you. Dean introduced me to him. I didn't want to say anything to you sooner and jinx my chances of getting the job. I did get the job, and it pays very well!" Gloria said with excitement. "He's the attorney we consulted about the infamous night I'll avoid speaking about."

"That is great," Janet informed Gloria. There was returned excitement in her voice.

"Is something else wrong, Janet?"

"It's just my head hurting. It's time for my pills, I think."

"Do you want me to go inside and get them? I will."

"No, let's go inside and sit for a while. We can sit in my bedroom and talk a bit more. I just want to be in my bed in case I suddenly feel an urge to rest," Janet suggested. "Being home is a lot of overwhelming excitement for me."

In Janet's bedroom, Gloria made Janet comfortable. Janet swallowed some pills and made a sour face because of their bitterness.

"Do you think Steven will stay here for a while once he's released from the hospital? He'll be needing care as well, and you make such a great nurse. I can vouch for that," said Janet with all honesty.

"Actually, I was leading to just that when we were outside," Gloria mentioned. "We've all been talking and wanted to run something by you. The Fox family is going to be leaving the area. I'm sure it has something to do with a witness protection program, but I don't know. Leo wanted to know if we would have any interest in taking over the security / private investigation business. There is a space for rent next to the alehouse, and Cheryl and I thought it might be a great way to get a start in our own business—with your help, of course. You could always leave the business once we get it up and running if you don't want to stay on.

"With all that has gone on, we feel a desire to help the community. You've done just such a great job at getting your art business up and running that we feel you have that much-needed business sense to develop a successful office. Steven thought it may be a great opportunity for him to move back here and be a part of it. His personal life really hasn't been going as well as we thought, not like he led us to believe when he got here. His personal relationship had ended, and he is alone in California. He can't take care of himself all alone like that, Janet.

"We are his family, and he needs our help. He needs a new lease on life. He viewed the shooting as a near-death experience and wants to look at life differently. I know it was nothing like a near-death experience, just a traumatic one. I'd bet your parents would love to have him back in Illinois too. What do you think? If not for you, for all of us. Will you think it over? It would just be a tiny financial investment for each of us and a bit of start-up work effort on your part."

Janet just did not know. "Let me recover for a bit, and then we can all discuss it. I think it might be a conflict with Dean's work, no?"

"We can discuss it in detail when you feel better. We just can't waste too much time, as we need the space lease signed before we lose the location. It's perfect!" Gloria said, really thinking so. "Money isn't even an issue if we all pull together and pitch in. It's only that we want you to be a part of it all—you, me, and Cheryl with the help of Steven and Dean. It reminds me of that old television program with the sexy private eyes." Gloria reminisced about the television series while making humorous, sexy poses. "I can be the prettiest," she suggested to make Janet laugh. "Who knows? Mignon could be a new crime-solving mutt like the one in our favorite cartoon."

"The only traits Mignon would have in common with that dog would be his cowardliness and addiction to food," Janet said while continuing to laugh. "Perhaps laughter is the best medicine, Gloria, but I need to rest now. Could you peek in and check on me in a bit? Don't wake me if I'm asleep, though. It was difficult to get enough sleep at the hospital. At first, they did not want me to put my head down because of a possible concussion. When I was managing to sleep, they made sure they awakened me for one stupid reason or another. Their beds were horrible. I'd forgotten what it was like to get a sound sleep with my head on my own pillow."

Chapter 20

Armani was sitting at his kitchen table, thinking of how things had become too quiet around town in the last few days. After the rush of activity within the neighborhood recently, nothing seemed to be happening in the world outside his door. Most days, he kept actively performing neighborly handyman tasks, just as people expected of him. That was a perfect cover for his otherwise sinister plans.

As he had thought, he realized handyman work simply was just not enough to keep him entertained in life. It was mundane and unexciting. Something inside him was squirming and was not melding well with the wild life he had been leading and had come to expect. He was not the type to sit still. With that thought in mind, he began thinking of the newest venture he had put himself in the middle of. It was a situation nobody would have ever expected of him. He was keeping a big secret in the cat-and-mouse game he was playing with his life: in his spare bedroom, Laura was staying as a welcomed guest.

Immediately after Laura was released from the hospital, she had been transported to Janet and Dean's to collect her belongings, which Cheryl had retrieved from their campsite. It only took a matter of minutes for Armani and his slick ways to win Laura over once she viewed him working in his yard. Janet, having previously spoken of Armani, had led Laura to believe he was a pretty good guy. He was even an ex-boyfriend of Janet's, Janet's neighbor, a friend, her handyman, and someone Janet had stated she had known her whole life. And Dean, the sheriff, had also known Armani for many years. They had been school chums back in the day. Laura believed Janet and Dean to be very good character references.

Besides, Laura was instantly attracted to Armani. Many women were. His rugged good looks and charm instantly swept her off her feet. She did not hesitate for a moment when Armani invited her into his home for a beverage and to become better acquainted. An indoor invitation was not something Armani offered to just anyone. Laura, having accepted his invite, felt so at ease discussing her kidnapping ordeal and situation with the captivating man who seemed to hypnotize her. Everyone had a desire to get ahold of Laura, and she had not known where to turn. Even reporters wanted to track her down as if her family, friends, the Mob, and authorities were not enough. It was overwhelming and caused her stress and paranoia.

Armani was a good listener and knew all the right words to say. As Laura perceived it, she was having a stroke of luck by running into the kind gentleman. Here she was in the quiet home of this mesmerizing man, in an environment she, for whatever reason, felt safe in. It helped to know a sheriff was only a matter of yards away in the next house. It was the perfect setup for her to keep a low profile while she sorted things out in her head and regained her sanity. Even her own family would not know where to find her to tell anyone. And Armani was so kind to cooperate by extending such a generous offer for her stay in his home knowing what kind of trouble she was in. What a kind stranger he seemed to be.

The situation was only anticipated to be temporary. Armani promised to help her obtain a private motel room just as soon as they felt they could work out the details and discretely transport her to one. Yes, any friend of Janet's and Dean's was a friend of his, he would say to her. While offering to assist her was his diabolical plan all along, Laura thought it had been her idea. She was just too confused and introverted to be so bold as to outright ask for help from people. When Armani had offered his assistance to her so genuinely, she couldn't resist taking him up on his offer.

Armani was just the kindest man to be helping her out, or so she thought. That was how manipulative and convincing Armani could be. In his home, Armani could keep her right under his thumb in case the Mob or authorities got on his back. She would be the perfect bargaining chip. Laura was a willing hostage, and she didn't even know it. Additionally, with

Cheryl in his rental property, all his pawns seemed to be falling into place to put him in a position he felt comfortable being in.

Laura was also led to believe she was helping Armani in return. Armani explained that Julie had been the love of his life, and now she had been confirmed dead. It had been a mentally excruciating year with him wondering why she had left him. He claimed to be alone and broken. The reason why was now all too clear. "The Mob took my love from me," he sobbed with his head upon Laura's shoulder. Laura's heart broke as Armani wove a tale of woe and lies to gain her sympathy and trust. She sympathetically listened to the words he spewed and quickly became his ally. He and Julie had never been more than acquaintances sharing a couple of sexual experiences, but Laura didn't know that.

"Then there was Janet. I knew I could not be the man for her like Dean was. I had to surrender her to him. I guess I am not a man destined by God to deserve the love of a good woman."

Laura was not a religious woman, but she did believe in a higher power and thought it admirable that Armani had religious faith. He did not. It was all a bunch of his bullshit to brainwash and win Laura over.

"I'm sure that's not true. There is a woman in this world for you," Laura lovingly assured him. "I'm sure we can get our lives on track if we help each other. I just knew we'd be good friends from the first moment I saw you. Janet and Dean speak highly of you, you know. I want to hide myself from the world until I am ready to face it. You are giving me that opportunity, and I am glad I am not dealing with this alone. Thank you for being here for me. Sometimes, the kindness of strangers means so much," she said sweetly as she leaned in to hug him firmly. As she did, the bathrobe she was wearing slipped open enough that Armani became distracted by the amber skin on a bit of cleavage.

"I understand," Armani responded in a soft and polite voice into her ear. He made certain she could feel his warm breath upon the side of her neck as he nuzzled her. It was a seduction technique he believed women attracted to him could not resist. As much as he wanted to seduce her, he knew Laura was in no mental or physical condition following her abduction ordeal to appreciate an aggressive man at this moment. While it was not his typical manner, which was to abruptly pounce on women, he was enjoying straying from his usual methods with this gradual seduction. Wanting to have sex with Laura while restricting himself from doing so was titillating. Usually, he always just took what he wanted when he wanted it, and willing women always let him.

Armani thought about his situation some more. Permitting Gloria and Cheryl to rent his home would allow them to be close by, where he could keep an eye on them at all times. It was an incredible concept that he would even have a landlord key to the property to discretely check on them anytime he felt the need. The organization was growing weary of waiting for many answers. It still worried him that recent events had affected his territory and that his Mob associates might not be telling him everything. As well, the authorities might not be telling people everything.

In reality, he felt as if he knew nothing when it was in his nature to be in control. Perhaps this time, ignorance was bliss; or it might be that this time, it would be his undoing. Not knowing made him realize that he needed to be more socially involved and interactive. Gloria and Cheryl staying on his property would be a good start. With Janet home, he could start visiting Janet and Dean more. He would observe them all more carefully. Planting bugging devices around their homes might be a way to start, he considered.

Soon came the day when Gloria and Cheryl were moving in. They were in the process of hauling boxes in their cars while a party appeared to be going on at Janet and Dean's. Armani recognized a car outside. It belonged to Janet's parents, Peg and Wes. Armani had not seen them in what seemed like ages. He rushed over to Janet and Dean's home to greet them.

Armani rang Janet's bell and took the liberty of walking through the open door. It felt like old times, when there had been an open door at the household at all times. Inside the house, a small group had gathered.

"Am I not invited to this party?" Armani asked Dean as Dean was coming to the door to greet him.

"It just happened to develop unexpectedly. Steven is home from the hospital, and we are celebrating. Peg and Wes came by to see him. You are aware Gloria and Cheryl are moving into your rental property today, and Gloria's parents came by to help. Gertty stopped in, and now you're here. It's an unexpected party!" Dean informed him. "Never a dull moment around here. I'd invite you in, but I see you've already found your way in."

Armani patted Dean on the shoulder and followed him into the living room.

"Hi! Have a beverage at the bar. Help yourself," Janet offered to Armani. "It's nice to see you. You've been elusive lately."

"It seems there is a lot to celebrate today," Armani understood.

"There is more. We just haven't made the announcement yet," Janet stated.

"Are you pregnant?" Armani asked jokingly.

"No, but I guess it is as good a time as any to make the announcement since everyone is here," Janet told him. "Hey, listen up, everyone. We have an announcement to make. Dean and I have decided to go along with a business opportunity Gloria and Cheryl want to pursue. We are backing them in a private investigation and security business they'll be taking over from Leo and the Fox family. Happier news is that my brother, Steven, will be moving here to work with us as well."

Peg and Wes were very happy to hear the news. "It will be so nice to have our son back," Peg commented. "Welcome home, son!" She was in her glory.

Armani wasn't sure what to think. He forced a smile in the confusion. It was good news, he thought. This could be an inside opportunity for him. He could really keep tabs on happenings. "That is good news," he claimed. When the space they would be utilizing for business in town was announced, Armani was quick to offer his handyman expertise with the build-outs. That would really make sure he had a foot in the door. "What brought about this business concept?" Armani wanted to know all about it.

"The Fox family wanted to unload their business, and we took a look into it," Cheryl took the liberty of answering. "We think it is a marvelous opportunity based upon the research we have done. It will be in honor of the friends we have lost. Maybe we can even figure out who Julie's killer was and where Caroline is while we are at it."

Even Armani did not know who Julie's killer was. He, too, would have liked to know. What had seemed to be a random killing had drawn the attention of law enforcement on his turf territory and put his department in peril. It also raised more questions his bosses wanted answers to. As for Caroline, he knew she had not been transported out of the country, as had previously been indicated by Dean. She was in Colorado, in the Denver suburb Aurora. He would never tell, though.

As much as he wished Cheryl, Caroline, and Laura had never met Janet, there was nothing he could do now. In his warped mind, he felt he was helping Cheryl and Laura now—Cheryl by renting to her and Laura by allowing her to stay with him. In some warped way, he considered that making amends for what had become of Caroline. He would never understand that his way of thinking was so very wrong. He could always manage to take any bad situation and think of how he could come out being the good guy.

Cheryl and Gloria left with Gloria's parents to start moving belongings into the old Irwin estate as soon as the moving company vans started arriving. Gertty suggested she should go home now, emphasizing to Armani that Janet's family was going for a boat ride. It was the first thing Steven said he wanted to do upon coming home from the hospital. Gertty thought it prudent to politely inform Armani of that detail, which he did not know. Armani and Gertty left together.

Cordially walking Gertty all the way home, Armani had the opportunity to talk with her. He loved talking with Gertty and had not really taken time to converse in some time. They strolled slowly, treading tiny steps. Gertty was not walking well due to her hips and legs, which were troubling her. They talked about that and the beautiful weather. They also spoke of any changes they had seen in the last year. Gertty was pleased with most all the changes, except those involving Julie, Caroline, and Laura. As far as

Gertty knew, there was still hope for Caroline and Laura. She would hope for a happy ending for the two of them, and she would keep thinking positively.

Armani was fishing for some information that he hoped could be beneficial, and Gertty did spill some beans. She mentioned how she had assisted in the rescue of their kidnapped friends, along with Cheryl and Gloria. No details of the murders were discussed, and Armani did not even think to question if these sweet women could be capable of such a massacre. But this revelation would still give Armani something to think about.

Gertty had always been like a mother to him, and he could not think of turning over that information to his bosses. The more information he would ever provide to his bosses, the more questions it would raise. Someday, he would need to provide some explanations, and they would likely not be truthful ones, not if he wanted to protect those dear to him. But it was good to know the real story. He suspected that the more he searched for answers, the more answers he would find.

* * *

The boat ride was very pleasant for Janet's family. The sun was shining and glistened upon the tiny waves of aqua water. It wasn't too hot, and the wind the boat travel generated felt invigorating. It was a perfect day and so reminiscent of the days when Janet was younger and her family went out on the boat together. It was the good old days all over again. How long she had waited to experience this with her family.

Peg wanted to venture over to where the mass grave was discovered. There, they bowed their heads in silence at her request. The Baskins' shop was nearby, and setting their eyes upon it began a discussion. The Baskin family still owned the property, and things would be awkward there now. How would it look for Janet to walk into the establishment after Mr. Baskin died in her arms? Dan would soon be released from the facility shortly. His incarceration time was coming to an end now that he had been cleared of murder and more. A mistrial would be declared. There were just a few details to be wrapped up before Dan would be permitted to come home. What then? How would any of them relate to seeing Dan again?

Janet had attempted to be in support of Dan always. They had remained in touch, and Janet always hoped she would be able to help clear Dan of his accused crimes. That seemed to be complicated now by the means in which that happened. What would she say to him? "I'm so happy to have helped clear you of your crimes and see you freed, but I'm sorry I had to be involved in the death of your father to do that." She considered it knowing it would not be a comfortable conversation to have.

Dan was incarcerated protecting his father, and now she had been the one to expose the truth. Everything exposed was what Dan went into confinement to try to keep secret. Perhaps Dan could understand that his father had attacked her and that she had reacted in the only manner in which she could. It was never her intent that he would die. She had no way of knowing how Dan was reacting to her involvement. She could only hope he would understand. However, to forgive and forget? Unlikely.

Following the boat ride, Peg sat Janet down privately in the kitchen back at the house. Peg explained how disturbed she had felt over the events that had taken place in the neighborhood and in their home. It would always be their home in Peg's thoughts as long it remained in the family and the family was together. Janet understood that much without question.

Until recently, Janet had avoided sharing many details of the previous year with her mother. Peg only really knew as much as the general public knew from news reports. Now she also knew Julie's skeleton had been discovered at the pier. She knew of an acquaintance who had shot her son. She knew her daughter had been attacked in the house by that same man, a local business owner whom they had long done business with. That man was now dead as a result of the attack and had died here.

This series of unfortunate events had Peg and Wes flustered. Janet assured her mother that these events could have happened anywhere and that they were not within her control or within the control of Dean. Unfortunately, being with Dean, there could be danger at times. It was not the perfect life Janet wanted to live, but it was her life to live.

"I like Dean a lot, Janet, but I'd have been much happier if you had hooked up with Armani. He's such a nice, mild-mannered, helpful young man," Peg told her. "He's not one to attract trouble and danger." Janet smiled knowing how ignorantly uninformed her mother was. "Whatever Dean is involved with, which brought Mr. Baskin to this house of death and pain, I don't approve of it one bit."

"The heart wants what the heart wants with regard to my relationship with Dean," Janet told Peg. "This danger of which you are speaking began before I moved in. It is rumored that Mob information was once hidden in this house before I bought it from you and Dad. What Baskin wanted was to get hold of that information.

"Everything bad that has happened in and around this lake is a result of that information and Mob dealings, so don't put the blame on me, Dean, or the house. This old house you and Dad sold to me came with a lot of baggage and issues attached to it. We are now just trying to clean it up. I know it's not your fault and you didn't know. Believe me when I tell you that I inherited a deep pile of shit along with this place, and people are cleaning it up for me. Now that I have informed you of that much, I suggest you and Dad be careful. We don't need this destruction of lives spreading to Prospect Heights. It is not public knowledge."

"Your father and I didn't know any of that. Please forgive us. We never would have sold you the house had we known there would be trouble here.

The events of last year were upsetting to us. Having heard of new events occurring now, I just had to speak to you about them."

"It is okay. I'm happy here, and I belong here. But I'm not your baby girl anymore, and you need to stop prying, including drawing your own inaccurate conclusions. Dean and I know what we are doing. I'll be okay here. If you ever fear for me, just call Gertty. She knows everything. Just know that there are some things Dean can't share with us. It's official business, and it all can be dangerous if not dealt with properly.

"Owning the private investigation company soon, I assume there will be some extent of danger in my life. I know that's not what any mother wants for her daughter. I know that you still think of me as your baby. But you need to know that I have grown up and I have changed. I can't sit still in a world of crime while my friends have disappeared and even been murdered.

"These problems were not something I created. They are something I and they became unwilling participants in. I can't just sit back someday as a quiet suburban housewife who pretends nothing is wrong. These problematic situations are not stopping just because I ignore them. It is not what you want to hear, but ignoring them will not make the danger go away. I must remain proactive," Janet lectured to her mother. "This is my life now like it or not!"

The men had come in from outside and joined the women in the kitchen. It was almost time for Peg and Wes to go back home to Prospect Heights.

They hated to leave and assured Janet and Dean they would be coming by more often. Janet didn't particularly want to hear that but expected that would be the case, though. Peg was one to worry, and she had reason to. Even if Janet couldn't discourage them from ever coming to town on her account, they would likely be coming anyway because of Steven. There was no stopping them now! Janet could only tell them under her breath how lovely that would be. "Well, we can certainly look forward to that."

Chapter 21

Cheryl and Gloria requested of Armani that he come to their new business to discuss decorating plans, as the business lease had been finalized. Armani showed up on time and complimented them on their choice of space. It was a modernized building, and the square footage was liberal enough for what they would need. They were still waiting for the business license and the IDFPR documents to come in to open the doors. They didn't figure that would take too long since Dean had clout with village officials and Armani was known for pulling many permits himself. They had connections in the community, and both would be of help rushing matters along. In a small village, people knew people, and that made all the difference. Since Dean and Armani had lived in Antioch their whole lives, they knew practically everyone and could accomplish miracles it would have taken Cheryl and Gloria forever to accomplish on their own.

Armani's work there would take a while to complete given that he still had other work responsibilities with various clients to tend to. Summer was a time when people kept him busy with jobs, and this was a large task to undertake on top of his regular workload. Winter would have been a better time for him to do this job. It was not by his choice to start this job at this time of year. He would need to work long, hard hours for a while. During that time, he hoped he would figure out a way to stick around the office once this work was completed. The information he would obtain could prove to be invaluable and would make a game out of the work. It wasn't gratifying enough to accomplish an earnest craftsman's living. The work now had to involve some secret element with hopes he would achieve some extra benefit to make it all worth his while. Otherwise, routine labor was just a plain, boring, and monotonous task that wasted his precious time

"I know you'll be busy here for a while. Before you become too wrapped up in this remodel, could you tend to a list of minor repairs Cheryl and I think you should look at back at the house?" Gloria requested. "They are simple things to be done. There is a list on our kitchen counter. Please look it over and do what you can for us. Cheryl and I could do some things ourselves if we need to and will compensate you for what is not within the scope of landlord repairs."

"Sure thing," Armani replied. "I can inspect the things you want done later today. I just need to get some measurements here so I can start these plans. How about right after lunch? That would give me plenty of time to get out of here and get over to the house."

"That would be great," Gloria said approvingly. "Let yourself in with your key if we aren't there. Take a look at the list we made and get back to us. If we aren't there, you know how to reach us by phone." Armani made a hand gesture indicating that was okay with him.

Trying hard to focus on his work, Armani's eyes kept wandering over to Cheryl and Gloria. He imagined what it would be like to engage in intimacy with the two of them. The thought of installing a hidden camera in their bedroom crossed his mind as well, but his thoughts were interjected by a mental image of Laura. No matter how hard he tried to focus on his work for Cheryl and Gloria, Laura became all he could think of.

He began wondering what Laura was doing. He wondered if she missed him while he was at work. Concluding his thoughts of her, he decided he should stop in the candy store on his way home and pick up a box of chocolates for her. Armani wasn't even sure she liked candies. He did know she would appreciate the thought and gesture. His act of kindness would surely help win her over even more. The whimsical candy store on the main street could provide just the right item to give to Laura.

When Armani did arrive back at his home, he found that Laura was anxiously awaiting his return. She had missed him and felt so lonely cooped up in the house all alone. The box of chocolates he presented her with did brighten her day. They talked for several minutes while Laura eagerly opened the box of candy and began picking out pieces to devour.

"Why do you keep a lock on your basement door?" Laura questioned while chewing on a milk chocolate-covered caramel.

"I keep valuables down there," he thought up as an excuse. "Nothing of value to other people, just things I have accumulated over the years. Honestly, I mostly keep it locked because I have a phobia of stairs and dark basements," he added with a false look upon his face, trying to express that he was embarrassed to admit it. "My good friend Irwin died from a fall down the stairs two doors down in my rental property. The fall contorted and mutilated him. I'll never get that vision of him out of my head as long as I live. As you know, Mr. Baskin also died from a fall down the stairs next door. That makes two people I knew. Death always comes in threes some people claim. I don't want the third fall to happen in this home. I feel secure keeping it locked. Just call me superstitious!

"There is nothing down there to concern yourself with. It's just a dank basement with some old work equipment and personal items. Before your being here, I worked and wasn't home often. Things are safer from thieves if they are locked up, wouldn't you agree? Last year, Dan was entering homes and stealing things. It happens, even here in the peaceful countryside. I wouldn't doubt if we soon have a crime rate equal to Chicago. The world is changing rapidly. It's frightening."

Laura did not pry any further with her line of questioning. She was satisfied with the answers Armani had provided her. "Caroline is very interested in the paranormal and superstitions. She believes in that stuff too. When we got to Antioch, she thought she had seen an Indian in the woods dressed in authentic garb. She claimed it was an omen, a warning of something bad. She was always trying to fill my head with superstitions. I miss her, Armani. Do you suppose she will be fortunate enough to be rescued?"

"If people are careful and do not screw things up with her abductors, there is a chance she may be," he said, offering her some hope. "I need to go back out again. I need to go to my rental property and check out some repairs our friends are suggesting. I'll be home as soon as I can, and then I will cook us an early dinner. Okay?" He phrased his request for permission in the form of a question to emphasize that he was taking her feelings into consideration, but she would not have protested, even had she minded. Who was she to make demands of him? And he cooked! He kissed her on the forehead as he departed the house.

At the rental property, Armani looked over the list of simplistic repairs that had been suggested. He spent only a few moments strategically installing a hidden special remote camera device in the main bedroom. Upon exiting the house, a young man came up the pathway to the door, where Armani stood with a key in the lock.

"Who might you be?" the young man questioned Armani with aggression in his voice.

"I might be the owner of this house. Who are you?"

"My name is Dale. I was informed that Cheryl lives here," Dale said sternly.

"She does. I'm her landlord. She's not at home right now. She is at her office, working, right now. She thought she might be home while I was here, but she hasn't returned yet. She could be home soon, or maybe not. I'm sure her schedule could change. I don't keep track of her."

"I called her cell phone and told her I'd be by. I didn't know she was working. Her parents gave me the address. I'm Caroline's boyfriend."

"So then you are the father of the baby she's expecting? I was sorry to hear of her disappearance. I had met her. She seemed like a fine lady. My friends speak highly of her," Armani told him. "Look, man, like I said, I don't keep tabs on Cheryl. But she was at this address in town earlier today. It's her office," Armani spoke as he wrote Cheryl's business information on a piece of paper in his notepad.

Handing the paper to Dale, Armani looked him in the eye and told him that he hoped Caroline would be found. Dale took the paper and thanked him. Having walked away from Dale, Armani smiled and shook his head. He was almost sure she would never be found. If she were, she would not be spending her future with him. *Poor guy,* Armani thought about Dale. From around the corner of the house, another man stood hidden in the bushes, listening in on the conversation.

Armani was passing Janet and Dean's house on the way home and decided to stop in for a friendly visit. Steven answered the door. Janet was home too.

"Come on in," Steven said with a smile. "Are you here to do work?"

"No, I'm just here for a friendly visit."

"Janet is home, sunning herself on the pier. Are you here to see her or me?" Steven questioned.

"I'll see anyone willing to look at me, but I probably have more to say to Janet," Armani thought likely. "I'll be back in a couple of days to perform some work. I'll finish any little tasks Janet has lined up for me then. For the time being, I'll just go outside to see Janet—not that I mind if you come with me and join us. I just came by to say hello to everyone."

Steven escorted Armani out to the pier. Upon seeing Armani and Steven, Janet and Mignon quickly jumped up and led them to the picnic table on her lawn. Janet assumed they would be talking for a few minutes and thought it best to talk there, where they could all sit comfortably while looking at the beautiful surroundings. Her garden was ablaze with color. The trees were full; and flower petals decorated their stems with a variety of blue, purple, and yellow tones. These colors attracted butterflies, and Janet adored them.

"Remember when I moved in and this yard was a mess? All crabgrass, weeds, and dirt. Just look at it now! The garden is so lovely thanks to you and your hard work." They each took time to take in the splendor. "I don't like sitting on the pier much these days," Janet confessed. "At first, I thought it was because of Julie. I then realized that was not it. I would feel comforted knowing she was near, dead or alive. I want to learn who killed her. Someday, we may find out, but it seems to me that most secrets become exposed later in the future, the finding of Julie's bones being one example. We spent a whole year not knowing her whereabouts when she was right under our noses.

"It reminds me of stories of people who die getting stuck in the chimney of their own home while trying to play Santa. In time, they are discovered. But Julie wasn't playing. Chaining her arms and legs to the posts of my pier was no ignorant action on her part. I'm off subject. It's not Julie's death in the water which has me spooked. It's all the other stuff in the water, along with so many dead people. I just can't help but envision dead people in the water all the time, and we have been swimming in that same water. It is sick and creepy.

"When they uncovered the mass grave in the lake and then pulled the dead guard from the water under my pier, I began to wonder how many other undiscovered bodies are in the lake. It is difficult for me now to sit on the pier and not imagine one isn't going to come floating to the surface or come drifting by. I can't help but wonder if I'll ever stop thinking about it."

Janet, Steven, and Armani all spoke of many things, including memories of Julie and how they all hoped her killer would be identified. Armani informed Janet of being at the office earlier and discussed some of his ideas for the remodel. "One other thing before I leave," Armani stated. "I met Dale just before coming over. He's Caroline's boyfriend." The remark was intended as gossip only. Janet and Steven wished they had met him too. Concluding the visit, Armani excused himself to head home. Again, from around the opposite corner of the house, a man stood isolated in the bushes. He had been listening to their conversation.

Slowly, the garage door to Armani's garage lifted automatically. He sat in his pickup truck, patiently awaiting the opportunity to pull his vehicle in. Coming down the gravel street was a car that appeared unfamiliar to him. Unrecognized vehicles usually meant sightseers, and he deplored them. As the car pulled up alongside his truck, Armani saw there was a group of four young men inside. They knew who he was and stopped to speak with him, but to him, they were strangers. Having identified themselves as Caroline's and Cheryl's brothers, they commented that they knew he must be Cheryl's landlord by the way he had been described to them.

The driver stated they were on their way to visit Cheryl at her home. Armani informed them she had not come home from town yet. They said they would wait outside her home for a while if Armani would not object. He didn't. The entire time they spoke, Armani was aware of a man trying to remain unseen in nearby trees. As the men drove off, Armani quickly jumped out of his vehicle and rushed over in the direction of the hidden trespasser.

The man remained still for several moments, assuming he had remained unrevealed. By the time he realized Armani was coming for him, he did not know which way to turn. The trees were too dense for him to run anywhere except directly into Armani, and that was exactly what he was trying to avoid. It was too late for him to make any rational decision. And then Armani was on top of him.

"What do you want with me? Why are you trespassing?" Armani then asked a few similar types of questions while grasping and shaking the man.

While the man tried in vain to come up with a false but logical excuse he could provide Armani, thoughts eluded him. "Armani, I know who you are. You don't know me. I was sent by our so-called friends to check things out around here. They wanted a report on you and what is happening around here. They are not sure they trust you. I do."

"You tell them that they are to lay off around here. They put a graveyard in a location where it could be discovered. I didn't," Armani claimed. "They chose to pick on young women with family and friends. I didn't," he added. "Now police, investigators, reporters, families, and tourists are crawling all over this lake day and night. I can't even walk out my door without being followed. You tell them to just stay clear from this area until the day I give them approval to proceed—that is, if I ever will. They've made a clusterfuck of everything here."

"I've seen that for myself," the fellow syndicate representative agreed. "My name is Damien. I guess I wasn't doing my job too well if you spotted me. Please don't tell anyone we spoke of this, and I'll tell them exactly what you want me to say."

From that moment, a new friendship began to form. It was one that would be a close bond as time went on. Armani felt relieved that he finally found a person with whom he could share his involvement with organized crime. The two took a walk and learned a lot about each other in a short matter of time. Neither wanted to be part of this syndicate any longer. Both felt trapped in it. Damien agreed he would help keep the Mob off Armani's tail as long as possible until the mess was cleared up. He was a man who could do that much for him.

"You are probably not someone I would have run up to today if things were different around here. Any other time, I would have ignored your presence. But my sense of awareness is overly heightened right now, and I've been on edge, so I ran to you. Sorry if I startled you and any feathers got ruffled. I'm glad we talked, Damien, and it is nice to have met you." Armani extended his hand for a shake.

By the time Armani entered his house, Laura had dinner started on the stove.

"That smells great! I love pasta," he admitted. "I didn't know you could cook. I was going to cook for you tonight."

"I cook fairly well. I learned a lot in scouting and school. Mom taught me a lot," she professed. She turned around from the stove and approached Armani. Unexpectedly, she wrapped her arms around him and provided him with a big hug. Her grasp clung tightly for a lingering time. Looking him in the eyes, she asked a very direct question: "Do you find me attractive?" He did and told her so. She continued to gaze into his eyes, and he could read her thoughts.

Upon lifting her chin, he cupped her head in his hands and placed a gentle kiss upon her lips. The kisses became more intense and passionate until their wet tongues were thrusting back and forth into each other's soft mouths. "There is time before dinner if you want to go to the bedroom," she suggested. He did not bother. He laid her down as their clothes were rapidly torn off and took her right there on the kitchen floor. His bulky, muscular frame was immense in size compared to her petite figure. She felt pinned under his sweaty, furry chest muscles, but she enjoyed it. He wanted to penetrate her hard, but he knew that might not go over well with her after her encounter with the kidnappers, so he slowed down and became very gentle with his touch.

Their eyes were locked, and they never stopped staring into the windows of their souls throughout the lovemaking session. Both climaxed together, and her juices poured and commingled with his seed. Armani lay on top of her for several minutes afterward, careful not to put too much of his weight down. He continued staring into her eyes and stroking her silky hair. He then realized that he loved this woman. It was a feeling he had never known before. There wasn't just an attraction between them. A natural bond had total control over them. It was not his choice, and he could not fight it. Laura felt the same.

Dinner was delicious, and Armani was feeling as if he was on cloud nine. His mood was elevated more so after receiving a call from his boss. It was obvious that Damien had reached the syndicate with his report and that all had turned out even better than expected. His boss told him that they were going to sever ties with him and the area due to all the commotion. It was unheard of that the Mob would ever do that. However, these were extenuating circumstances, and the Mob did not want to deal with him or the problems. Someday, they might call upon him again, but someday might never come. One was never really out of the Mob, and only the future would tell. Again, Armani related it to a game in which he could not make a play until his opponent made their move. This was no time for any moves to be made in Antioch. It was wise to leave the playing board undisturbed until another day.

Later that evening, Armani tossed around ideas in his head. While he considered them to be complex, they were really quite typical of his usual thought process. He knew the Mob would be leaving him alone for the interim. That would be leaving him with much more free time on his hands. He would be bored. His life was all about the unusual and taking risks. Yet on the other hand, he felt a need to run and get away. That might have been hidden insecurity that came with not believing the Mob was, in fact, backing off. All things considered, whatever he was going to choose to do with his life, he would conclude that it was all for Laura's sake.

It would be nice to get her away from Antioch before she was discovered. Being that Laura missed Caroline, Armani had a thought. As were most of his thoughts, he considered it to be another potential personal accomplishment to help humanity. Really, it was to make up for his own feelings of guilt—guilt over what had happened to Caroline. Having fallen in love with Laura, he was experiencing a sudden greater appreciation for humanity and the suffering of people he had come to know and those he had hurt. That feeling was new to Armani. He was becoming a more compassionate person with every passing day. Laura could be to thank for that.

Sadly, Armani dreaded telling his clients that he would be going away. They often depended on him, and he had never let them down. In a different train of thought, he had never even taken a vacation. He was due one. He would announce it as being a vacation. As soon as he finished the build-outs for the girls' business, he would leave. His whole life had been spent working while saving his money, and he had inherited quite a lot from Irwin and his parents.

Technically, he was wealthy. He could go anywhere or do anything he wanted.

His decision was to go to the Denver area and search for Caroline. That would take him away, get Laura away, and give him something exciting to do. But he did not want to leak too much information too soon. He did not want word getting out that he was planning such a trip. He would make the announcement that he was going to take a road trip and discover America without specifically mentioning Colorado. Secretly, he would take a month-to-month lease on a home there while telling the agent he would be visiting the area for an undetermined time on business.

By the time he finished working on the build-outs for the girls, winter would be approaching. Things were always slow in winter, which was when tourists and part-timers left upon the arrival of colder weather. About the only work he would be missing would be house-sitting, autumn leaf removal, and any early-snow removal. His clients would just need to make do without him this year. Although he knew that life could always take an unexpected turn and he might never return, he hoped that would not be the case. This was his home and the only home he had ever known.

Not knowing how Laura would take the news, Armani was happy that she took it well when he finally decided to tell her. When planning all this in his mind, he knew there was a chance she would not be accepting of his idea to get away. Fortunately, she was willing to follow him anywhere. Her life was with him. Of course, he had not informed her that this plan in any way involved Caroline. Denver, she thought, was just a random place he told her they would be going. She could pick the mountains, suburbs, or urban city for all he cared. He hoped she would pick the mountains, but he would not limit her choice.

Her only downside was that she would have to wait a whole month, cooped up in his home, before they would get away. Perhaps by then, her newly developed agoraphobia would subside, and she would feel less fearful of leaving the house. He assured her that the month would pass quickly and that she could research and pick any home in the Denver area where she wanted to stay. A small cottage to a grand mansion—all were available possibilities. The more he spoke about going away together, the more excited she became. It was hard for her to believe that any man would be doing this all for her. She was under the delusion it was all about her.

Chapter 22

The weeks that followed in Antioch seemed normal for all the neighboring friends. Armani kept the busiest. He worked hard and kept his lover entertained. The day came when he finished the requested repairs in his rental home, and he removed the camera from the bedroom of Gloria and Cheryl. During the time in which it had been installed, he only found limited pleasure in their bedroom antics. They didn't excite him as much as he thought they would.

In his past, when he had been alone, masturbation was a pastime he frequently engaged in. Such voyeuristic visuals used to excite him. Now with Laura in his life, she turned out to be a nympho with a sexual appetite even he had trouble keeping up with. After the first time he engaged in watching Gloria and Cheryl be intimate, he had been there and done that, but Laura was the real deal. As for the Mob, they didn't come around or call. Armani felt free from them and somewhat believed he was leading a normal type of life.

The agency build-outs were coming along swimmingly and were almost finished. Janet, Dean, Cheryl, and Gloria were all wrapped up in their new security and private investigation business. They even had some clients inherited from when the Fox family had owned it. Client needs never ceased being tended to between ownership by the Fox family and the new owners taking over. Business was already busy before the new office space had open doors, but the owners all managed just fine working from their homes or in the business space while Armani sawed and made construction noise for hours on end. Nobody complained.

Dean, Cheryl, and Gloria continued their regular jobs. Janet continued running her art business. Perhaps that would only be for the time being. It seemed likely some would leave those jobs and commit full-time to this business someday. Everyone was excited to see what the future held. Any nightmarish events that previously occurred at the lake were rarely spoken of, but that did not mean they were ever or would ever be forgotten. These events were not behind them, and never would they be. They were just treated like a dream of the past unless some happening caused them to rear an ugly head. That was to be expected and unavoidable.

Steven was still trying to make his move to Illinois. It was taking him time to close the door on his life in California and wrap up details. He was anxious for all the relocation efforts to be over. The exertion he expended was taking a toll upon his health. He would survive it. It was just difficult for him to get through. The family members of Caroline, Cheryl, and Laura stopped coming around after they snooped for a few weeks after Armani first saw them. They did not uncover any enlightening details and departed the area. They came, and they went, but it would probably not be the last that Antioch would be seeing of them.

The newest face on the block to come around was Chuck from Baskin's. He managed to become friends with Cheryl, Dean, and Janet. Armani came to know him as the guy who assisted him when he went into the Baskin Boat Shop. Somehow, Armani knew he and Chuck would someday become better acquainted as well. At this time, Armani did not want anyone else prying into his life. That was nothing personal against Chuck. But Chuck noticed the intentional distancing and did take it personally. All the other lake people treated him very well, and Armani was always very polite but short with him. The harder Chuck tried to win him over, the more Armani backed off. Chuck eventually took the hint.

Dean managed to keep the authorities under control if or when they came around. He would remind them that people had rights and that they best not harass them. When possible, everyone kindly cooperated. There were some unresolved crime issues, and everyone concerned still wanted answers, mostly to pacify their own curiosities. With respect to those particular crimes, nobody ever had anything new to say. Anything previously undisclosed still remained secret. One misappropriated word could send everything into a tailspin. Basically, authorities all knew Dean and avoided wasting their time researching and rehashing the same old details over and over. Those investigators just hoped that something might turn up and that there would be a break in any of the many cases.

An example was the case of who killed Julie. The more time that passed, the more the trail grew cold, and the less investigators and reporters came around asking about it. Anyone could tell that they only came around because someone higher-up had directed them to follow up. They seemed to know they had been sent to perform a useless task from which nothing new would be disclosed to them. Often, those being questioned became more irate each time with the repetitive disturbances.

Gertty's life did not change much. Barring any unusual events, she always spent each day as she had spent the day before: she gardened and baked. Rarely did she venture off her property while not being escorted because she still did not want to risk falling. But all this did not mean to imply she was lonely or did not appreciate life. She preferred to be a loner in her own home. And all the neighbors stopped in almost daily. Gertty considered them to be her family. It seemed that one of them or another was coming or going from her house. Sometimes, it was too many visitors, she thought. She would be in the middle of something and would need to stop to answer her door several times a day. They might even interrupt her naps. But they loved her, and she loved them. God forbid the day people stopped visiting, she thought.

Armani spent the most time by Gertty's being that he helped with many of her chores. She knew him better than anyone. He knew Gertty would be the one to miss him most of all while he would be gone to Colorado. He dreaded telling her the news. Today was the day he would tell her that he would soon be leaving. She would need advance notice in order to find help in taking over his work chores around her home once he left. The others would more easily manage without him.

What Armani was going to find comfort in telling her was that he could tell her much of the truth about Colorado. Gertty was the one person with whom he trusted secrets—not that he always told her everything or that he always told her the truth. He was simply able to divulge more information to her than to anyone else he would be telling about his departure even if it wasn't the whole truth.

Sitting Gertty down, he explained to her that he was going away and that any details shared with her were to remain their secret. Armani told her about the trip and that he thought he had a lead on Caroline's whereabouts. He wanted to look into his suspicions while on an extended vacation. Nobody was to know because he didn't want to get anyone's hopes up or have them asking too many questions. In general, it was his private vacation, and not everyone needed to know his business at all times.

Gertty thought that was a bit mysterious but didn't question his motives. He deserved a vacation. If he could figure out where Caroline had gone to, that would be wonderful. Since she didn't know any of the details, she did not realize that Armani could be in danger. She would be sad to see him go, but something she would never do was stand in the way of one of her *kids* experiencing all life had to offer them.

Within a matter of days after talking with Gertty about his vacation, Armani's remodeling work at the agency was completed. The once vacant large space had been transformed into an impressive, modernized workspace. Carpet and plants softened the environment. Janet's original artwork hung on the walls. The last detail was to hang the signs. They read in large print Village Agency with smaller print below reading Security and Investigative Services. *Not a lot of ingenuity,* Armani thought, but it did get the point across without any confusion. It had not been easy getting everyone to agree upon a name.

Upon completion of this large job, Armani felt it was time to inform every one of his intent to depart town for a while. He explained that it was part personal business and part vacation. While he had no particular date in mind to return, he assumed it likely would not be until after winter. The whole country was his to explore. He stated that he wanted to stay away while snow fell upon Illinois. That was a good reason for anyone to stay away if they had spent their whole lives dealing with Midwest winters. Little did his friends know that he would mostly be in the Denver area, where it snowed.

Before he could depart, his friends insisted on throwing him a party to say goodbye. While Cheryl and Gloria considered being the ones to host it, Janet insisted she and Dean throw the party and combine it with a grand opening celebration. Cheryl and Gloria would be hosting a more businesslike opening party at the office after Armani left town. He was sorry to be missing it.

Come the party night at Janet and Dean's, everyone had a grand time. The celebration was exquisite. Armani wanted to cry knowing that he could be away from his friends for a long time. He had never been away from home for long, and it might be that he would never come back, he thought. He never knew what life would throw his way.

Chapter 23

On a dark night shortly after Armani and Laura departed town, intruders smashed a backdoor window to his house and made their way in. It was not uncommon for kids to break into homes they knew were unattended and throw party gatherings, but this was not the instance here. Armani had a very advanced, sophisticated security system installed by his Mob associates, and kids or just any common street person would not know how to bypass it. Nobody would know the details of its installation except those involved in installing it.

The intruders searched his home high and low. They had never done anything such as this before at his property. Upon a complete search of his home, they set it ablaze, leaving none of the main structure or the garage standing by morning.

That night was devastatingly upsetting to Janet and Dean. Their home was positioned so closely that it was in danger. Amber flames accented with every color of the rainbow raised to the sky in the hour after midnight. Dean was away at work when the arson began. Mignon pawed Janet, who was sound asleep, forewarning her about the strong smell of smoke in the air. Janet's medications had her zonked-out cold. Mignon's effort to awaken her was eventually effective, but by the time Janet got around to phoning the fire department, the fire was raging out of control. It did not take much to burn smaller, aged wooden homes at Lake Marie, such as Armani's home.

Dean heard about the call from emergency dispatch. Rushing from his desk and to his vehicle, he drove until he eventually pulled onto the street with their homes. At the same time, firefighters and other emergency vehicles were arriving. Janet was safely sitting in her car at the entrance to their street with Mignon and Cleopatra. They would remain a safe distance away until receiving approval to return to their home.

Dean's correct observation based on his experience was that it was too late to save Armani's home. The vicinity was engulfed in billowing black smoke. By the time the smoke had cleared, the structure had been reduced to a pile of rubble. At least the fire department was able to stop the fire before it spread off Armani's property line. Most of the ash had blown toward and into the lake, not toward the other surrounding properties. By the time the fire was fully extinguished, Gertty, Cheryl, and Gloria had parked their cars behind Janet's and were conversing with her until such a time when they could return to their homes. They were weeping over Armani's loss.

Armani was on the phone with Damien as the fire was at its peak. Damien had called Armani to inform him that the syndicate had broken into his home looking for the memory stick or any other incriminating information they could find to use against him. Mostly, they wanted to retrieve any evidence that Armani could later use against them. Lucky for Armani, nothing was found. The syndicate did not care about having the memory stick information in their possession as much as they wanted it destroyed. It could be too dangerous in the wrong hands. Armani commented to Damien that he did not have the stick and had assumed the actual existence of it was only a legend.

"It is not a legend," Damien explained. He knew that Irwin had been murdered, but this was news to Armani. It had been suspected. It was never proven. "Before the fall down the stairs, Irwin informed his murderer that the memory stick did, in fact, exist," Damien claimed. "Irwin once had it in his possession before hiding it behind a freezer in the home Janet and Dean now reside in. Before Irwin could retrieve the item, someone had been there and removed it from its hiding spot. Irwin wasn't able to say who that person was. The Mob was upset when the person sent to confront Irwin didn't return with a name. Was it that Irwin wasn't able to say because he didn't know or because he was afraid to say? Nobody will likely ever know.

"The Mob was further upset by the murder taking place. The person sent to confront Irwin was not sent to murder him. You have taken his position by default. That is another reason bosses have gone easy on you with all that has happened. They may also fear you do have the memory stick and could use it against them someday. The burning of your home by them is only something I am confirming with you. They are not to know I told you. On the other subject, not all the lake residents have been declared clear of having the stick. They'll always be continuing their search for it."

"Let me guess," Armani said. "The Mob thought I had it because I had access to the home before Janet moved in."

"That is correct. They didn't push you for it before because you were one of the gang. With recent events, they didn't want you walking with it. They wanted to do a bit of digging around your home. As you know, they came up empty-handed. They burned down the home in case they had overlooked it. The good news is that they are going to back off now. They believe you know they burned down your home and will not mess with them.

"I want to mention that while Irwin did not know how to get ahold of the memory stick before he died, his last words were that he knew it was still on the block. Everyone thinks he meant the block your home is on. They'll still be looking for it—I mean, anyone who believes it exists. So one last thing I want to say before I have to hang up: keep Laura away for now. I know she is with you, but they don't." The call was then disconnected.

Armani was shocked by the last comment. Immediately, the phone rang again showing Dean's number. Dean had phoned as soon as he could. Armani answered and acted surprised to be hearing from Dean, but he wasn't surprised and had been expecting a call. Dean informed Armani that his home was gone. Acting distraught, Armani pretended to take the news hard. Dean wanted to know if Armani would be coming back soon in lieu of the news. Armani responded, "It doesn't seem I have anything to come home to right now. Thanks for calling."

Laura wanted to know what all the late-night calls were about. Armani told her the Mob had burned the house down. He wanted her to be alarmed, making her more reliant on him. "They were looking for you. Someone tipped them off that you had been there," he told her. "Don't you worry, though. We got away in time, and you are safe here with me. The Mob has given up for now, I've learned. I may have lost my home, but I have you." Laura felt terrible for his loss and held him close to her. She felt so loved by his efforts to help her. He was her hero and savior.

Armani wanted to cry. He thought of the wonderful party his friends had thrown for him before he left. He recalled a moment during which he thought he might be away for a long time and of the thought that maybe he would never make it back to Lake Marie. The fire confirmed his thoughts as being a real possibility. Perhaps it would be best for his friends if they never saw him again. He only seemed to attract and create trouble. For the time being, he would avoid contact with them. He would tell them he was off the grid and wasn't getting phone calls.

Chapter 24

Colorado was beautiful, and Laura and Armani couldn't wait to get settled into a stylish mountain cabin home Laura had selected. It wasn't a mansion by any means. It was, however, large enough and well-appointed. The mountain views were breathtaking, and a bubbling stream out back was an interesting feature. The mountain air was so fresh and clean. Leaves were changing colors.

"I'm so glad you suggested Colorado, Armani. It's so lovely here, and I feel completely refreshed," Laura proclaimed.

"There is something I should tell you, Laura. I wanted to wait until we got here. It may not be accurate information. I didn't want to get your hopes up," Armani began saying. He paused for a moment while composing his words. "I did some investigation into Caroline's whereabouts. I also hired people who wish to remain anonymous. They discovered that she may have been brought to an area nearby here. That is why I wanted to come to Colorado. I hoped for your sake that we could do something to help locate your friend.

"I don't know if we will be able to help at all. It just felt right to try. I didn't even want to tell you because it could be a wild-goose chase. Now that we are here, though, I think you'd know something is up if I seemed to be distracted with something. I'm telling you now that what I'm going to be working on is trying to help rescue Caroline. Are you mad at me?"

"Do you think there is really a chance we could rescue her?" Laura was elated. "Mad at you? You are such a sweet man. I can't believe that you would do this for me and for Caroline too. You are so special."

Armani knew that was how she would react, and he wanted her admiration.

"Now let's christen this home with some nooky," Laura said with a seductive smile Armani couldn't resist.

* * *

Armani passed out shortly after making love. He was tired, and it had been a long, adventurous excursion from Illinois to Colorado considering all the stops they made to go sightseeing along the way. It was while he was sleeping that Laura began really thinking about what Armani had told her about Caroline possibly being in that area. Laura began to feel guilty that they had wasted any time on the road getting to Colorado if her friend was suffering somewhere. They should have rushed straight through to Colorado had she known.

* * *

The following morning, Armani awakened early. Laura was up to greet him and immediately questioned why they had waited to come look for Caroline. Armani already had the answer in case she asked. "The Mob can be around any corner. There was too much at risk. The time had to be right. Even if we had arrived earlier, it would have done us no good. I needed those calls you asked me about to advise me on how best to act on this. Remember, I told you there are to be no questions. You are better off if you don't know anything at all. Don't you trust me?"

"Yes, of course, I do. I'm sorry for questioning you. I could just bite my tongue off. I guess I was just excited last night over the possibility that Caroline could be rescued. You were sleeping, and I was in a strange house. My mind wandered. Don't think ill of me for questioning you. I promise I will not question you ever again," Laura said with disgust in her voice over doubting his ways.

Armani assured her not to be so hard on herself for it. He would let it slide this time, he told her. As soon as he returned from going to pick up some groceries, they would have breakfast. Then he would take her for a walk. It would be refreshing for her to get out after being locked up in his home for a month. The walk would clear their minds and help them think about how they could go about locating and helping Caroline. After that, Armani would set up his computer system so they could get started on locating her. It was already panning out to be a busy day ahead.

One thing he mentioned to Laura was that it could take months or even years to track down her friend. There were no guarantees. While Laura would be free to invest whatever time she desired in the task, he was not obligated to spend every minute of his life at it. He wanted some normality and peace in his life, which Laura understood.

The grocery store was large and confusing to Armani. He was familiar with the smaller stores in Antioch and knew his way well around those. But this store had a different layout, and the change over-whelmed him. When he was done with the shopping, he was glad to have completed his task and exited the establishment. Upon loading the groceries in his truck, he turned to find Damien standing behind him.

"What are you doing here? Are you following me?" Armani demanded to know out of fear the Mob was tracking him.

"Chill! I'm your friend. I'm not here to cause you trouble. I'm here to help you," Damien informed him.

"Why would you want to help me, and how did you know I have Laura with me?" Armani questioned.

Damien explained many things to Armani until Armani was pacified by the discussion. "Listen, my friend, not everyone wants to be involved with the Mob. Many are involved against their will. I was blackmailed into becoming involved. There is a group of us who have banned together. We secretly help each other in combating the syndicate. We rescue people they have wronged. We are sort of an Underground Railroad. The UR we call ourselves.

"People are still bought, sold, and traded all over the world. We know you are not hiding Laura for kicks. We know why you are here in Colorado. Fortunately for you, the Mob doesn't know anything. They know nothing of my dealings. They know nothing of your dealings. I'd like to help you. Correction, the UR would like to help you. In return, you can help us someday. In a way, you could call us the anti-Mob—double agents, if that helps you understand more clearly, just like you, only you haven't seemed to relate to what you are yet.

"You don't want the Mob finding out your secrets. You'd be a dead man. You are lucky they let you live through all you have been through. The fact they have left you alone tells us that you are someone special. I think by now you have noticed that you can trust me too. I've risked my life telling you everything I have told you. You need us, and we need you," Damien expressed. "To respond to your earlier question, no, I did not follow you here. We knew you were headed here before you arrived. We know our business and the business of everyone in the Mob.

Even the corrupt divisions of the Mob don't know as much as we know. I can help you get to Caroline. It won't be easy, and I don't think you can get to her without us."

Armani wanted to know what he should do. "Wait for me to call you," Damien requested. Concluding their conversation, Armani wanted it known that Laura did not know of his previous involvement with the Mob. "Of course," Damien understood. "This is not an organization one usually announces their involvement with. We all keep our identities and involvements secret. I assumed you understood that." Armani nodded.

Armani went to the cabin he was now calling home and cooked up a nice breakfast. Laura had always been impressed by his ability to cook. It was something he had to do for himself since an early age. It was his responsibility to cook for himself and his father ever since his mother passed away. Conversation about Caroline ensued after dining. What he thought had been a made-up excuse in answer to Laura's earlier question now seemed to fit right into the factual status of life. He explained that he had heard from his sources while he had been out shopping. They advised everyone to sit tight until they contacted him again. Laura was excited by this news. She had not initially expected that anyone was going to be helping them locate Caroline. That gave her even more hope that her friend could be located and freed.

* * *

Two days went by before Armani heard from Damien again. Damien had located Caroline's exact location and assured Armani she was alive and unharmed. She was being kept at a mountaintop ranch not far away. The question would be how best to get her out of there. The ranch had armed guards, and prisoners were not allowed to mingle with any guest invited onto the ranch. An open-door invite was an absolute impossibility. Business meetings conducted by the staff there, including illegal adoptions, are handled out of an off-site office in Arvada, several miles away.

This was not the first time the UR was attempting a rescue. They had attempted many in history. Sometimes, they succeeded. Usually, the best way to retrieve any person was to buy the captive their freedom by claiming to be another slave owner or syndicate dealing in such criminal activities. The Underground Railroad group had staff able to help arrange that if desired, but it would not be cheap. A woman like Caroline, who was already impregnated, could bring upward of $200,000 or more. Much of that value was for the baby. If they waited for her to give birth, they could possibly get Caroline out for a generous $75,000. Negotiating for any lesser amount would be tricky.

Another way to get Caroline out would be a rescue sting. That could put a lot of people in danger and mean that Caroline would be on the run if she did get away. The last known option was to leave it all in the hands of law. But the government was known to waste time and botch jobs, and they would only play by the rules. It was never known which side the officials involved were on, and any inside tip would result in failure. There was a good chance captives would be removed from the ranch before a rescue could be made. In such a case, Caroline would likely never be found again.

This ranch group was in no way part of the Mob that Armani and Damien were associated with. The ranch organization was their own organized worldwide human trafficking organization. That meant no matter how Caroline would come to gain freedom, there was a potential that an enemy could be made with this or some other completely different syndicate ring.

Armani would have been willing to spend money on Caroline alone, just not the baby too. He could easily afford the $75,000. Most likely, the ranch syndicate already had a buyer waiting for the birth of the child. It would be sad if Caroline needed to wait so many months to gain her own freedom. So much could happen between now and then.

Armani explained a few of the pitfalls to Laura. One fact was that the sale could likely occur more quickly if Caroline lost the baby. If the ranch wasn't waiting for the baby to be born, the sale could possibly happen immediately. Considering the possibility of buying the baby along with Caroline, Armani was not going to put up $200,000 himself, assuming that would be the agreed-upon sale price. Caroline had never even been sure if she wanted to keep the baby in the first place. Paying for something she didn't particularly want seemed ridiculous.

At the first sign of any trouble, guards at the ranch were ordered to shoot all hostages and anyone not authorized to be there. It would be dangerous. Caroline's life was in enough mortal danger daily. Time could be of the essence, as Caroline could be transferred out of there at any time. Attempting to negotiate for her life or expect her to be rescued legally by the law could waste time. Armani and Laura did not have any proof or know where Caroline was being kept to go to the police. They debated the pros and cons of all options.

Laura did not know what to request. She was in no position to pay for the freedom of her friend. She didn't want her friend to get harmed. She did not want her friend to be kept anywhere against her will for even a minute more. If Caroline were to escape, Laura knew firsthand that being on the run was no way to live. There just had to be an adequate solution. But what was it?

Chapter 25

It had been another couple of days before Armani heard from Damien again. Damien called, and Armani answered promptly. "The UR has a plan. It is dangerous, but similar plans have worked before in like circumstances in other locations. There will be a meeting a week from today. The UR wants you and Laura to attend. This will require the help of both of you, along with several other people.

"Meet me in the lobby of the famous hotel in Estes Park at 7:00 p.m., and I'll tell you which room to report to. Don't loiter in the lobby, and don't talk to me. I'll just tell you the room number. Knock on the door and wait inside for me. I'll show up when everyone else has arrived. I've staggered the times others are to arrive. Don't get impatient there, as a bar will be set up with refreshments. Help yourselves." Damien's instructions were explicit and fully comprehended.

* * *

A week to the day, Laura and Armani showed up at the designated rendezvous. Damien was there on time. "Room 217. Knock only four times, and quickly," he instructed. They did as they were told. In room 217, several people were there, making idle conversation. Nobody seemed to know the next person, couples knowing their mates excluded. The people all seemed polite enough to Laura and Armani.

"Try the appetizers," one woman suggested. "They are to die for!" Armani and Laura loaded a plate to share and accepted beverages before finding places to sit upon the edge of a bed. The suite was on the smaller side and just comfortably accommodated the dozen or so people there. After they waited approximately half an hour, Damien showed up.

"Hello," one of the other men said. "I'll be hosting this meeting today. You've each been carefully selected to help the UR with a mission. It is imperative you keep this information top secret. I assume I do not need to tell you what will happen if a stool pigeon is discovered. It would be the last time they say anything." Several people in the room chuckled.

"As each of you know, there is a ranch near here buying, kidnapping, and harboring a group of young women. The hostages are pregnant or impregnated there, and the babies are sold in illegal adoption transactions. Our informants tell us there are six or so women currently there. Our mission is to rescue them and get them to better places. We will offer them some advice, as freeing them could put them in danger. First, we just need to worry about getting them out of there. You know we do our best to keep them protected." Everyone in the room was sitting quietly and following along with the conversation.

"We've been monitoring the ranch and have come up with a plan to break the hostages out. It will be dangerous. We hope nobody we care about gets injured or killed in the process. For some of you, you may know the routine or know how our missions can go. Of course, each one is always different and specific to its nature." The man walked over to Armani and Laura. "We have a few newcomers here. I'd introduce all of you more formally; but it's best you not know too much about your fellow comrades." Laura and Armani glanced up at him. "I'll let Damien take it from here."

"I know each and every one of you to some extent. We all have something in common: we want to see those women freed. The basic outline of the plan is simple. To protect each of you, you will only be provided with information as to how to complete only your own specifically assigned task. Some may be given backup tasks in case of emergency. I'll give you the general rundown now," Damien said. Then he began describing the mission.

"We've been tracking a delivery truck which shows up there daily. We've obtained a duplicate model of the truck and have had it painted to resemble the delivery vehicle. One of you will be a driver. Several of you will be dressed as guards. But all of you will be armed. We will get the truck into the gates with each of you in it. Then you each will be expected to perform your designated tasks to the letter. While we can't predict unforeseen circumstances, we can assume each of you is capable of following the instructions provided to you.

"Within the next week, I will be in touch with each of you. Don't worry, I know where to find you. You will be instructed as to any details which pertain to you. Come the day we act, you best be at your best. Any screwups could cost us and the hostages our lives."

* * *

On the ride home, Armani thought he should break the ice with conversation and interrupt Laura, who was quietly lost in thought.

"You didn't know your man was a secret agent, did you?" She looked at him and smiled. "Are you going to be up for this?" he questioned.

"Yes. I just can't believe they are trusting me with a gun. I'll need to control myself with it. All those bastards upsetting Caroline and those other women deserve to be shot. You may need to teach me to fire it, but I'm ready to use it. I'll do whatever it takes to get her out of there," Laura assured him. "Honey, there is something I haven't told you. You know that ranger, the one they found dead? I killed him. I said I didn't know what came over me to do a thing like that, but I do know. He hurt me, and I sought retribution. I'd do it again if I have to."

Armani turned to look at Laura with an evil grin. He had been thinking all along that he was actually Satan when he had never even murdered a person. This seemingly darling young lady had outdone his own wickedness. Had he cared about the ranger, he might have been more upset. His only negative concern was that the death of the ranger had reflected poorly upon him. Then again, so had Laura's escape. He got over that. He would get over the death of the ranger too.

Her confession intrigued him even more, and his admiration for her became grander. The death of the ranger was no basic, quick kill. It had been brutal. He knew that and never would have thought Laura had it in her. "I'm impressed," he said, his evil grin turning into an innocently boyish smile.

Chapter 26

A few more days passed. Laura was sitting at her kitchen table while Armani was taking his shower. She heard footsteps behind her, and then two manly arms gently wrapped around her chest from the rear.

"I thought you were in the shower, honey." The bathroom water was definitely running.

"I'm not your honey," Damien said as he removed his arms from around her. "I just thought I would see how on guard you are these days. You seem pretty relaxed given all that has gone and is going to go on. While that is good that you are so relaxed, you should be more alert."

"It's early morning, and I've not had my caffeine. I'm not alert until I have downed my beverage. How did you even get in here? Did Armani let you in?" Laura questioned. She assumed he must have.

"Let's not discuss unimportant details. I have your mission instructions and supplies," he stated while handing her a canvas bag with contents within it. "You are going to replace the main nurse. She is often seated at a work desk outside the rooms the women are being kept in. Her real name is unimportant because many people in this industry operate under false names. She has dark hair, and you can identify which nurse she is by that trait. There is a wig in this bag which matches her hairstyle. She wears a specific type of dress. One just like it is in the bag. Shoes too. Size 6, I'm sure, is your size."

He is correct, Laura thought. Also in the bag was a cassette tape in a mini recorder, a vial, a syringe, and a gun. Laura examined each item carefully while pulling them out one item at a time.

"You'll be in the back of the truck with other people when it arrives at the ranch. As the rear doors to the truck open, you are to make a run inside the building. Don't worry about what is going on around you. Hopefully, for your sake, it will be a peaceful environment up until this point. Our guards we will be sending along with you will have you covered, or at least they will cover you until you are at the desk post. Locksmiths will unlock any locked doors for you. Assume you will be requiring their services.

"Get inside that building as soon as that door is opened. With any luck, you'll probably head directly to what looks like a nurses' station desk in the center of the building. Your objective is to find the nurse with dark hair and jab that syringe full of that fluid in the vial into her neck. Don't accidentally stick yourself with it, don't let her trigger any alarms if you can help it, and don't let her out of your sight until she drops to the ground and appears immobile.

"Take over for her at that desk, and don't leave your post until you are taken away by our guards. Try not to shoot anyone. We don't want gunshots or unnecessary noises drawing any attention. That tape contains a sample of the nurse's voice. Try to impersonate it. If you observe any personal traits she has, try to impersonate those as well."

"I understand so far. What will this injection do to her?"

"Don't worry about that," he advised. "It will keep the nurse from getting in the way, if you know what I mean. That's all you need to know. Your job will be to sit at that desk and look and act as much like the nurse as you can. If any alarms are sounding from that station, figure out how to turn them off immediately. Answer phone calls in her voice. Assure anyone calling that all is fine and under control. You do whatever is necessary to keep that post under control. Got it?"

Laura understood, but she had not swallowed much of her coffee, so she was experiencing a head rush from this discussion. The rush was making her feel flush, and the blood was pulsating swiftly through her veins. How she wished she had been going on the mission right at this moment. The less time she had to think about what she would be doing, the less time she would have to dwell upon her personal feelings about it.

Entering the kitchen, Armani walked in naked with only slippers on his feet. "I didn't know we had company. I would have dressed for company. This is awkward. Please excuse me," he said almost bashfully.

"Didn't you let him in?" Laura asked Armani.

"No," he replied. "How did you get in here?" Armani asked Damien.

"That is not important. And don't be shy, Armani. I've seen your sexcapade films before. There is nothing you've got to show me now that I have not already seen of yours," Damien informed Armani. "It looks like mine anyway."

"What are these sexcapade films of which he speaks, Armani?" Laura wondered curiously.

"Why all the questions with you two? I haven't the time to tell you each of the lives you've been leading," Damien responded. "Now, then, Laura has already been advised. Here are your instructions, Armani. We need a strong man such as yourself to assist with the removal of the hostages. Some may not be in a condition to walk out on their own, and you may need to carry them. I hope you have a strong back. As I already informed Laura, you two will be picked up here at your home on Tuesday at ten in the morning. Don't even think of not being ready on time. The weekday seems to be a less active day at the ranch for us to penetrate the fortress." After stating that, Damien discussed specific details.

"You'll be very quiet in the back of the delivery truck when instructed to be. The moment the back of the truck opens to let you two out with others, you'll make your move to the building entrance door with the rest of the crew. Once inside, you'll be given the go-ahead to head toward the hostage rooms mid-way through the structure. There will be a couple of people with you to unchain or untie any hostages. Help them rush their task if you can. But remember, your job, Armani, is to get those women out and into the truck as swiftly as you can. There will be at least one other person doing the same in tandem. Here is a bag for you. It contains the clothes you are to wear and a gun. As I told Laura, don't use firearms unless you must. We don't want any unnecessary firing alerting our opposition. Understand?"

Armani understood.

"A few other things I want to say to you two. I am happy we are working together. I hope our mission will be a successful one. I need not remind you of the consequences should you not follow through with the mission. You are both expendable to protect the others." Damien turned to walk out of the kitchen. He spun around momentarily to address Armani. "Nice cock, you dog!" He smiled and then headed to the main door and out.

Laura followed behind and locked the door behind him before checking all the other window and door locks. "How did he get in?" she wondered, scratching her head.

In the large master closet, Armani dressed. Laura came to the doorway and leaned her back against the door frame.

"What is this about sexploitation films of which Damien was speaking?" Laura was still curious.

"Long ago, I appeared in a few local stag films. That was Irwin's business. He was like a father figure to me. He left me the house Cheryl and Gloria are renting from me. It is obvious that Damien has seen a film I appeared in. Apparently, the man knows a few things about us. We should not ever underestimate him," Armani assumed.

Chapter 27

Come Tuesday, the truck arrived right on time to collect Laura and Armani. Damien was alone inside of it in the cab and was pleased his assistants were ready for the mission. "I was able to pick you two up at home because it is just me in the truck right now. We will be picking up the others along the way at various designated locations. I would never disclose your address to anyone," he assured them. Damien predominantly spoke of necessary details en route. Other topics were also discussed. One included that Damien was not his real name. "Most people in this business don't go by their real names," he declared. "I think I may have mentioned that to you before." He assured them this would not be their last mission together, assuming they did well and survived it.

"The UR has future plans for you two. Don't worry, they are not too overly demanding. But they have put a lot of money into this mission, and they will expect some reimbursement in the form of favors. The good news is that they will keep you protected from the bad side of the Mob and its more unsavory members. At other times, it pays very well financially—sometimes in cash and other times in fringe benefits."

Armani asked some questions, which Damien refused to answer. "I'll talk if you want. No questions are to be asked of me, though," Damien stated. Armani considered that perhaps even less talk was more favorable. He didn't want any of his twisted stories to be unraveled by Damien in front of Laura. Laura sat quietly without knowing what she could possibly ask of this stranger or an organization she had no real concept of.

As the truck rolled on, picking up people, Armani and Laura got shuffled to the back trailer with Damien and the others as more came aboard. A new driver had taken the wheel, and only one other man sat up front in the cab with him. The back of the truck was dark and totally enclosed with only a couple of small lights on the roof section to create a dim glow. It was, however, enough to allow for what was needed to be seen, and that was nothing.

It was when all the people had been picked up that Damien made mention of a helicopter that would be deployed to the ranch, but only if they needed it. As with any gunfire, they did not want to draw any attention with machinery flying overhead. It was then requested by Damien that everyone remain quiet so any guards at the ranch gate would not be alerted as to their presence in the trailer. In the dimly lit truck, they sat while the temperature became more sweltering by the moment.

Eventually, the truck doors were opened, and the crew hiding inside made a mad dash out. By the entrance door to the ranch building, one ranch guard was sprawled on the ground. It was difficult to determine if he was dead. The crew all naturally assumed he was. A locksmith was quick to pick the lock and allow access to the invaders. An opposing guard was quickly overtaken in a corridor upon their entry. Laura was pushed ahead of the group to scope out the nurse staff area. It was all clear, except for one person.

Sitting at the desk with her face buried in a book was the nurse Laura was to confront. The nurse didn't even look up from the pages until Laura was near her. Seeing Laura, the nurse began asking quick questions. "Who are you? What are you doing here?" The nurse briefly looked away from Laura and saw a guard in a uniform coming. She didn't look closely enough to see it was not one of the ranch guards but turned her eyes back to Laura. "Who is this woman?" the nurse shouted, expecting the guard to answer her. "I don't think she should be here!"

The nurse stood up from her desk and took a few steps backward to back away from Laura's impending approach. Clumsily, her chicken legs wobbled, and she tripped over her own large gun-boat feet. Laura chuckled at the awkwardness of the nurse as she lunged on top of her victim and jammed the needle into her neck. The woman attempted to fight back for what few moments she could, but it was hopeless. Laura's weight on top of her was too much for the nurse to fend off. The fluid in the needle began acting rapidly. The nemesis went limp with an occasional twitching of the body as foaming white drool spewed from her lips. Laura calmly picked herself up off the woman and shoved her under the desk before seating her own butt in the desk chair. She could still feel the warmth the nurse's ass had left on the vinyl cushion.

Laura's comrades were already in their positions. She could see people down on the floors in the hostages' rooms. She could not determine if they were the enemy guards, nurses, or administrative staff. It didn't matter to her. One rival was as bad as the next. She could not determine if they were dead or unconscious. It was of no importance to her. It was unlikely any would be left alive, and Laura had her own responsibilities to do, including making sure her post was secure, which she did. Just as she had been instructed, no alarms were sounding, no phones were ringing, and no switches had activated any silent alarms; so Laura relaxed slightly.

She looked down at the book that the nurse had been reading. It was some thriller about a lakeside murderer. She smiled and thought, *People actually read this stuff? I live it!* She found humor in the thought. Then she took the nurse's purse from off the chair. Taking out a wallet, Laura noticed that the name on the identification was Darlene. *Such a pretty name for a pretty lady. She looks just like me with dark hair. It's always the pretty ones who get it,* Laura thought as she let out a quirky laugh while looking down at Darlene. *Now I know what the fluid in the vial can do. I'll have to ask Damien to get me some more of that stuff. One never knows when that stuff could come in handy,* she silently considered while continuing her quirky laugh.

Laura placed Darlene's credentials and any valuables she could scavenge from the purse into her own pockets. She then hung the purse back on the chair's back. Reaching down to Darlene, she removed Darlene's wedding ring and pocketed that as well. Laura looked up and saw Armani coming out of a room with one of the women being rescued. It was not Caroline. The woman looked exhausted, and she was wrapped in a plain pink blanket. It was evident that the hostage was naked underneath the wrap. It reminded Laura of when she had been rescued—naked and upset. She could remember that time frame well. Laura's heart went out to the scared woman. Behind them was another man, who was escorting another woman out. She was also not Caroline. The woman seemed to have trouble walking, and her escort was attempting to hustle her along. Soon, a third woman was being led out. Again, the hostage wasn't someone Laura recognized.

Armani returned from outside and blew a kiss to Laura as he passed by the desk. She motioned, pretending to catch it in her hand, but the desk phone rang and distracted her. Laura answered, "Darlene here." She did not know if there was another way that would have been more appropriate, but the person on the other end of the receiver was none the wiser that it was not Darlene herself. It was a guard calling to say that he would not be at work that night and to pass the message on. Without saying much, she indicated she would do that.

While Laura was on the call, Armani exited a hostage room with Caroline. Her friend looked dazed and lost. Laura waved at Caroline. Armani, not wanting to speak with an active receiver in Laura's hand, did not promote any sounds. Caroline did not pay attention and had not recognized Laura in the dark wig. After Laura put the phone back into the cradle, she could hear Armani telling Caroline that it had been her friend in disguise at the desk they just passed. Caroline would have liked to stop in her tracks and thank Laura for her rescue and tried to turn around and go to her friend, but Armani prevented her from doing so and nudged her toward the exit door.

As Armani and Caroline stepped out the door, gunfire could be heard ringing outside. Laura became alarmed and jumped from her seat. All the crew and the remaining women were coming out of the rooms. Laura headed for the door, leading the rest. At the door, her hand reached for the handle, but a guard halted her from going outside. "No! It may not be safe," he declared. The guard exited instead, and the door closed behind him.

As Laura reached for the handle again, the door was pushed open from the outside. On the lawn,

AJ LEBERGÉ

three people Laura did not recognize had been shot. The mission crew was rushed past the motionless bodies and quickly assisted into the back of the truck. The doors closed, and the truck took off at top speed. The passengers were jarred by the sudden acceleration of motion. Damien announced that some unexpected visitors had to be taken down on the lawn and that their helicopter had to be dispatched. The chopper was to remain with their vehicle until the coast was clear.

Explosions could be heard in the distance. Those booming noises couldn't be identified by most of the crew. The men who had been responsible for planting bombs around the ranch building and property knew the noises were the sounds of detonating explosives. The ranch building and other areas on the property were up in flames. It had been the intent of the UR to leave the building nonfunctional and to destroy the remains of any persons killed during the acts. The mission was successfully accomplished.

Laura sat beside Caroline and held her closely while Caroline trembled with fear. The crew was hyped at their success, bellowing whooping cheers. Meanwhile, the rescued women were all weeping. Armani was positioned on a bench seat several seats away and across from Laura and Caroline. He blew Laura another kiss. It was dimly lit inside the truck and even more cramped with the extra bodies than it had been going there, but Laura could see his lips motioning the sentiment. She thought of how proud she was of him and of his heroic actions that day and every day. Never had she personally known anyone to be that brave, and he had done it all for her and Caroline—once again, or so she thought. She would be forever appreciative unless the day ever came in which she would find out he was one of the people responsible for putting them in this situation in the first place.

Most of the hostages rescued approved of being dropped off at a hospital. They would need to walk in on their own and would be dumped there with little knowledge of the rescue to be divulged. A couple were taken to predetermined drop-off points where people were expecting them. Caroline declined going to the hospital. She felt well, as the ranch staff had provided her and her future baby with quality medical care. If anything, it was her emotions that needed caring for.

Caroline, at this moment, felt as Laura once did. She just wanted to go someplace she would feel safe and where she could think. She was not in a position that she could have ever prepared herself for. It was comforting enough at this moment that Laura was with her and she was away from the ranch. How Laura longed to tell Caroline so much at this moment. Instead, Laura sat quietly with Caroline. Laura had previously been warned against saying anything to Caroline until Damien had discussed what he needed to with her. Nothing could risk being said that should not be.

When all the others had been dropped off, Damien took over the wheel, and Armani sat by his side in the front cab. Damien advised Armani of how Caroline's future could best be handled. If she would ever take anyone's advice, her decisions would yet remain to be seen. Fortunately for Caroline, Laura already knew firsthand what it was like to be on the run. She was certain she could someday speak of her firsthand experience to Caroline, and then Caroline would perhaps not feel so unique. Today, though, due to the amount of carnage left in their path during this rescue, people would not be turning their heads and looking the other way.

The destruction today was on a much grander scale than that in Antioch during the small-town rescue her friends had implemented to save her. The Mob involved in Antioch could have been a small operation compared to the syndicate they had just tangled with. Most likely, this rescue would be adversely retaliated against. The crime family attacked today was unknown to most all individuals involved in the rescue. They could be big or small. Damien assumed they were not a large conglomerate based on what he knew of their past. Then again, he might not know all there was to know.

Ideally, Caroline could be of great use to the UR and could be kept well-protected if she would agree to be a part of their institution. Presenting that idea to her would be Damien's challenge. Yet it was a common challenge he and the UR faced when recruiting. Caroline would need to be properly primed for it. He knew how to do that sort of thing. And there was the baby she would likely be considering come the day she would make her decision. That made her different from Laura. Caroline had never murdered anyone. That, too, made her different from Laura. Nobody yet knew if Caroline was cut from the same cloth as Laura and if she would be able to handle responsibilities.

"Let Caroline rest until she can think clearly. Just make certain she doesn't do anything stupid in the meantime," Damien warned. "Don't let her know the UR exists until you are sure she is vindictive enough to swear her allegiance, and I'll instruct you as to how to proceed with her. We know how to deal with women and girls like her in her condition and in this situation. However, if she screws up, we'd have to kill her to keep our secrets. That would be a shame after all we've done to rescue her, wouldn't you agree?"

Armani nodded.

"Of course, she can walk knowing nothing and do as she pleases. She could just walk away right now," Damien offered as an alternative. "But if she knows anything, anything at all, or is too smart for her own good, she won't be alive much longer. Nobody walks away from the syndicates and the UR with secrets. None of us is as forgiving as the Antioch Mob you are familiar with was with you aside from the burning down of your house."

Armani wasn't sure if it was meant to be comforting or a threat.

Damien went on to say, "I'll be keeping an eye on Caroline myself. As a matter of fact, I'll be around to keep an eye on all of you. Consider me your unseen babysitter. You are all my responsibility right now. Don't any of you do anything unusual or skip town until you hear from me again. Just sit tight after today's adventure and relax. I'm counting upon you not to screw up like you did in Antioch. I know that wasn't something you could have helped, but the Mob still debates if you are reliable and accountable or not. You still skate on thin ice. Don't worry, you are all perfectly safe and can feel free to lead relatively normal lives right now—I mean, as long as all three of you do as you are told. The UR doesn't think we are expecting too much out of you."

Armani understood the directives. Then there was a final conversation that took place between the two men. Damien took a moment to describe finances.

"The UR takes in funds from numerous sources. Sometimes, they get reward money. Sometimes, they get donations from rich philanthropists supporting their causes. Insurance companies provide payouts. Other times, funds are earned from other illegal activities. No matter how funds are obtained, the UR believes the ends justify the means. Today was a very costly rescue mission," Damien said, stating the obvious. "This all started in an effort to help you, Laura, and Caroline. The powers that be agreed to take this cause on," he continued.

"Several women and their future babies were rescued. You know that. Being that was the case, the UR felt you and Laura worked hard to put forth a lot of charitable effort. You laid your lives on the line for people, and that is commendable. They didn't want you to walk away empty-handed today. There is a briefcase of cash on your bed at home. It's not as much as you could be earning with the UR. It's just something to help carry you through."

Armani had not been expecting such a reward.

Chapter 28

Having almost reached their mountain home destination, Laura and Armani switched places. Armani
now sat in the trailer with Caroline. He did not know
what Damien and Laura were discussing up front in
the cab. He rather wished he could be a fly on the
wall. He did not mind keeping secrets from Laura,
but it did bother him that Laura was likely keeping
secrets from him. Likely, Damien was lecturing Laura
on the same topics that had been discussed with him
earlier.

Armani did all he could to comfort Caroline in
Laura's absence while trying not to scare her. He had
been provided permission by Damien to discuss some
matters with Caroline if she was up to it. She was,
and Caroline listened intently. In particular, Armani
requested that any rescue details involving him and
Laura remain confidential. He informed Caroline of
the trouble she was in for having escaped the ranch.
On the flip side, he comforted her with the knowledge that she would be protected and safe for the

time being at the mountain home he and Laura had been living in. She could rest there and think. That was all she needed to hear. Her words in exchange were few, but she made sure they sounded gracious.

It was late when Damien dropped Armani, Laura, and Caroline off at the cabin. The indirect route had taken longer due to them going out of the way on a few occasions in order to be certain they were not being followed. Despite the long, difficult day, they were all hyped with adrenaline rush, which had not yet worn off.

Getting situated inside, they showed Caroline where things were in the house so she would not feel as if the house was a terrifying and unfamiliar place. Laura drew a bath for Caroline to soak in and provided her with a robe and slippers to slip into when she was done. Caroline relaxed in the tub and prepared many questions she would be inquiring about.

Laura and Armani sat in the bed in their bedroom and had a quiet discussion. Armani was less involved with the talking and would have preferred releasing some pent-up anxiety on lovemaking. Laura held him off in lieu of conversation.

"Okay," Armani agreed as he put his forearm across his head and fell backward onto the bed in disappointment. "But you owe me after what I did today!"

"What's in this case on the bed?"

"Damien didn't tell you? We received modest compensation for our work today."

Laura opened the case. "Wow!" she exclaimed. She gazed down at the wads of cash. "It's full. The bills are all small, but the case is full. I'm assuming they use small denominations of unmarked bills," she figured. "I want to take some of this money and take Caroline shopping when she is ready if you will let me. She'll need some clothes now—that is, if she will be staying with us for a while. I assume she will be. It is okay with you if she stays, I assume?"

"Damien told me that we are to keep an eye on her until we are sure she is stable and on our side. Then he said to make sure we keep an eye on her until we hear from him unless she wants to go her own way. Then we are not to stand in her way. She is in danger, and it would be stupid to let her go into the world on her own right now. Damien advised me as to what I can say and cannot say to her right now. Did he have that talk with you?"

Armani was cautious about what he was saying to Laura. Also, he was anxious to question her regarding anything Damien might have shared with her and not with him. That would need to be discussed at a more private time, as Caroline would soon be out of the tub.

"We can have a casual conversation with Caroline when she is done in the bathroom. I'd like a quick shower myself. At least for tonight, I'll insist I sleep by her side to keep her from flaking out on us. I can observe her actions better if I am with her," Laura commented. "Damien suggested that."

Armani laughed. "Can't I sleep with you two? You know I will be sleeping all by myself tonight. Maybe I want you near me. Now I'll never be able to protest anything you tell me or ask of me because I don't know if it's you talking or you following UR instructions. Damn that Damien!"

"That's right," Laura said as she jumped on him in bed for a quick kiss before rolling off and heading into the bathroom. "I'll shower first and get back to Caroline. I don't want her to be left on her own for too long."

Armani laughed aloud. "When you just jumped on me, I had a vision of you on top of that nurse at the ranch. Seeing you in that chick-on-chick action made me hot! That reminds me of something. They had you kill that woman, didn't they?" Armani questioned, thinking back through the day.

Laura peeked her head out of the bathroom and shook her head around before disappearing out of sight. She never answered his question one way or another. "That nurse you are speaking of had a name. It was Darlene," Laura informed him. "Damien and I did some talking about identities. What do you think if I dyed my hair dark and started calling myself by her name, at least by her first name, Darlene. I thought I could just assume her whole identity since I took her identification from her purse. Then I thought about it and realized I don't know what kind of trouble she may have been in. I don't need her problems. I have enough of my own. If I ever need to present her identification instead of my own, I could. I've taken it from her. Any thoughts?" Laura waited for Armani to respond.

"Do I have a say in this, or have you and Damien worked it all out for us?" Armani spoke in jest. "I'm only joking. Just as long as the carpet will match the drapes, I'm okay with it."

"No carpet. Hardwood floors all the way, Honey!" She followed that up with a giggle knowing he would be smiling about that. She wished she could see his face in the other room.

Once they all gathered in the den and savored poured cocktails, they let conversation take a natural course. It seemed wise to start at the beginning and tell Caroline about the events that had led up to Armani taking Laura in. So as to keep her updated, they told her of the lives of those she had last seen in Antioch before her abduction. Then Caroline told Armani and Laura all about her experiences during the abduction. It had been unpleasant for her. Most of the trauma she endured was more mental. Her abductors had treated her physically well considering. There was just a lot of mental manipulation and fear that she would not ever get out of the ranch alive. She had come to love the baby she was carrying and thought of Dale often.

Armani told her of meeting Dale and her brothers. "They started coming around shortly after your abduction, and I had the chance to meet them," he told her. "They eventually stopped coming. There was nothing in Antioch for them. Your family is fine, though," he assured her. That led to a further discussion that opened the door to a conversation about her future plans.

"If you return, you will put your loved ones in danger. Don't think about that tonight. We have some thoughts on how to help you. You have options, and we know some are ones you would not think of on your own. Just take some time for yourself to breathe. We can help you when the time is right. Laura and I will support your decisions. We just need you to know that what you decide will affect us too. You are in a lot of danger. Laura is in danger. I am in a bit over my head too."

Surprisingly, Caroline was rational and figured as much.

"I think you should call your family tonight. Dale, too, if you want to," Laura suggested. "You can't discuss any details, though, and you must be very careful about what you say to everyone. You can't speak of the rescue. You can't tell them Armani is here with us. Inform them that you can't say much more because you are still in a rescue situation after having been kidnapped. Tell them you are with the friend who gave you your favorite necklace for your sixteenth birthday. Don't speak my name and ask them not to as well. Keep the conversation short.

"Assure them you love them very much and will contact them again when you feel it is safe to do so. Tell them you have a lot of thinking to do and don't want to put anyone in danger. You can't say much more because the phone could be bugged. It's not really, but let them think it could be." That should be sufficient for now, Laura felt. "They just will want to hear your voice and know you are unharmed. And when you are done calling them, we can call Cheryl."

Caroline was happy to finally be having some contact with those she loved. Her mother answered the phone. It was late, and she didn't bother to check the screen on her landline receiver as the call came in.

"Hello," Caroline's mother said, slurring her words while half asleep. "Have you any idea what hour it is here?"

"Mom, it's me. It's Caroline. Listen carefully. I can't say much." Caroline continued saying only what she could.

Her mother listened, speechless, crying. "I'm so sorry, dear. We'll wait to hear from you again soon. Can you at least talk to your father for a moment? He'll want to hear your voice."

Caroline's mother shook her father from his sleep. Her dad accepted the receiver and was in a dither over the call. In his excitement, he started asking too many questions. He was always the sort to take charge and be helpful. Caroline handled the conversation perfectly and managed to end the call as well as anybody could have. She was crying tears of joy just hearing voices she so recently feared she would never hear again.

As for Dale, she wanted to wait to call him. It was so nice that he had visited Antioch to look for her. It was nice he was concerned about her and the baby. Until she could decide what she was going to do in life with Dale and with the baby, she didn't want to be forced into an uncomfortable conversation. She knew what he wanted for their future. Under normal circumstances, that might have been what most normal women in normal life situations would want. But she was not normal, and her life wasn't normal any longer. She could deny that if she didn't already know differently. Nothing would ever be normal again.

Upon Caroline composing herself and shutting off the waterworks, they called Cheryl. Cheryl was elated to hear the good news. "Your friends in Antioch and I are here for you if you need us. Please stay in touch. We think about you always. We miss you. So much is going on here. I can't wait until I see you two again. It will be like old times," Cheryl was certain, but Caroline knew differently. After getting off the call, Cheryl prayed. It was something she had rarely ever done until Caroline and Laura were initially kidnapped. Ever since, she said a prayer every time she thought of them and figured it could not hurt. Despite not being the organized religion sort of person, she still had some faith in positive affirmation. Cheryl wanted the driving force of the universe to know that her friends were loved and in need of help.

The next day, news reports were still reporting on the ranch explosions. Investigation into the causes for this disaster was still being looked into. It was unlikely that any complete determination of the reasons for the events that had taken place would ever be discovered or disclosed to the public. Nobody involved would dare speak of it to outside sources. Any official information would either be kept secret by government agencies or misconstrued as a total fabrication of the truth. Anything true or not to please people and get paperwork processed would be the end determination.

Laura and Armani felt confident that nobody would ever label them as being the perpetrators. It was Caroline they worried about. The opposition knew they once kept her there and would not want her walking away. They would know she had information on them and the rescue. But since they had not discussed the UR with Caroline per Damien's instructions, they knew Caroline would have no choice except to join the organization. While they had been informed she would be able to make choices, only one would be the right one to guarantee life. It would have been kinder had the UR come right out and told her that themselves right away. Apparently, they wanted Caroline to realize it for herself and let her think the decision was her own reasonable choice.

Chapter 29

It was a long process getting Caroline to make the decision that she would slip into obscurity with the UR people protecting her. Her first thought was that she wanted to go to authorities with information pertaining only to her abduction and nothing of the rescue, but in a short time, she learned that the other kidnapped women and their families had to enter a witness protection program. She did not feel it was right to upset the lives of those she held dearest. Her brother, her parents, and even Dale would be uprooted into a program; and it would be all her fault. Dale was a nice guy. He was just not someone she would want tagging along.

The UR promised Caroline that she and her baby could lead a rather normal life if she cooperated with them. She would not be involved in anything dangerous in the front lines. They would give her a lucrative desk job and allow her to develop a new life under an assumed identity. Basically, it was the same offer the witness protection program would have presented to her without involving her innocent loved ones. It was the right choice for her to make. Sadly, it would likely prevent her from seeing her friends and family ever again. Her last request before leaving with the UR was that she would be able to make one last visit to see Cheryl and her own family again before she would be whisked away into oblivion. Her wish was granted as long as she understood the potential risks she would be taking by going back home even if it was only for a few hours.

Antioch was especially lovely this time of year. The foliage was still rich and colorful. The sun shone brightly. Armani drove Laura and Caroline to the home of Cheryl and Gloria. Passing by the now-empty lot where Armani's home once stood, Armani paused for a moment to see that which had been wiped out. Many sad thoughts came to mind as he thought of memories he had growing up there. "Time marches on," he said, turning to look at each of the women.

The visit was to be unexpected for Cheryl and Gloria, who had only been informed that an unexpected surprise was to be expected that day. He made sure they would be home. They were expecting a delivery or something else along that line. The delivery of Caroline and Laura to their doorstep was the greatest delivery they could have ever hoped for. They were blown away not only by the sight of Caroline and her baby bump but by Laura as well. Laura was now coiffed with dark hair and officially announced that she was to be referred to as Darlene.

The women were briefed on what they needed to know. They were asked to accept with grace and understanding the unusual situations their friends were in. To turn a better phrase, they were asked to try to understand the synopsis being described to them—mostly truth with a few false twists. Darlene she now was, they all agreed. While they might not have agreed with the decisions made by Caroline and Darlene, they also knew that much information was being kept from them for safety reasons. It was not their place to decide or judge the lives of other people. With only a short time to spend, they didn't want to waste it on disagreements and serious talk. Having things back the way they had been before this whole mess had taken place was what they all wanted to experience most of all during this short time together.

"Before we get underway with the festivities of today, there are a couple things we need to do," Armani stated. That included everyone. "First, we need to get Gertty, Janet, and Dean over here. They all agreed with that. Gertty, Janet, and Dean should share in the excitement; and they should all go over to get them as a group. That would work out well because Armani had a surprise waiting afterward, and it was outdoors.

Gertty was usually always at home, and today was the same as usual. She didn't think to ask questions and just went along with the crowd as they escorted her next door by Janet and Dean. She was up for the walk and would not complain. Janet and Dean had been informed earlier by Armani, as Cheryl and Gloria had been, that a surprise was to be expected today. Janet and Dean were anxiously awaiting to find out what it was. Steven had since temporarily moved in with them and was anxious too.

Since it had been Armani who had notified them to expect the surprise, they suspected that he was returning to town and that he wanted them to be home to greet him. To the surprise of Steven, Janet, and Dean, the whole lot of them showed up at the door at once. Even Mignon was overjoyed with Armani's return. Armani scooped Mignon up in his arms, and Mignon licked his face with joy! Meanwhile, Cleopatra just leisurely laid by the table, twitching her tail in a relaxed manner.

Dean was thinking along another line as the group exchanged hugs and greetings. His professional mind was at work. Armani knew it would be. The idea of this event being a surprise wasn't solely for the purpose of entertainment. Armani did not want Dean to have time to get the notion that this gathering was law enforcement related and to use some ability to act upon legalities Caroline and Laura—now Darlene by name—had dodged. Armani needed to see Dean face-to-face to explain first. They had enough of a past that Armani knew he could count on Dean to prioritize being a friend and confidant over acting in authority. Dean could be a reasonable man.

They all went inside for a group discussion. Damien had advised his friends well, and they stuck to the script. However things had been described, Gertty, Steven, Janet, and Dean could relate and agreed to go along with whatever was being told to them. Those being newly advised only understood it all to mean that everything happening was over their heads, was beyond local authoritative jurisdiction, and was being handled by the high-up and almighty government powers. It was secretive. For the safety of everyone, they were to always be cautious.

Gertty, Steven, Janet, and Dean were not informed of the UR or the real story behind Armani, Laura—now named Darlene—and Caroline being where they were today in their lives. As far as they knew, the UR was the government. Duped, Gertty, Steven, Janet, and Dean were now playing along. In all actuality, they probably would have gone along with anything for their friends, even had they all known the truth. That was the type of friends they were—as long as they understood why they needed to go along. It was best they not know the whole truth at this time. If information was withheld but the rest of the stories still seemed plausible—and they were—the stories would be accepted. It would not have been the first time if they had gone along with fabricated concepts for friends and kept the real truths buried. Friends were family, and they came first.

Dean informed Darlene and Caroline that the Mob had claimed responsibility for the deaths of the gate guard and ranger at the campsite. They hadn't actually committed the murders, obviously. The Mob really hadn't claimed to be the murderers either. Only the UR division staff had spoken on behalf of the entire Mob when making such a public confession. The Mob, as a whole, was still trying to figure out who had committed the murders and who within the Mob had spoken out to claim responsibility for doing the deeds.

Authorities could not have known this was the case. Few people knew the Mob had a secret group of UR members defying orders from the inside and running things their own way. It all meant that Darlene, Caroline, Cheryl, Diana, and Gertty were not being held accountable for the murders. Of course, authorities still would have appreciated questioning them about that night, but legal counsel action had prevented that. As far as their lawyers were concerned, they could not touch the women, and they couldn't. To date, Diana had not said a word. It was doubtful she ever would. She had not witnessed the murders of the guard and ranger and wouldn't have had anything to say on the subject except speculation.

Darlene, Caroline, and Armani already knew the aftermath developments. Damien had been keeping them abreast all along. He had arranged for the Mob to take the blame. Unless Darlene or Caroline filed kidnapping charges, the least that any accused Mob member could be charged with would be a civil suit claiming unlawful detainment of an individual. The state could potentially file felony kidnapping charges, but laws to do that without the victim filing a formal complaint varied from state to state. It would be difficult to get any convictions if Darlene and Laura did not cooperate. Realistically, the only men they knew to be involved had been murdered. Who would they be able to point a finger at? The state would not even know who to prosecute should they try. It would all be pointless. Speaking out against the Mob in any fashion would only put them in danger. Everyone understood why nobody was saying anything.

Raising a wineglass and urging the others to do the same, Armani made a toast from the bottle of wine he had selected and brought along for the occasion. "I have another secret, and I wanted us all to be together when I make this announcement," he said with a smile as the others raised their glasses again as well.

"Darlene is pregnant!" Dean joked. Everyone laughed. They recalled when they had last toasted together, and that same assumption had been blurted out about Janet and Dean.

"Better," Armani said, still with a laugh. "We need to take a short walk together just down the road. I have something you all need to see." The group assumed he would be taking them by his obliterated dwellings and accommodated his request shortly after downing their libations.

Surprisingly, Armani was leading them the opposite way down the street, away from where his home had been. They passed Gertty's home next door. They passed the home of Gloria and Cheryl next door to Gertty's. They walked until they reached the last house. Since the burning down of Armani's home, only the four homes remained off the gravel road.

"Why are we here at this property?" Janet asked. It was a huge home, very aged. The home had been that of a wealthy family for many years. The family was rumored by local folklore to be cursed. When the son of the family was left alone in the world, he was the only heir left to inherit it. The problem was that he was not a normal young man. He was in a special care center and could not care for the house. A trust fund kept the household barely running. It had sat vacant and had been slowly deteriorating for a long, long time. Irwin and Armani had done what they could to barely keep it maintained with a maintenance allowance provided by the trust fund until Irwin died, and then Armani had taken sole care of the property—that is, until today.

It was a menacing structure. Iron gates and the brickwork on the property had become overgrown with vines just during Armani's short absence from town. There had once been a day, many years ago, during which Gertty suspected trouble within the walls of the home. She had called the police. Upon entering the vacated home, two missing girls were discovered. They had been drained of all their blood. It was a memory Gertty did not appreciate recalling. The house still haunted her nightmares and gave her chills when she looked upon it.

Armani pulled Darlene into his arms and said, "Darlene and I now own this home. We will be moving in and fixing it up." Armani had seen fit to buy the place. The sale details had begun before he even left town. He had helped take care of the grounds as a caretaker since he had been a young boy and knew the estate well inside and out.

Damien approved of the belief that Armani and Darlene should not flee from Antioch. Running could make Armani appear guilty or scared of something, and the Mob and the people of Antioch had never really known Laura to make any correlation that this Darlene creation was actually Laura incognito. They should stand their ground in Antioch.

Damien knew Armani and Darlene would soon be of great use to the UR in the Illinois village. With Laura now being known as Darlene, only their friends and her family would know what she had been through and who she had been. They were all being sworn to keep her new identity a secret, and they gladly obliged thinking it was officially government security related. It was either that, or she would be taken away from them forever. Precautions were in place to assure she would be well-protected should she agree to stay.

Damien was even sending over a couple of government officials working undercover for the UR to make the setup appear to be official. The past was literally being buried, and the future was a fresh start for Caroline, Cheryl, Darlene, and Armani. Gertty was given a clean slate as well given her involvement with the initial rescue at the camp. This was all thanks to the help of the UR, to which Armani felt indebted.

Darlene appeared thrilled with the idea. Armani had sensed some hesitation on her behalf and had assured her it was all approved. She knew what he meant. The UR had approved the living arrangement. With UR approval and Armani beside her, she was more than fine with the place. The group offered their congratulations.

Heading back up the street, the clan reached Gloria and Cheryl's house. A large black car was parked in front of Armani's truck. Two men got out and approached. The men were earlier than expected, and Armani felt saddened. Flashing badges, they identified themselves as government agents and asked if everyone could be invited into the house to talk. They were friendly enough and handsome—not that their appearance mattered. Their covert purpose was to speak to the group on behalf of the UR while posing as the government officials they actually were.

The talk was brief. They explained the situations and dangers. They justified Darlene and Armani being there. In short, they confirmed what Armani, Darlene, and Caroline had already been telling everyone. The badges just seemed to make it more official. They asked that everyone help in maintaining the anonymity and privacy of Darlene and Armani. Additionally, they requested that if anyone suspected that anything unusual was going on with any of them, they would call them first before involving local authorities.

"The local authorities would not understand the situation as we might. They are not informed of government matters at our level," the men emphasized. "Here are our cards with our numbers on them in case you need to reach us. If you suspect any trouble, please call anytime, day or night, right away. We can advise you promptly and even get the appropriate help right over to you." Trouble really wasn't expected, and talk was just part of the act.

In conclusion, the entire conversation was a roundabout way of telling the group of friends to mind their own business in an effort to keep them from asking too many questions or becoming involved in private affairs in the future. Armani and Darlene could do as they needed, and the friends would hopefully respect that there were things they should not know about. Even Dean was supportive.

This was also the time during which Darlene and Caroline had to leave. The women would be taken to visit their families before Caroline would permanently be taken away by the men. Darlene would now be around Antioch regularly if not away on an assignment and would be able to spend time with her family as she pleased. The official men were still escorting her during this initial reunion to make sure there wasn't any sign of trouble.

While there, they would be flashing their badges and having the same talk about confidentiality and safety with the family members just as the friends had received. Their professional appearance would hopefully encourage the family to act appropriately around Darlene and speak properly with reference to her new identity. Her family, too, would come to learn to respect her privacy if they wanted to still be a part of her life, just as her friends would.

Their family visits were short. Darlene wanted to spend the majority of the remaining time with Caroline and her family since they would be disbanding. This gathering was bittersweet. Watching Caroline say goodbye to her family was heartbreaking for Darlene. Darlene had also known the family almost her whole life and could only imagine the emotional upset they were feeling. As a parting gesture, Caroline handed Darlene the scrapbooks from her past, which she had shared on the camping trip, and asked her to keep them for her. Her scouting badges and mementos of her past had no place in her new life. Touching the necklace Darlene had given her on her birthday, she informed Darlene she would always wear it and think of her.

Caroline hugged Darlene and whispered in her ear, "I'll always think of you as Laura. May Darlene find peace, joy, and serenity."

Darlene could not hold back her tears as she said goodbye to her oldest and dearest friend. "Thank you for the scrapbook, Caroline. Just one thing I want to give to you to also have as you depart," Darlene said as she flipped through pages in the book. "Remember this badge? It was for bravery. I want you to take it with you. You are one heck of a brave woman, and you deserve this badge now more than ever," Darlene claimed as she pinned the award to Caroline's lapel.

Caroline nodded and smiled through her tears. She hugged each of her family before the men with their car took her away for good. Darlene took some comfort in knowing that her mutual involvement in the UR with Caroline could someday bring them face-to-face again in life.

Outside, Armani stood leaning against his truck while waiting to take Darlene home. She called him inside for just a moment to introduce him to Caroline's family. He was concerned she would want him to meet them, and he felt terrible doing so. The abduction of Caroline was something he could have prevented, and it was his fault they were losing her and her future baby. At least they did not know that much.

Armani had already met Caroline's brothers the day they came to his neighborhood, but meeting her parents was tough. They were still crying over the loss of Caroline from their lives. It was an awkward situation to be in. It was also one of the rare times in which Armani began to cry too. He did not like to cry and rarely showed emotion.

Darlene was in awe of his sensitivity. She would likely never know the whole reason he was saddened by this meeting. As for the father of the baby Caroline was carrying, Dale was not there. She wasn't speaking of him to her family or friends.

Chapter 30

Back at the old neighborhood, Armani and Darlene stopped back in to visit Cheryl and Gloria. They talked way into the wee hours after midnight. There was talk of the party Janet and Dean were throwing as a celebration of life for Julie in a few days. It had been a postponed event due to all the chaos. A lot of miscellaneous talk and gossip was also said during the night. The last conversation topic was how happy Cheryl and Gloria were with their new business.

Initially, most of their inherited accounts were local security service assignments. They had to hire several new security staff and patrol guards to fill the positions. More recently, since the discovery of the mass grave, they were receiving more work looking into mysteries and past missing persons reports. Armani and Darlene tried to act as though this was all impressive to them, but they shared a playful exchange of facial expressions, during which Armani and Darlene looked at each other and tried not to laugh aloud. The security business was nothing like the rescue job Armani and Darlene had pulled off and of which they could not speak. In comparison, life with the security company seemed lame.

Cheryl and Gloria were unaware of the private joke. They attributed the occasional glances and smiles to be those of two people in love. "Look at you two," Cheryl finally commented. "Get a room! We insist you stay the night until you can scope out that horror castle you are now referring to as your house. Take the last bedroom on the left." With that said, they all retired for the night.

* * *

The next day, Armani took Darlene to pick up her car at her parents' home, where they had been storing it for her. He thought it would be wise if she did not drive her old car from now on in case someone recognized it. They took the sporty car into a local car dealership, where they traded it in and plunked down cash for the remaining cost of a classy, luxury German automobile.

Next, they went shopping. They bought some new clothes for each of them. Darlene liked picking out clothes for him. He picked out some stylish and fancy clothes for her. They were very different from the school clothes she had always picked out for herself. They enjoyed a pizza for lunch. He preferred the same toppings she did, and that appealed to her. It was just one more thing they shared in common.

After lunch, they went to buy some furniture. Some of the furniture had to be ordered, and delivery would be delayed. Some could be delivered the next day. They settled on taking with them a queen-size mattress and box spring set to be slept on until their furniture arrived. The bedding taken today would remain in the guest bedroom in the future. Armani loaded it onto his work truck, which they had been driving. Darlene ran into a service station mart and picked up some beverages and treats to satisfy any munchies they might be getting later during the night. Until the refrigerator and kitchen appliances could be delivered, there was no reason to stock up on too much food yet.

It would have been nice had the home been ready to be moved in. Being that it wasn't, they would make do. Darlene could easily rough it. She even had a thought that they could borrow the gear from her brothers that had been used on the camping trip if need be to get by, but it was just a thought. For tonight, they would get along just fine without it. They could count on the neighbors to provide them with refrigerator space and anything they might have forgotten.

So much had happened since Darlene got to town that Armani had never even showed her the inside of the house. She did not know what to expect of it. When at the stores, Armani told her what types of items to pick out for now, which she did. If her selections were too not in style with the house motif, he steered her away from them. For now, they had only ordered the beds, a couple of chairs, and a coffee table.

They had picked up blankets and sheets. Tomorrow, at least the appliance company could deliver their new refrigerator. Armani told her she could decorate the rest of the place a bit at a time as soon as she had time to decide upon what she could use and would like. It would be all up to her. She loved him for that.

But tonight, she was exhausted. It had taken every ounce of energy she had left to get the purchases from the day inside the house and make the bed. All she wanted was to get some of the snacks. Looking around the house could wait until she was well-rested. Her excitement over the house was certainly there. She just did not have the energy. Armani could completely relate to the feeling.

The couple ate their dinner and relaxed on their new bed. Armani had an ounce of strength left and wanted to woo her. She did not want to disappoint him after all he had done for them and their home today. He wanted to "christen the pad," as he put it. She begrudgingly participated. He did not even notice that she was not giving it her all. As long as he was getting off, he didn't care if it was in an old dish-rag. She did, however, enjoy reaping the benefits of the pleasure. She just couldn't get together the energy to do much of the work. In the end, the act was complete, and Darlene wanted to take a bath. The long, hard day of physical exertion left her feeling less than clean and worn.

"Best call your friends next door. I haven't had time to start the water heater or clean the tub," he informed her. I could use a shower too," he said as he lifted up his arm and exposed the sweaty, musky fur under it. He made a stinky nose face. Then shoving her face into his armpit, he laughed. Darlene enjoyed the smell of a man's armpit and didn't resist his advances. "You're one sick lady," Armani said to her. "I love you for it!"

"For you, I'll lick anything on you at any time," she said. She knew certain things might gross him out. Normally, she loved his armpits. Tonight, the conversation reminded her of her friends and how they would try to outgross one another on a topic until it was changed. Now that seemed to be what she was trying to do. She really was tired and just not in the mood. She needed restful activity, not that of the playful sort.

Cheryl and Gloria were not at home for the evening. They reached Gloria on her cell phone, and she instructed them to use Armani's landlord key to get in if he still had the copy. He did have it. As they approached the home, a figure in black departed out the other side of the house just as they got to the door.

Darlene wanted to take her relaxing bath, and Armani opted for a quick shower in another bathroom. He finished long before her and looked around for anything to occupy his time. In what would have normally been a guest bedroom in the house, the women had an office setup. Not being able to resist snooping, he searched the desk and file cabinet drawers. Some were locked, but they were easily picked. Armani had been learning a trick or two from UR locksmiths.

In a bottom drawer of the cabinet, he found a file labeled UR on it. Looking through the folder, he found a lot of very interesting data. It made sense that the UR had gotten to Cheryl and Gloria after that night at the woods. There wasn't much unknown data of concern to Armani at this time. He never knew if or when any of it would come in handy, though. He copied each page on their copier and took the copies home with him under his shirt. After her bath, Darlene checked out the refrigerator and took cold cans of soda with her.

Back at their own home, Armani showed Darlene the papers.

"Those sneaky bitches!" she proclaimed. "What do you think they are up to?"

"I don't think we will ever know," he answered. "But they sure had us fooled, didn't they, sitting there all ignorant like, talking about their security guards the other night? I'll bet they knew all along who those UR men were who came to see them when we got to town, and they never said a word. They played it so straight. I'll bet even Janet and Dean are involved in the UR as well. Dean didn't hesitate one bit not to haul you or Caroline in for any questioning." Armani pondered this turn of events. "It may not mean anything to us tonight, but l would bet we are in for an interesting future here together in Antioch."

"Suddenly, I am not so tired," Darlene said to Armani. "What do you say we make a quick stop to see Janet and Dean? We can tell them how sorry we are that I had to leave yesterday with the men and thank them for having us all over. I'll tell them about our day out shopping. I want to have some fun at their expense," she said with a wicked grin. Armani liked the way she was thinking.

* * *

Mignon barked as the bell rang. Janet was a bit more apprehensive about opening the door these days since Baskin had forced his way in. "Who is it?" she yelled out before getting near the door.

"It's Armani and Darlene," Armani announced. Janet opened the door. "Say, I could put some security cameras around this house for you. You seem to be in need of them." Janet seemed flustered.

"Is anything wrong, Janet?" Darlene asked.

"I just had an experience again. Come on in," Janet said invitingly. "Let's sit in the four-season room. I was just sitting in there before you arrived, and I had another vision of Julie. If you don't know, I have been seeing a ghostly figure of her out by the water—a glowing apparition of green usually but more purple these days. I used to see her pointing at the water. It's something I haven't seen since her remains were pulled from the lake. Dean and Gloria had me go to the doctor to get my meds adjusted. Know that I am not the only one who has seen it.

Anyway, I just saw it again. This time, it was all purple, and it was looking back at me through the window there. I was just going to check it out when the bell rang," she finished saying.

"Where is everyone else?" Darlene asked.

"Steven is above the garage, and Dean is at work."

Armani and Darlene went to the door and opened it to go out to the lake and check the area. It was dark outside, and Janet flipped a light switch for them to see better. "I don't think you'll find anything out there. Nobody ever does," she yelled after them. They searched the area while Janet stayed inside and sat in her favorite chair with Mignon on her lap.

Armani went around the house to see if anything or anyone had been there or had gone away. Darlene stayed in the area and paced the waterfront back and forth. Looking into the water, she saw a purple glow, and a naked man floated to the surface with his eyes open. It seemed to her that he was perhaps swimming by. He was doing the back float with no intentional arm or back muscle movements. He was just doing a relaxing float by with the small currents within the water moving his appendages. Then he went under the pier and never resurfaced as the purple glow diminished. Darlene stood there waiting and watching for him until Armani came onto the pier to get her.

"Everything okay?" he asked her, noticing she seemed distracted.

"I saw someone. It was a naked man. He floated to the surface in a glowing purple light and then went under the pier and disappeared."

"Perhaps it was just the evening light and your reflection in the water," Armani suggested, looking down at the lake surface.

"Do I look like a naked man to you? There was a rather intense light, not a reflection of the sky."

"No, I suppose not. You know something? I'm glad you don't look like a naked man. You look beautiful just the way you are. In this lighting tonight, you look perfect to me." His words stopped as he took her into his arms and kissed her passionately. "Grrr," he growled with a purring roll of his tongue.

Back at the house, Janet continued waiting in her chair while petting Mignon. The dog was a mooch for attention, and he got every bit of it he desired. Armani and Darlene entered the home, and Mignon barely made an effort to lift his head from his comfortable massage.

"Nothing?" Janet asked—not that she expected they had found anything.

"Darlene thinks she saw a merman. That's about it."

Darlene slapped him on the shoulder and explained. "It was not a merman. It was a naked man swimming with some sort of light under the water. It was giving off a purple glow. He was on his back, staring up at me with his eyes locked open, and then he went under the pier. He never resurfaced," she described.

"What did he look like?" Janet inquired.

"He had dark hair. He was shorter than Armani and on the firm, stocky side. I'm not sure. He was under the water surface most of the brief time. He had an uncut dick and large nuts. I saw that much," Darlene hated to admit that was what her observation had been focused upon.

"So this is one of your sexual fantasies you are playing out?" Armani said, making a joke out of Darlene's experience. Darlene slapped his shoulder again.

"Was he on the right side of the boat?" Janet inquired.

"Yes."

Dean entered the room after having quietly entered the other end of the house. "I could hear you all talking when I came in. That man sounds like a description of the guard Baskin murdered here after Darlene was kidnapped," he informed them. "Don't tell me you all believe in ghosts now. Do you?"

"I've lived here my whole life, and I've never seen anything," Armani proclaimed. "If you want spook stories, go see Gertty. She knows them all. She thinks our new home is haunted. The previous owners didn't die in the best ways. Then those two dead girls were found in the house. It's always been known by local kids as being haunted.

"That is just great!" Darlene exclaimed. "About what I just saw? I know what I saw in the water. Nobody is going to convince me otherwise!"

"Thank you, Darlene. See, Dean, I'm not nuts, and my meds are not out of whack. Thank you very much for standing your ground," Janet insisted, happy that someone else could now back her reports.

"I don't know about any ghosts, but I will protect you, Darlene," Armani assured her as he grabbed her and began passionately kissing her.

"Get a room!" Dean said in response to their horny behavior.

"Funny that your neighbors told us to do the same thing. I may not know anything about ghosts, but I know quite a bit about the UR," Armani stated aloud to the shock of Darlene. "Fess up, buddy boy! What do you two know?"

Janet and Dean stared at him. "UR? I don't follow," Janet replied with a dumbfounded look.

"Seriously, Janet? You and I have been through a lot. You'd not be lying to me now, would you?" Armani looked serious.

Janet shook her head and raised her hands up as if saying, "What gives?"

"Uh, Armani, let's you and I speak privately in the other room. I've had some business on my mind, and I need to run something by you," Dean requested in an insisting tone.

Armani followed Dean to a room at the other end of the house and began questioning him. Armani asked questions in return. Dean admitted to knowing about the UR as part of his job. He had some dealings with them over time, and they had helped in cases involving the Mob. Janet would not know that.

She didn't even know what the UR was. Dean would rather she never learned. Armani did not disclose his affiliation. He asked if Dean knew the government men who had come by the other day. Dean admitted to knowing them as government men. Dean had not reacted when they came to indicate that he had or had not ever met them before.

"So? There are many aspects of my job I keep private," Dean mentioned.

"And what about Cheryl and Gloria? What's their involvement with the UR?" Armani wanted to know.

"I didn't know they were involved with them," Dean honestly professed.

"Well, they are. Don't ask me how I know. Darlene and I just came from there, and I discovered as much," Armani informed Dean, swearing him to secrecy.

"And what of you and Darlene? What's your affiliation with the UR?" Dean asked knowing he shouldn't be.

"All I want to say is that the reason our friends were rescued from the Mob is that I turned to them for help. They freed our friends, and now I am indebted to them. So far, I have not heard from them. I'm sure they will call upon me one day. That's our secret." Armani made Dean promise to keep his secrets too.

"I'm glad you are telling me all this. At least I know where people are coming from when they speak to me. I'll not say a word to anyone. I can only say it is a dangerous organization dealing with the

Mob. If you know the right people with the UR, they do mean well. They often function outside the law, though. They do what the police and even the government sometimes can't because of the laws and procedures they are bound to. Their members are fearless," Dean informed him. "Don't ever mention the UR to Janet. She knows nothing of this. Don't involve her please."

"She may already be involved if you are part owners of the security company and the security company is involved with the UR. Think about that," Armani warned. "Could Janet be so clever that even you don't know she's already involved?" Dean only raised an eyebrow but said nothing. "It is time Darlene and I go," Armani mentioned as he reentered the room where the women sat talking about Janet's apparition sightings. "Thanks for an interesting evening, Janet. And don't you worry, I'm sure there is a logical explanation for what you have been seeing. If we can be of any help getting to the bottom of the sightings, we'll be here for you." Janet thanked him.

Walking in the moonlight, Darlene couldn't wait to ask, "Are they or aren't they, and why did you risk exposing us by speaking first?"

"If you ever need someone to turn to, run to Dean. I hold a few things over his head and know he can be trusted. He knows of the UR and secretly works with them at work. He declared he knows the government agents who had come by when we got to town but not necessarily as being UR people, at least that is all he would tell me. He also insisted he did not know about Cheryl and Gloria being in any way involved with the UR. He insists that Janet knows nothing at all about the UR or anything. Being that she is a partner in their security company, I questioned that. Dean only raised an eyebrow at me when I told him what I thought," Armani informed her.

"You think they know more than they lead on?"

"I don't know. I just know that the UR is playing games. If we are all working for the same organization, don't you think we will someday find out? I don't like being toyed with. If anyone does the toying, I'd like to be in control of that. Right now, I feel like a pawn," Armani admitted.

"There isn't much we can do, is there?"

"Not that I can think of. As of this moment, we are being left alone. I don't imagine we should react to anything unless we have need to. We just need to realize that the UR will forever control us unless we make a run for it," Armani concluded. "And I'm too tired to run."

Darlene agreed.

Chapter 31

Weeks passed peacefully. Armani and Darlene believed they were leading normal lives, but were they? Armani was repairing the home section by section. Darlene cleaned and decorated. He tended to the traditionally manly chores. She tended to the traditionally typical feminine chores. Sometimes, they shared responsibilities. Darlene's most enjoyable tasks involved tending to her man. She loved spoiling him. Marriage was on her mind although she hadn't been pushing the *m* word topic. When she could casually get away with it, however, she would drop hints.

He picked up on her subtlety. Hidden away, he kept an engagement ring. It was there for the right moment when he would be ready to ask her to marry him. He wanted to surprise her when she least expected it, along with a box of her favorite candy from the candy store downtown.

One cold, dreary day, in the early morning hours, Damien showed up in their garage when Armani was sawing lumber. "I hope you two are up to your new assignment. I should discuss it with the two of you together," he requested. "It will save time."

Armani led him into the house, and they confronted Darlene. She didn't like the fact that they could be called upon at any time and their home intruded upon. She could now understand why Armani had addressed such matters of UR undesirability with her in the past. "Look who showed up," Armani announced. "He has a new assignment for us."

Damien explained that it would be similar to what they had done last time at the ranch. There were a few children being held hostage in a child sex trafficking ring. As in the last rescue mission, Darlene and Armani would be assisting in getting them out of the building they were being held in. "Here are your bags of supplies," Damien said, handing bags to each of them. He then explained the details. The job was to take place up north, in Sister Bay, Wisconsin.

* * *

On the designated date and time, Damien pulled up in a van. He explained he would transport them to a motel, where they would gather with a group of individual comrades. They would be provided a motel room to stay in and be performing the rescue the next morning. Unlike last time, there was no time to waste before the event would be taking place.

Come the morning of the rescue, everything went as scheduled. A group was placed in the back

347

of a delivery truck and taken to the hostage location. This time, there was a second delivery-style vehicle accompanying them. A woman in the truck with them mentioned that there would be several children being rescued and that the other van would be needed to transport everyone to safety. It sounded like any routine UR mission, just as Damien had mentioned.

As the mission progressed, the crew was delivered to a specific location. Darlene made it to her post and handled her responsibilities accordingly. This time, she encountered and killed a couple of her opponents along the corridors, which did not faze her. If truth be told, she was hyped by the thrill of it all and hated the people she believed were scum. It also turned her on to the point of orgasm when she killed—very sick and twisted.

Armani escorted the children out. Sometimes, he carried them two at a time with one in each arm. When he passed by the post Darlene was occupying, he managed to blow a kiss at his beloved. As happened during their last mission, gunfire started sounding outside the door just as Armani had stepped outside. Darlene attempted to depart her post to see what the commotion was about. She was worried that her man was in trouble. A couple of her companion guards stopped her in her tracks. One of them ordered that she sit back down at the desk and perform her responsibilities. Another pointed a gun at her and threatened her for thinking of going outside.

Darlene did as she was told and sat quietly at her post until other guards came along and escorted her and the remaining team members to their trucks. She was worried, as Armani was nowhere to be seen. As she exited the door, there was a lot of blood on the concrete slab outside. It looked dreadful. Much of it had run off the cement slab and into the grass alongside it, making it difficult to tell how much there actually was. She looked all around her and did not see Armani. The other truck had already departed, and she was lifted into the one remaining vehicle. Damien was not inside it with her either. All she was left with in the back of the truck was a bevy of strange faces. She couldn't recall any of them.

Nobody was talking, and Darlene sat quietly too, along with her teammates. She knew they were not to talk until they were informed the coast was clear. When she was granted permission to speak, she finally got to ask about the guard shot outside the door. She was informed that multiple people had been struck down outside. When she asked where they might have been taken for medical help, one person responded, "Only those still alive are taken for medical care to a secret location. It's too late for the dead."

It was UR policy that nobody would be left behind. No evidence should be left at the scene of the crime. Removal of bodies was not one of Darlene's assignments, and she did not know the policies pertaining to that. Their conversation did not pacify her. When asked if anyone had seen the man shot outside the door, who had possibly been loaded into the other truck, one guy responded, "Our team had loaded him up. He wasn't moving or responding."

Back at the motel, Darlene sat silently in her room. Filled with worry, she wondered if all this was all worth it. Damien entered her room and had a glum look upon his mug. Her heart sank, and her jaw dropped open. Tears filled her eyes. "He's alive," Damien said. "He's just barely hanging on. We have the best medical experts with him, and I've known them to work greater miracles," he assured her. "The bullet itself wasn't too bad. He hit his head on the cement step outside the door when he dropped. You should have seen him. It was as if he saw the bullet traveling through the air and put himself in harm's way to protect the children he was holding. Have faith!"

It was not commonplace for Damien to express feelings for his help. This time, it was different. He, too, wanted to weep for Armani and Darlene. Darlene had been through so much and was one of the few working these missions with a loved one to worry about. It took a special person to share potentially deadly experiences with the one they loved. Darlene and Armani were a rare breed. Damien wished he could have someone to love. He didn't dare.

Sitting on the bed next to Darlene, he wrapped his arm around her and drew her into him tightly. She sat silently and motionless. "When you are ready, I can take you home. First, rest if you need to," he told her, but she was ready to go.

Chapter 32

Darlene awaited the return of Armani through lonely weeks of sunrises and sunsets. Her days seemed empty, and life pointless. The UR had asked her to perform a couple of simple tasks for them now and again. She did what they asked with little thought. She did not even know why she was doing the labor. Each grind seemed unimportant and trivial to her. She knew they somehow were not. The UR needed them done because they played some role in their needs, and she did them with no questions asked.

To pass her time at home, she eventually began wallpapering the kitchen. The pattern she picked was rather simple. She hoped Armani would live to some-day see it. She hoped he would appreciate her selection. At the very least, it gave her something to do with her time. Normally, she would have been capable of doing so much more in a day, but depression hampered her functionality quite a lot.

After many days of scraping off the old paper and applying the new to the walls, she stepped down the work ladder after having applied her last sheet. Armani was discretely standing in the opposite corner of the kitchen with a smile upon his face. She didn't say a word when she turned and finally saw him standing there. Moving swiftly, she joined him and began kissing him obsessively. His right shoulder had been injured, and his arm seemed lame, but nothing mattered to her at this moment except that he had finally come home to her.

Their lips continued pressing together until Armani pulled back for air. Neither had still spoken a word. He took her hand and led her to a chair, where he sat her down. Reaching into his pocket, he pulled out the engagement ring. He never asked her to marry him. She never said she would. Their unspoken words were sufficient to imply what they wanted to say. Armani slipped the golden ring onto her finger as they kissed passionately again and again before finally speaking.

There was a lot each had to say. Armani spoke of his ordeal and the pain he experienced. They had taken the best care of him, he informed her. Darlene filled him in on the lives of their friends. She showed him the remodeling work she had accomplished in his absence. And then when he was up to it, she gave him the best physical loving she could. All he had to do was relax, and she took care of everything. Her mouth traveled over his body from head to toe until she satisfied him with a happy ending. It went without saying that he was happy to be home again.

Darlene allowed him to rest in quiet comfort for a couple of days until he was up for any socializing. Janet and Dean had been planning a homecoming party in his honor. They had still held off on the celebration in honor of Julie. When Armani was up to it, the party took place. Everyone was happy to see him and glad he was feeling better. Darlene never divulged to anyone what the real cause of the injury had been. She lied. She said he had fallen off a ladder at home and injured his head and shoulder. The injury was reportedly severe enough that they transferred him out of town and had admitted him into a special clinic where he could not receive visitors. His head injury had prevented phone conversations, she told them.

Gertty had made friends with Darlene in Armani's absence. Often, Gertty had provided her with the most elaborate baked goods, and they talked for extended periods of time. Gertty was very pleased with Armani's choice of women. The older woman had known him his entire life, and she never thought he would find just one woman to keep him satisfied. It was with Gertty expressing her thoughts that Darlene slipped on her ring of diamonds in front of everyone and made the engagement announcement public.

Gloria and Cheryl also made a wedding announcement. "We decided to make it official too," Gloria said with pride. "We are planning a pretty big wedding celebration. Both our families want to be in attendance. Business associates and friends will attend as well," she said happily. They were not boasting. It just surprised them that so many people from their social circle cared and were in support of their female matrimony. The party would be large enough that they were hoping to rent a private banquet hall at a local alehouse.

While engagement rings were being shown off, Cheryl inquired about a lovely necklace Gertty was sporting. She seemed to always wear the same piece around her neck. It was a tarnished silver-toned chain with a smaller-sized, intricately cut antique key on it. "It is the key to my heart, I always tell people," Gertty described. "Someday, when I am dead and buried, I have no doubt one of you here will be able to say that they possess the key to my heart and all it accesses. I'm still thinking of which one of you will be deserving." Jokes were made in lieu of her comment, and the people laughed.

Janet had been keeping busy with her artwork since Armani had last seen her. She was looking forward to producing prints of her works and selling them online. As for the security company, she distanced herself from day-to-day operations now that she had set up the computer systems and business strategies. That was all she had ever intended to contribute to the firm. Her work was done there. Rarely, she would attend a board meeting, but she really didn't care. She put all her trust in the others to handle the business adequately.

Dean shared that he had been busy at work, as usual. The mass grave discovery had opened a can of worms within the community. Tourists were flocking in, even after tourist season usually concluded, just to see where it had been discovered, and with more tourists came more trouble. His job normally kept him busy, and these extra work issues made for extra work hours. He would have the winter to rest, however, when many residents left the area and fewer tourists rarely showed up around town. Perhaps, he thought, this might be the start of Antioch becoming a more year-round destination, or maybe it was just a temporary fad.

Steven had news. He had found an apartment suitable for rent and was ready to move in within the next couple of days. He had been occupying the coach house above Janet and Dean's garage and felt it was time to give them their personal space and privacy back. Janet was almost sad to see him leave the property. She knew he would be remaining close by, though. That kept her from weeping. "Dean and I may need to consider creating another person to fill the void around this house," Janet hinted. "Dean might be ready to try as soon as you all go home." Dean simply blushed.

One conversation intrigued all the guests, and they all had something to say on the matter. Janet causally mentioned to Darlene that she had been seeing the apparitions outside on dark nights. Gertty was absorbing the conversation and told her stories of the strange and unusual events that had been reported to afflict the lake area over time. The stories were not new to anyone. Everyone listened to Gertty speak.

They knew this topic was always bound to be the entertainment at local parties from time to time. The tales Gertty entwined always brought about such differences in opinions. Some people did not believe in the stories. Some found humor or disgust in their sick and warped nature. Other people believed in them wholeheartedly.

"I do believe you, Gertty," Janet spoke.

"I do too," Gloria said. "I've seen the glowing spirit of Julie one night from Janet and Dean's window and another time from my pier when I looked over here on one dark night."

"I have seen things too," Darlene confessed. "As some of you know, I saw a man in the water by the pier here one night. I never debated anyone who did not believe me because I really wasn't sure what I had seen. It was just freaky."

"Would you recognize him again if you saw him?" Dean inquired of his guest.

"I'm sure I would. The image has stuck with me. It haunts me. I mean, I am sure a lot of other guys could look just like him, and I'd be hard-pressed to assure anyone it was definitely the same man. If I saw him naked again, I'd have an easier time identifying him. I never forget a cock," Darlene wisecracked.

"It just so happens that I have a picture of the patrolman on me now. Here it is." Dean pulled it from his wallet.

Darlene would bet that was the same man. Dean informed Darlene that a couple of nights after Darlene reported seeing the figure in the water, the dead man's body went missing from the cemetery. "It's been the first reported grave robbing I have heard about during my reign here," Dean mentioned. "That is why I have his picture with me now."

"Hey, Darlene mentioned that she has seen things, as in a plural sense of the word. I'm curious what else she has seen," Janet said, scrutinizing Darlene's choice of wording.

"It's all too weird to talk about. You will all laugh at me," Darlene worried. "I know Armani would for certain."

"No, he won't. We will not let him," Gertty said. "You can tell us. I'll make sure Armani sits here respectfully."

"If you promise, well, okay." Darlene sat on the sofa as Gertty handed her a fresh glass of Chardonnay. "While Armani was away, I saw and heard things in our home. I attributed it all to stress, being in a new home, alone and all, including worrying about Armani too. Perhaps even what I had seen in the water and the tales I had been hearing around here were causing me to have an active imagination. There's been a lot of stuff I've seen. I just didn't want to admit to it."

"Go on," Gertty encouraged her. "What?"

"A couple of times, I have seen a figure cloaked in black. Nobody should have been in the house. I often heard of shadow people in horror movies. I would joke to myself that it was the shadow people playing with me. On one stormy night, I thought I saw a man hanging from a rope inside the foyer.

Lightning flickered a couple of times, and a couple of glimpses of him dangling in the air flashed before my eyes. He was there, and then he wasn't between the bursts of light. I blinked a few times and wiped my eyes in disbelief. I haven't seen him there again."

"Are those the only incidents, Dear?" Gertty inquired with interest.

"Since you are asking me, I'll tell you. There was another night, it was late, and I could not sleep. I got up and went to the kitchen for milk. As I walked past the room on the main level with all the built-in shelves in it, out of the corner of my eye, the room appeared to be furnished as a quite lovely library. I just knew all along that those shelves were bookshelves and that it just had to be a library at one time. It had heavy, ornate curtains on the windows. Books stocked all the shelves. Elaborate furniture and decorations adorned the space as I saw it. Mind you, it was late at night, and I was overly tired. I didn't even think at the moment I was walking by that we had not furnished that room yet. I probably would have just kept walking right on by, except..." Darlene stopped speaking.

"Except what?" Janet asked as she went and sat down next to her on the sofa.

"Except I was sure I saw a woman in a chair with her head looking as if it had been removed. Perhaps it looked to be blown off. It stopped me in my tracks just as I stepped past by the doorway. I came to a standstill and contemplated what I thought I had seen in that room. I was scared upon the realization.

When I calmed myself down, I reluctantly backed up and turned my head to look into the room. It was just an empty space, as it should have been. That's not all," Darlene stated as she looked around to see the expressions on all the faces. She wasn't certain she should say more if anyone was thinking of mocking her.

"Please don't stop," Gloria requested. "I'm appreciating hearing about this."

"I was hearing voices in the house one night. They sounded like two people bickering. The voices sounded like a marital spat. They were just barely audible enough to hear vaguely. When I'd open my bedroom door to check, they'd stop. Lastly, I saw two young women on the floor. Gertty had told me two girls had been found dead, drained of their blood. I thought it was some sort of hypnotic suggestion toying with my brain.

"That's what they looked like, only one of the girls looked as if she had been severely bitten on parts of her body. Her arm had been severed midway up, and her hand was completely gone," Darlene said, concluding the events. "I haven't seen or heard anything in the few days since Armani has returned. These events don't happen all the time. Armani had been gone for a while, and these were isolated incidents," she wanted her friends to know.

Armani was looking concerned because he knew that the scenes Darlene discussed were at one time accurate down to the last detail. He didn't know what to say. These stories were not available to read about in such detail online. They had happened so long ago, before computers were popular. The small-town newspaper had always been hesitant about printing any really gory details in those days. How could she have known all this down to the last detail?

Gertty looked alarmed as well. "That house has always given me chills when I have gone by it. If not for you living there, I would not think of going near it. I should tell you, Hon, you've mentioned things you should not know about. Yes, I had told you about the two murdered females having been found there, and they had been drained of their blood. What I know I have not told you is how I led the police there to the house to find the girls."

"It seems you will be telling us now," Darlene commented with a trembling in her voice.

"Old man Irwin had been taking care of that place after it became vacant following the murder and suicide of the owners and their son having been taken away." Gertty went on to say more. "Irwin had not been seen or heard from in a coon's age. I thought I'd check out the old house to see if he had injured himself there while taking care of the place. He could have been dead, and we'd not have known. The front door was open when I first arrived there. What I saw was a pack of coyotes coming out of the house. One had a human hand in its teeth. The other animals in his pack came out after him. They were snarling at me. I got scared and took off for home.

"It was my lucky day that I made it home safely and called for help. I was with the police when they found those girls. They were in a huddled position on the floor. They looked weird having been drained of their blood. I never heard how long they may have been dead. Be assured that it smelled. The girls had been there for some time. The coyote had chewed one of the hands off a girl clean off." Gertty told more of the story. She never liked getting into gory detail, but this time, she shared every last fact.

Most of the guests believed that what Darlene had seen was due to haunting phenomenon. One guest believed she was making up the stories to spook everyone. A couple of people believed she had seen something, but they were unclear as to what. Those people were Armani and Dean, who believed there must be another, more realistic explanation. "We've lived in Antioch our whole lives, and we have never seen anything as supernatural as you claim," Armani stated with Dean in agreement of his claim.

Armani still found it perplexing that Darlene knew the man of that house had hung himself in the foyer after shooting his wife in the head. That story, along with the other details of the death in the house of which she had spoken, was completely accurate. Armani did not know how she could have known—unless Gertty or someone had filled her in. He went with that conclusion and just pretended to go along with her belief in the stories while not believing she had really witnessed these scenes.

Steven hadn't lived in Antioch his whole life, but he had spent a great deal of time there while growing up. He reminisced about an evening long ago when he had brought friends along for a weekend at the family vacation home. While playing with the other boys, they dared him to go knock on the door to the empty big old home Darlene and Armani now owned. When he got to the door, it was slightly ajar. He pushed the door open all the way and saw a dark figure standing in the foyer. There was no description he could provide, except that he thought it was a shadow person, just as Darlene had described. That had been enough to scare him from ever going back there.

That experience didn't help him gain a macho image with his friends. It seemed, he recalled, to be the start of them calling him a sissy. It was a stigma he could never shake. Worse, the names he was called were more vulgar as he aged. It didn't help that he had actually been trying to hide his homosexuality. That event in his life was enough reason for him to never have any affinity to that particular home. He blamed that house for his diminishing popularity with other kids.

"Maybe the next adventure will be to have the new detective agency in town look into all these reports," Armani said. "That is, if you're all not too busy to take on another job."

"Or too scared," Cheryl said while making an excellent rendition of an eerie whistling tune through her lips.

Chapter 33

Come the following day, all the couples were still talking about the party at Janet and Dean's home. It had been the best gathering any of them had attended in a long time. That included the day their friends had returned to town. Some attendees had too nice of a time and were suffering unpleasant hangovers come the dawn, which was seen as a pink-orange line of light along the horizon.

Gertty, being a loner living in her dwelling, sat quietly in her home alone until she felt it was time to do some work. Removing the old key pendant from around her neck, she walked over to an antique grandfather clock in her foyer and used the key to open the front wooden cover. Reaching in the open door and contorting her fingers behind the brass pendulums, she removed a computer memory stick. It was something Irwin had asked her to retrieve from Janet's home before his untimely demise.

Using the memory stick, Gertty navigated the files on her computer and printed off just a few pages of data from just one of the files. Much of it was in code. Other bits and pieces were spelled out more clearly. Unfortunately, that which was spelled out would be very incriminating to people she loved and cared for if their opposition should ever obtain it. She knew she could never hand the evidence over to authorities without hurting so many people. It would hurt a great many people if the Mob obtained it as well. In the hands of a stranger, one could only assume what they might choose to utilize the information for. For whatever good it was doing in life, she found it enjoyable to use the information as she saw fit for herself. In her otherwise boring, mundane world, it provided her a sense of power and importance.

Sometimes, Dean was mailed information anonymously by Gertty, which he could pass on at work to other investigators. Gertty's mailings had helped investigators quickly identify many of the decomposed bodies from the mass grave. Some information was sent to the new investigative office in town owned by her friends—again, anonymously. They were able to use the information to further investigations and get a jump on the police who were trying to solve the same crimes.

The information made the sleuths look good to the public. It gave an indication to the public that the investigative services the agency was providing were actually doing some good in their field. It delighted her to know she could be of help to other people and control how the information was best being used to serve mankind or, if not, how it was best being used for how she saw to be appropriate.

Thumbing through a few pages of papers she had printed off her computer, she sat perplexed. Not all the data was clear. Some of it was documented in riddles and codes. Deciphering the confusing notations was how she loved spending her lonely times. Doing so made her feel intelligent. She had learned and was learning so much. For example, some of the code had been based upon ancient Native American symbols carved into trees on the island sandbar near the middle of Lake Marie. These symbols had been suspected to be linked to local crimes.

One such crime was when the body of Eli had been found murdered in his charter boat. The symbols had been carved into Eli's flesh, and his blood had been used to draw them on his boat. Janet provided Dean with information pertaining to those symbols based on information she had found in an old book on her bookshelf. Gertty later studied that book and learned a lot from it. She also learned a lot from all her friends, as they often divulged other secrets to her. She could usually see through their secretive lies and piece together the real stories. Whenever her contribution to crime solving led to a victory, she felt she had won said victory.

Damien, confidentially, had been a good friend to Gertty for many years. In the early years of having met him, he was a friend of Irwin, and she had often caught him snooping around in the neighborhood. She even caught him in her own home once and shoved her shotgun into his face that day. It wasn't until she had deciphered a particular code on the memory stick that she learned of his involvement with the UR and forced more extensive truths out of him. He was reluctant to divulge some secrets at first, but she finagled them out of him.

To prove he could trust her, she provided him with some information he later concluded to be accurate and informative. They became good friends over the last year. She had informed Damien of where the ranch in Colorado held pregnant women. She informed him of where the children in Door County had been kept. Obviously, she did not know if the places were still in operation or held the people he sought to see freed. It merely gave him leads on where to look. Her leads to date were 100 percent spot-on.

Now Gertty hoped to unravel another mysterious code on the memory stick to help Damien and the UR with yet another lead. It amazed him how she could know any of this information people would have killed for to keep secret. She jokingly told him that she was clairvoyant and that such information would just come to her in a trance when she least expected it. He had no other choice except to believe her.

Then she would do a bit of research online. She would look at old news reports, maps, or any information she could use to substantiate her claims and provide him any information she could. It was not always just him but anyone she felt the information could most benefit in the way she assumed they would use it to achieve her desired end result. No matter how the information was being provided to them, Damien and anyone else obtaining it were definitely appreciative.

When Damien next showed up at Gertty's home, she let him in, as she normally did. He was dressed all in black with a hoodie on. His clothes were soaked with rain, and Gertty asked that he remove them while she got him a bathrobe to slip into to keep warm and dry. She excused herself only momentarily while she placed his clothes in her dryer. When she returned to his side, he had already poured himself a small glass of bourbon. It was not unusual for him to make himself comfortable in her home. He, too, these days could be considered a son she never had, so much so that he called her Mom when nobody else was around.

"Mom," Damien said, "I have some bad news, I'm afraid. I heard that Diana has been kidnapped again. We believe it was not the Mob who found her. We suspect it was the party who wanted to get their hands on her in the first place as retaliation against Fox. As you know, it was not the UR who had placed her in their own witness protection program. It was the government and authorities who did the placing. The authorities probably screwed up again. There are always too many people involved on their end and too much red tape. Too many leaks from those people. Can't trust any of them."

Gertty felt sorry for the young girl. Diana had been through so much, and those getting their hands on her would knowingly not be kind, if they allowed her to live at all. Unfortunately, the memory stick had been in Gertty's possession for a year. Any crimes of today were too recent to have been included on it. She didn't think there would be any way she could be of any help to Diana now. If she could, she surely would.

"I will let you know if I have any premonitions of Diana," Gertty mentioned as the only suggestion she could muster. "On the bright side, I do have some information to provide you with. It may not be as big of a rescue as you've been accomplishing, but it is something nonetheless. During some lunar cycles, there is a satanic cult that gathers and commits human sacrifices during their rituals. Their selected offerings do not usually come from around here, but the human trafficking sector of the Mob provides the cult with their victims.

"One such ritual will be taking place in a month. The rituals always take place here in Antioch, in the woods surrounding Lake Marie. My visions tell me that during the ritual next month, a man with his pregnant wife will be killed. They will cut out the hearts of the man and woman and cut out the fetus as well. Those parts will be cooked in the devil's fire and consumed. The cult members believe it gives them extended, eternal life. Here is a note I have typed for you. I thought it best to involve you, as the authorities have known of this practice for centuries and have never once been able to prevent the ritual from taking place. That makes me wonder."

As a side thought, she mentioned, "Keep an eye out for people who appear younger than their age. The members of this cult may not actually achieve youth through the ritual. I suspect that they rely upon cosmetic surgery to maintain a youthful appearance and create the illusion their beliefs actually work for them. They are delusional and dangerous. Some may be church members to further disguise their identities. Their dishonesty and complicity are dangerous. Some resort to drinking human blood between rituals in the belief it helps maintain the reported benefits."

Damien looked over the information with great concern. "It looks as if we have something else to put a stop to. I'll get started on this right away."

As Damien departed, Gertty had a brief image in her head of Diana in trouble.

About the Author

During the 1970s, AJ LeBergé was privileged to spend his youth at a family-owned lakeside vacation home on Lake Marie. Life in the small village of Antioch was even more peaceful in that era given that the area was considered countryside. Home computers were not yet something commonplace, television stations were limited, and the reception required rabbit ears. Having been mostly an unoccupied summer and vacation home dwelling much of the year, newspaper delivery was not ordered to that address. Instead, entertainment and news were passed on by family, neighbors, and friends. More often than not, information was fictional, or facts had been embellished upon as stories were conveyed down the line. People told the stories the way they wanted and believed what was told and heard by them as they deemed appropriate.

AJ finds interest in sociology and people. His writings clearly reflect that in the development of his books. The Lake Marie characters are created in such a way so as to express that they each have their own feelings, beliefs, ways of life, and morals. In that respect, it is assumed that readers will interpret the characters and story lines differently depending upon the reader's personal viewpoints. Rarely does he prefer to paint exact pictures and be specific but would rather leave a lot to the individual reader's own imagination. His story lines are reminiscent of conversations he heard as a youth.

Horror and mystery have always been AJ's passion. Even when he was growing up, ghost stories, late-night television horror shows, monster magazines, and horror movies at the local theaters were then and have now remained a source of entertainment. It was with those passions in mind that AJ started writing books that paid homage to those affinities and relive in his mind the experiences at Lake Marie.

Despite his writings being fictional, readers often state that they get so caught up in his tales that they start believing the stories are factual. That is easy for a reader to do, as Lake Marie and Antioch have actually had their share of horrific and unexplained events over time. Creating such a belief that his stories could actually be based upon true events is his intention. Using an actual physical location, such as Antioch, adds credibility.

AJ hopes all his readers continue to enjoy his stories. Look for *Lake Marie*, the book that started it all, in softcover and hardcover at fine book retailers worldwide. The next books he intends on publishing are the next novels in the *Lake Marie* series and a holiday sci-fi thriller.

As a prolific artist, his fine canvas works can be found at art galleries. Check online at ajleberge.com or other supported sites to see where his masterpieces are currently available. Information can be easily found on the websites pertaining to his books, art sales, and upcoming projects.

Milton Keynes UK
Ingram Content Group UK Ltd.
UKHW011815010124
435301UK00001B/20